FINDING *her* JOY

BOOK 1: HEART OF A FAMILY SERIES

FINDING *her* JOY

A Christian Romance Novel

DONNA WITTLIF

This is a work of fiction. Some of the places are real, but not all. All the characters and events portrayed in this book are fictional, and any resemblance to real people or incidents is purely coincidental.

ISBN: 978-0-9992543-0-1

Published at Amazon.com

Editor: Debra L. Butterfield (debralbutterfield.com)

This book is dedicated to all those who are carrying an unwanted child for whatever reason, but especially to those who have been raped by a relative or friend. May you know God's love for you and your unborn child and find peace and joy.

Jesus said, "Whoever receives one child like this in My name receives Me; and whoever receives Me does not receive Me, but Him who sent Me" (Mark 9:37, NASB).

CONTENTS

CHAPTER 1

Leaving Mama

"Della."

"Yes, Mama." Della rubbed the top of the cold hand clutching hers, feeling the sharp bones under the thin skin. "What is it?"

"Go, child." She coughed and raised the towel in her other hand to wipe the blood-streaked sputum from her lips. "Today, July 4, 1964, is your liberation day."

"Go where?"

"To your Aunt Marie's in Puttersville. She'll take you in."

"But who will take care of you, Mama? Cook your food? Wash your clothes?"

"I won't need anyone. I won't be here."

"Mama!" Fear tore through Della, ripping at her heart.

"Go, Della. You must be gone before he comes home."

"I don't think Aunt Marie likes me. She won't take me."

"She's kin. She has to take you in." Her hand shook as she turned toward Della and reached out to stroke her daughter's long, curly blond hair. Heaving a sigh, she dropped her hand. Tears filled her eyes. "You're all I have. I won't lie here and watch Gus destroy you."

"But Mama—

"Look in my bottom dresser drawer. A jar..." A hard cough racked her worn body. "A jar with some money is in the back. Take it."

Della opened the drawer, felt toward the back, and pulled out a small pickle jar filled with bills and change.

"It isn't much. Maybe twenty-five dollars. Enough money to get you to Puttersville."

"Where does Aunt Marie live?"

"One thirty-six Grant Street. Write it down. Her phone number is—"

"Wait!" Della searched for a slip of paper and wrote down the address and the phone number her mother dictated.

"Now take my suitcase and put as many of your clothes in it as you can. Remember, you won't be coming back." She closed her eyes and pulled the threadbare blanket over them.

Della stared at the still form, then reached under the covers and wrapped her hand around her mother's cold fingers.

"Go, child. Before it's too late."

"But Mama..."

"You have to go. Give me that one last revenge. Now hurry."

Della pulled the suitcase out from the bed, forced the rusty hasp open, and threw her clothes inside. Dirty jeans on top of clean dresses, socks with holes in the heels, and two worn sweatshirts. Tears streamed down her face. The world swirled around her in slow motion as if she were on the outside looking in.

"Are you ready? Are your clothes packed?"

"Yes, but Mama—"

"Then go. Take the Old Mill Road to the downtown bus stop."

"Mama, when will I see you again?"

"You won't in this life. Now go before he gets home."

"Mama, I love you."

"I love you, too. Always have, always will. Now go and never look back."

Mama hadn't let her tell the thing that nagged and worried her. A sob tore Della's throat as she threw her purse over her shoulder and grabbed the suitcase. She opened the door and turned for one last look at the still form in the bed, then closed the door and ran to the old maple towering above the yard. Leaning against it, she spied the speck of a vehicle making its way down the road. Daddy's truck? She held her breath, fighting the fear that gripped her. In a few minutes the vehicle passed, leaving her alone in the shadows cast by the trees.

Lifting the suitcase over rocks lining the familiar path descending to Old Mill Road, she directed her steps toward downtown Morgantown. A thousand times she'd walked this road. A thousand times she'd stopped off at the small grocer on the corner. A thousand times she'd waited for the school bus in front of it, but no more.

Her feet knew the way, and she followed the route etched in her mind, past the gas station, past Chafe's Hardware Store that smelled of bags of oats and grains mixed with molasses for horses, down the alley that led to Church Street, and around the corner to the First National Bank. The bus stop loomed across the street from the bank.

Pausing to check for cars before crossing, she set her suitcase down in front of the old brick building housing the bus station and pulled on the doorknob. The door didn't open. Stepping to the window, she brushed the dust from the pane and squinted, trying to see inside the darkened room.

"Aint' no bus service nights."

Startled, she turned and eyed the man standing in front of her. "What?"

"No bus service. They cut out nights."

"I need to go to Puttersville."

He jerked his head toward a yellow and black car parked up the street. "Might try the taxi. Owner Bob's probably in the tavern over there."

"Thanks."

Della picked up her suitcase and crossed over to the taxi in front of the tavern. It was empty. *Never been in no tavern. I'll just sit here and wait a bit.* Glad for the jeans covering her legs, she sat down on the raised curb and leaned against a tree growing through the walk. *Here I am, sittin' right where everyone can see me, right in plain sight. If Daddy'd happen to drive his truck down Main Street, here I'd be. And he'd stop and make me git in. I don't wanna see Mama dead!*

Tears filled her eyes. *No more Mama. No more sitting on the back porch singing hillbilly tear jerker songs with her. No more watching Mama making her fiddle strings sing like the wind in the mountains and hearing her talk about joining some band. Then she'd be famous, she'd said, and she would have pretty dresses and travel, and some day, they'd move into a nice fancy house, just like Patsy Cline.* "I'm sorry Mama," she whispered. "It wasn't my fault Daddy had to sell your fiddle to buy me school shoes 'cause he drank up all the money. Wasn't my fault you got sick and then Daddy said it was cancer, and we couldn't afford no medicine or doctors or anything to help you. Wasn't my fault, Mama, it wasn't."

She had tried to help Mama. Every day she gave her aspirin for her pain, but then the aspirin ran out. "Please buy Mama more aspirin," she begged Daddy.

"Ain't making her well, is it? I'm saving up my money to take her to the doctor and get her some real medicine. Next week I'll have enough." With that Daddy slammed the door on the way out to his truck, and she didn't see him until next morning.

That week she quit going to school to stay home with Mama. She'd wake up early every morning, check on Mama, cook oatmeal for their breakfast, and pack Daddy's lunch pail. Two fried egg sandwiches and a thermos full of coffee. Every day he'd leave for work in the coal mines, and she'd settle down to bathing Mama, changing her bedding, washing clothes, sweeping, and cooking dinner. Every day.

Daddy never came home for dinner, but she knew he'd be home after she went to bed, because in the morning his truck sat in front of the house. He came into the kitchen, fresh from shaving and combing his hair, and he'd eat his oatmeal without looking at Mama, and then he'd pick up his lunch pail and leave.

She heard the familiar rumble and looked up. Daddy! His old blue truck turned the corner and headed down the street toward her. Like a cat slinking under a car to hide she was in front of the taxi, hunched in front of its right tire. She trembled as the truck rattled up behind the taxi and parked. Daddy got out and headed toward the tavern without looking her way. As he entered, another man came out.

Della stepped up onto the sidewalk and picked up her suitcase.

"Going somewhere?" the man asked.

"I'm waiting on the taxi driver."

"I'm Bob, and I drive the taxi. Where can I take you?"

"How much to Puttersville?"

"Usually twenty, but tonight, half price for a pretty little girl like you." He took her suitcase and put it in the back seat, then held the door open for her.

"One thirty-six Grant Street," she said as he pulled onto the highway.

"Big July 4th party?"

"No."

"Family?"

"Yes, my Aunt Marie." She glanced to see if Bob was watching, then unzipped the suitcase, pulled out the pickle jar, and counted out ten ones.

"I hear they're hiring down at Puttersville's No. 1 Mine," Bob said. "Might give up this taxi and get a job in the mines."

"Daddy works there, and he ain't said nothing about that."

"It's been in the newspaper for a week. Surprised you haven't seen it."

"We don't get no newspaper. And Daddy...well, he just don't say nothing."

"What street did you say?"

"Grant Street. One thirty-six Grant Street." She stared out the window until he turned the taxi off the highway onto a street, turned a corner, went right onto another street, and stopped in front of a house.

"Here we are."

"Here's your money. Thanks for driving me."

He opened her door, and when she got out, he reached for the suitcase and set it down on the sidewalk. "Hope your Aunt Marie's home."

She picked up her suitcase and started up the driveway. A sign standing in the middle of the yard read *House for Sale*. Large black letters saying *Price Reduced* filled the bottom half of the sign.

CHAPTER 2

Sister Bess

The door knocker landed with a heavy thud as Della let it fall for the third time. No answer. Leaving her suitcase on Aunt Marie's front porch, she strolled to a little gate on the side of the house, reached over it and undid the latch. A stone-paved path ran into the back yard, and she followed it to a covered porch with pots of red and pink geraniums hanging from its eaves. She went to the back door and banged on it.

"Aunt Marie, are you here?" she called. "Aunt Marie, can you hear me? Aunt Marie!" Again she knocked and shouted as loudly as she could, but no one answered. Going back to the front, she banged her fist on the door and dropped the knocker several times.

"I'll sit here and wait awhile. She's probably visiting," she muttered. The smell of wieners and hamburgers grilling in the back yard of a house across the street wakened hunger pangs. Down the street a fire cracker hissed as it soared into the dusky sky with an explosion of light.

A fireworks show? She picked up her suitcase and walked toward the falling stars. About fifty people gathered in an empty lot behind a small church building, and she approached them slowly. She stopped. She didn't know these people. No one had invited her.

A young Negro man ran toward her. "Hey, who are you?" He looked at the suitcase in her hand. "What you doing here?"

"Just lookin', that's all. I'm leavin' now."

"Leaving? No, you're not leaving." A matronly Negro woman took her by the arm. "You just come on over here and join us. Let's get you a hot dog and a drink." She turned to the young man. "Danny, you stash this lady's suitcase while she eats. What'd you say your name is, dear?"

"Della."

"I'm Bess Huston, but everyone calls me Sister Bess. Where you from, Della?"

"I came from Morgantown to visit my Aunt Marie, but she doesn't seem to be home."

"Are you hungry?"

"Yes, Sister Bess."

"Then you come right over here, and we'll get you something to eat." Sister Bess slid a hot dog onto a paper plate and gave it to her. "Here's catsup, mustard, onions, relish, all the fixings. Just help yourself."

"Thanks." Della covered the wiener with catsup and relish and picked up a glass of iced tea.

"And have some cookies," Sister Bess said, stacking four on her plate. "Now, you just sit over here and enjoy your food while Sister Bess talks to you."

"I appreciate it," Della said. "I am really hungry." She sat down and devoured most of the hot dog, all the time listening to Sister Bess.

"We're members of the South Side Church," Aunt Bess said. "The black congregation in town. But we do have some white folks who don't want to drive to North Side because it's so far. Now tell me again. Who did you come to see?"

"My Aunt Marie," Della said between bites of oatmeal cookie. "She lives at one thirty-six Grant Street."

"The house with the For Sale sign in its yard?"

"Yes."

"Oh, honey, I drive past that house every day, and I must tell you, I haven't seen anyone there for quite a while. Are you sure your aunt is home?"

"We don't have no phone, so Mama couldn't call. But she said Aunt Marie would be here. And she said she'd take me in when I got here."

"Where's your mama?"

"At home in Morgantown. But she's real sick, and she told me to go live with Aunt Marie, and if Aunt Marie ain't here, I don't have no place to go."

A perplexed look crossed Sister Bess's face. She stood with her hand cupped around her mouth. "Danny, hey, Danny," she called toward a group of young people twirling sparklers.

"Yes, Sister Bess," the young man said, running up to her.

"You take this woman's suitcase and put it in my car trunk until we find out what to do." She handed him her car keys. "Thank you, Danny."

"But..." Della said, watching her suitcase disappear toward the parking lot.

"You don't say a thing," Sister Bess said. "You don't have a place to stay, and Sister Bess has an empty room in her house. There's no more to be said, understand?"

"Yes, Sister Bess."

"Now let's go watch the fireworks. You like fireworks, don't you?"

Della nodded. *If only Mama was here. Mama loved fireworks.* She followed Sister Bess to the crowd of people sitting on the ground. Bess threaded her way through family groups, then stopped and pointed to a worn quilt spread over the grass.

"Sit down here," she said, pointing to the quilt.

Della sat and stretched her neck to try to watch Aunt Marie's house. *What if a car pulls into Aunt Marie's driveway? I'll just have to ask Sister Bess to give me my suitcase.*

The sky lit up with a burst and a boom of light, followed by a series of pops and hisses as more rockets sped skyward in streaks of light. Explosions turned the heavens into a candelabra of stars cascading toward the ground. Before they evaporated, another round of fireworks flew into the air and burst into a crescendo of colored lights.

"Aren't they beautiful?" Sister Bess leaned her head next to Della's ear. "I never get tired of them."

Della smiled. "They're real pretty." *But hope they don't last too long. I'd like to check to see if Aunt Marie's home before it gets too late.* She squirmed through the next fifteen minutes, trying to keep an eye on the fireworks and checking Aunt Marie's house every other minute. *It would take her a minute or two to get out and go in the house, so I'm bound to see her if she comes home.*

When the last volley of fireworks exploded, a huge sparkling star formed a canopy over the field. Different sections of the star went from red to blue, then yellow and white. The people oohed and ahhed as burning stars floated to the ground.

"Are you ready to go? There's someone I want you to meet."

"Yes. But could we stop at Aunt Marie's house so I can make sure she hasn't come home?"

"Sure. Just help me gather up a few things I brought." She walked to the tables and picked up a plastic container, which she handed to Della. Then she gathered an empty cake pan and pie plate. "These sure went fast."

In a few minutes she stopped the car in front of Aunt Marie's house.

"Just gonna check," Della said, getting out and running up to the front door. She knocked and let the door knocker fall several times. Tears filled her eyes. "Aunt Marie, Mama said you'd be here to take me in and take care of me. Where are you? Why can't you be here when I need you?"

"She'll probably be here tomorrow. I'll check again tomorrow," she said as she walked back to the car and got in. "Does your husband live with you?"

"No. The mines got to my man. He died of black lung disease four years ago."

"I'm sorry. It must be hard."

"It's okay. I still have my job teaching down at Puttersville High School. I have a son and daughter-in-law who live nearby. The Good Lord is taking care of me." She glanced at Della. "Now what about you? Why are you leaving your sick mama?"

"She told me to. She made me go." Tears slid down Della's face. "I didn't want to go and leave Mama, no I didn't. But she sent me away. And now Aunt Marie's not here."

"You poor child, stay with us tonight. Tomorrow we'll ask around about your Aunt Marie."

"Us?"

"My mother lives with me."

They pulled up in front of a wooden house with blue shutters and a front porch surrounded by white wooden railing.

"Come on, child. Let's get your suitcase." She opened the car trunk, and Della took hold of the suitcase.

"I don't want to be no trouble, Sister Bess."

"No trouble. Come meet my mother. Mother Carrie, as everyone calls her."

Della followed her through the door. Sister Bess turned on the light, and Della glanced around the living room. "Where is she?"

"Mother?" Sister Bess walked into the kitchen, then turned and passed down the hall. "Mother? You in here?"

Della was right behind her as she yanked the bathroom door open.

"Mother!"

Peering over her shoulder, Della saw the sprawling figure of an elderly woman. She lay on the floor with her head against the tub. A small pool of blood gathered under one side of her head.

"Della, call the police! Tell them 112 Garden Street, and tell them to hurry."

Della grabbed the telephone book and looked up the police, then dialed and relayed the information.

"Is your mother breathing?" the woman on the line asked.

"Is she breathing?" Della stretched the phone line down the hallway as far as it would go.

"Yes. Breathing, but she can't sit up," Sister Bess replied.

Della relayed the information. "They say they'll be here in a few minutes," she said.

"Oh, Mother, it'll be all right. We'll get you to the hospital, and you'll be okay." She turned to Della. "Please go out in the driveway and wave when you see them coming."

Della ran out the door to the bottom of the driveway. In a few minutes she heard the wailing of the police car, and she waved her arms as it drove onto the street.

"In here!" she yelled as two men jumped out and ran toward her. She led them into the house and down the hallway to the bathroom.

"Help her, please help her," Sister Bess said, wringing her hands.

"Let us through, Ma'am." They picked Mother Carrie up and carried her to their car, where they laid her in the back seat. Della watched as they sped down the street.

"Come, Della, go with me to the hospital," Sister Bess said. "Oh, if I'd only stayed with her instead of going to the fireworks!"

CHAPTER 3

Mother Carrie

Della sat in the Waiting Room beside Sister Bess. *If only Mama was here. Mama would know what to do.*

"It's all my fault. Never should have left her alone." Sister Bess rocked in her chair, then took a tissue from her purse and wiped her eyes. "But then," she continued, more to herself than anyone else, "Never was a problem before. Nothing ever happened."

"It's not your fault," Della said. "She could've fallen if you'd been home. But why didn't she go to the fireworks show with you?"

"She said her feet were swollen and she was tired. Oh, if I'd only tried a little harder to get her to come." She rocked back and forth in her chair. "Only God knows how long she lay there on that cold bathroom floor hurting with no one to help her."

"Mrs. Wagner?" A man in a white coat approached them. "I'm Dr. Richards. Your mother suffered a cut on the back of her head and a concussion. She'll be okay, but we'd like to keep her and run some tests."

"May I talk to her?"

"She's in Room 24."

"Thank you. Let's go, Della."

They made their way down a hallway to the room.

"Mother, I'm here." Sister Bess dropped into the chair beside her mother and stroked her hair. "I'm so sorry you fell."

Mother Carrie opened her eyes and smiled. "I'm good," she whispered, then closed her eyes.

"I owe her so much," Sister Bess said. "I was a pretty wild young girl, but she always kept me straight. Without her, I'd probably never gone to college, got my teaching degree, had a career. Mother made sure all that happened."

"Mama wanted me to finish school." Della bowed her head as tears filled her eyes. "Ain't her fault didn't happen."

"Still can happen. Don't give up."

"Maybe someday," Della said, shrugging. "When I find Aunt Marie."

"Let's go home and get some rest," Sister Bess said, letting go of her mother's limp hand. "She's asleep."

"Will you drive past Aunt Marie's house? Just so I can see if anyone's there?"

"We can check again."

They left the hospital. In a few minutes Sister Bess turned onto Grant Street and slowed the car down as they passed the house. No lights shined through the front window.

"She's not here." Della swallowed the lump in her throat. "I don't know where she is. Mama said she'd be here."

"You can stay with us until you find her," Sister Bess said as they turned off Grant. "You can use Mother's bathroom. Towels are in the linen closet."

"Thanks. I'll make it up to you."

"There's no making up, Della, just doing unto others. Just like Jesus said. All that counts is doing what God and Jesus said."

When they entered the house, Della grabbed some newspapers and headed for the bathroom. Kneeling, she soaked up the spot of blood and scrubbed the tile floor.

"Thanks for cleaning that up," Sister Bess said, sticking her head into the bathroom. "I appreciate your help."

"I'd like to take a shower. Is that okay?"

"Of course. Use the soap and shampoo in here if you want. I'm going to bed so we can go see Mother early. Good night."

"Good night." Della went to the bedroom Sister Bess had given her and opened her suitcase. No nightgown or pajamas. She sorted to the bottom and found some clean panties and a long shirt and took them to the bathroom. Turning on the shower, she stepped into the tub and relished the warm water running over her body. Picking up the bar of soap, she scrubbed, then washed her hair with the lilac-scented shampoo. *Nice. Daddy never bought any nice soap or shampoo, just that old green slimy stuff.*

She turned off the water, got out of the tub, and dressed. Back in the bedroom, she stood in front of the dresser mirror and brushed her hair. A pang of fear swept through her chest. *I'm late. Ten days late. Maybe just the stress of everything that's happened lately.*

She crawled into bed, and even though the night was warm, pulled the blankets over her head. *Oh God, if there is a God, please don't let it be. It can't happen. Not now.*

She awoke to the sound of singing coming from the kitchen. Getting out of bed, she pulled the blankets up and slipped into a pair of jeans. As she walked down the hallway, she spied Sister Bess in the kitchen.

"Good morning, Della. Sleep well?"

"Yes, ma'am."

"Good. Here's some muffins and jam for breakfast. Hot coffee in the pot, or you can have some milk."

"Thanks." Della poured herself a glass of milk, then broke a muffin in two and spooned jelly on each half.

"I'd like to go see Mother as soon as we eat," Sister Bess said. "I hope she can come home today."

"Okay." Della ate, then went to the bedroom and slid her feet into her worn sandals and changed her top. She joined Sister Bess in the living room.

"Ready?" Sister Bess asked, picking up her purse.

"As ready as I'll ever be," Della said, tearing the unraveling threads from the bottoms of her jean legs as she followed Sister Bess out the door. On the way to the hospital, they passed Aunt Marie's house, but it looked as empty and forsaken as it had the night before.

"Where did you graduate from high school?" Sister Bess asked.

"I didn't graduate." Della hung her head. "I was a senior, but then Mama got sick, and I had to take care of her."

"I see."

They pulled into the parking lot at the hospital, and Della followed Sister Bess into Mother Carrie's room. Dr. Richards was standing beside her bed, making notes on a clipboard.

"We ran some tests on your mother last night," he said without looking up. "She has had a minor stroke. She suffered no lasting damage, but a small stroke is often a sign that a larger one will follow. I'm going to dismiss her to go home, but she will need to rest in bed for a few days."

"What will she be able to do? Can she get up at all?" Sister Bess asked.

"She can sit up in bed, but don't let her get up to use the bathroom without someone by her side to support her. She will need help with bathing and dressing."

"We'll take real good care of her. I'm glad she can go home."

"If you're ready to take her, I'll send a nurse with a wheelchair. Here's a prescription she needs to take." He tore the small sheet from the pad and handed it to Sister Bess.

"Thank you." Sister Bess turned to her mother. "We'll get you dressed and have you home in no time, Mother."

Della handed Sister Bess her mother's clothes from the bag in the small closet in the room. After they finished dressing her, Sister Bess rang the bell for the nurse, and one appeared with a wheelchair.

"I've been thinking," Sister Bess said after they tucked Mother Carrie into the car. "I'm going to need some help with Mother. Will you stay on and help me for room and board?"

"Yes. I mean I can stay until I find Aunt Marie."

"Good. Next week I have to attend training sessions for my teaching job. I'll be gone most of the day, and Mother will need help. You can care for her, and you can do something else I have in mind."

"What else?"

"You're going to school and getting your GED."

"I am? What's a GED?"

"A General Education Diploma. Same as a regular high school diploma."

"How do I go to school if I'm taking care of Mother Carrie?" Fear pounded in Della's chest.

"Night school at Puttersville High School. They offer classes and tutoring for free. I'll help you. And the high school is within walking distance."

"But—"

"No buts. I won't allow you to stay uneducated and ignorant."

You're not my mother. You can't tell me what to do, and you can't make me.

"So we have a bargain? Help with Mother during the day and classes at night?"

"I...I guess so." Della swallowed the lump of rebellion in her throat and looked out the window. "I'll try."

"Then it's settled. I'll call the school and get you enrolled as soon as we get Mother home."

Taking care of Mother. Going to school. Doing homework. I won't have time to look for Aunt Marie and ask her to help with Mama. No,

I won't do it. No matter what Sister Bess says. The car pulled into the driveway, and Della got out and went to help get Mother Carrie into the house. But her mind stayed with Mama.

CHAPTER 4

Caring For Mother Carrie

Mama, my Mama, I want to be with you, helping you. Della bent over Mother Carrie, washing her face and neck with a warm washrag. "How do you feel this morning?" she asked.

"Bess, is that you?" Mother Carrie opened her eyes. "Where's Bess?"

"She had to go to work this morning. I'm Della, and I'm going to take good care of you."

"I have to use the bathroom."

"Here, let me help you up." Della pulled back the covers and put her arm around Mother Carrie. "Easy, just turn around and stick your feet over the side of the bed." She watched as Mother Carrie sat up and inched her legs toward the side of the bed, then held onto her as she slid onto the floor. Holding onto Mother Carrie, Della unfolded her walker and turned it toward the bathroom.

"I can get myself to the bathroom, thank you." Mother Carrie pushed her away and swayed as she headed out the bedroom door.

Della ran to catch her.

"I told you I can do it myself. Don't tell anyone Carrie Huston can't get herself to the bathroom."

"Yes, ma'am. I'll wait for you outside the door."

"No need." She scowled and shut the door behind her.

Della sighed. *Mama never acted so ornery.* She heard the toilet flush, then waited for Mother Carrie to come out. Several minutes passed, and no sound came from the bathroom.

"You okay?" she yelled.

"Course I'm okay." The door opened. "Just washing my hands."

"I see." Della followed her back into the bedroom and watched as she sat down on the bed and struggled to turn around and pull up the blankets.

"Well, you going to help me or not?"

"Yes, ma'am." Della reached across her to grab the blankets and pull them up, but Mother Carrie moved her feet, and they got tangled in the sheet.

"Might as well do it myself. Can't get good help these days."

Tears stung Della's eyes. "What do you want me to fix you for breakfast?"

"Can you scramble a good egg? Can you make me some toast without burning it?"

"I believe so. Anything else?"

"Some grape jelly on that toast and some coffee."

"Yes, ma'am. I'll be back with breakfast in a jiffy." She hurried to the kitchen, glad that Sister Bess had made coffee, still hot in the pot. Finding a small skillet in the drawer under the stove, she lit the burner and swirled some butter in the bottom of the skillet. She cracked the eggs into a small bowl, scrambled them up with a fork, and poured them into the skillet. "Just pretend you're doing this for Mama," she told herself as she put two slices of bread in the toaster and stirred the eggs. Finding the tray Sister Bess had set out, she arranged the food and took it into Mother Carrie.

"Here's your breakfast, Mother Carrie." Shall I put it over your lap, or would you like to sit in your chair?

"I'll sit."

Della held the tray and watched while Mother Carrie eased herself out of bed and took the two steps to a stuffed chair. Setting the tray down on the foot of the bed, she placed a small table in front of the chair and placed the tray on it. "Anything else I can get you?"

Mother Carrie stared at the food. "Some pepper for my eggs."

Della ran to the kitchen and whisked the pepper shaker from the counter. "Anything else?"

"That's fine. What'd you say your name is?"

"Della."

"And what do you do, Della?"

What an odd question. "Right now, I'm helping you."

A bit of steam from Mother Carrie's coffee wafted toward Della, and her stomach turned somersaults. "Excuse me," she said, grabbing her stomach and running into the bathroom. She heaved into the toilet, but nothing came up. *Good thing I haven't eaten breakfast.*

"You okay?" Mother Carrie yelled.

"Fine," Della said, wiping her mouth on a piece of toilet paper. She smiled as she returned to Mother Carrie. "Don't know what got into me."

"Maybe something you ate." Mother Carrie pushed the tray back. "You can take this. If I could get up, I'd show you how to scramble some decent eggs."

Della carried the tray into the kitchen. Mother Carrie had eaten a tiny bit of the eggs and a half slice of the toast. Della picked up the untouched piece of toast and took a bite, but her stomach roiled, and she tossed it into the garbage can.

"Della!"

"Yes, ma'am?" she said, scurrying back into the bedroom.

"Help me sit up. Where are my pillows?"

"Here." Della picked up three pillows from a nearby chair and arranged them to support Mother Carrie's body.

"Turn on my television. Channel 4."

Della turned on the television and switched the channel. Loud enough?"

"Yes. That'll be all now."

Della returned to the kitchen and filled the sink with hot, soapy water. She opened the trash can to scrape Mother Carrie's plate into it, and again, a wave of nausea swept over her. She sat down, her heart racing. Images of Mama, when she was expecting the baby brother that they lost, raced through her mind. *Maybe it's only a touch of the flu.*

"Della!" came the plaintive cry from the bedroom.

"Yes?" Della asked.

"I need you to help me get comfortable."

Della rearranged the pillows, lowering Mother Carrie to a half-lying position. "There, how's that?"

"Better. Can you turn off the television? I'm going to rest."

"Have a good rest," Della said as she turned off the television. She pulled the door to as she left. After finishing the dishes, she found a rag and dusted the end tables, the mantel, and the television in the living room. The phone rang just as she finished, and she picked up the receiver.

"Hi Della, this is Bess. How is Mother?"

"She's resting now. She didn't eat much breakfast."

"That's okay. She never does."

"What should I give her for lunch?"

"There's a bowl of chicken soup in the refrigerator. You both can have that. Need to get back. I'll check in later."

Della hung up and went into the kitchen to look for the chicken soup. She opened the refrigerator door, and a plaintive cry from the bedroom assailed her.

"Yes, Mother Carrie," she said as she entered the room.

"Was that Bess on the phone?"

"Yes."

"Next time she calls, I want to talk to her."

"Okay. If she calls again."

"Is it lunch time yet?"

"It's only 10:45." Della pointed to the clock on her night stand.

"Oh, I see. Is it too early to have some lunch?"

"We can have some lunch. I'll go fix it." She poured the soup into a pan and put it on the stove.

"Della! I want to eat at the table."

Della hurried into the room. "I don't know if you should."

"What's the difference between sitting here in a chair and sitting in a chair in the dining room? Help me up."

Della wrapped Mother's robe around her, then supported her as she slid her feet onto the floor and toddled behind her walker into the dining room. Della eased her into a chair and ran to the stove. The soup was steaming, and she found two bowls and filled them.

"Here you go," she said, setting a bowl in front of Mother Carrie. "Sister Bess's chicken noodle soup." She brought her bowl to the table and sat down.

Della lifted a spoonful of soup to her mouth. Mother Carrie blurted out, "Dear Lord, thank you for this awesome soup that my Bess makes, the best soup in the world. In Jesus's name. Amen."

Relieved that her stomach had calmed, Della ate all her soup, picked up the bowl and drank the broth, then emptied the remaining half cup into her bowl. "I was really hungry," she said as Mother Carrie glanced her way. "And this is the best soup."

"My Bess is the best cook. Over there in the canister are some oatmeal raisin cookies. Could you get us each one?"

Della brought the canister to the table. After giving one to Mother Carrie, she sank her teeth into a cookie's chewy sweetness.

"This recipe is one my mother taught me. Of course my Bess made them."

"They're good." Della waited for Mother Carrie to reach for another, but when she didn't, she carried the canister back to the cupboard.

"I'm tired. I'm going to visit the bathroom, and then I think I'll take a nap.

Della hovered by Mother Carrie's side but didn't hold onto her as they made their way to the bathroom. When she emerged, she walked with her to her bed and helped her into it.

"You stay close by in case I need something," Mother Carrie instructed.

"I will." Della edged her way to the door and looked back before closing it behind her. Mother Carrie's eyes were closed.

After washing the dishes, she found a magazine on the coffee table and sat down. The phone rang as she flipped through the pages.

"How are things going?" Sister Bess asked.

"Fine. We ate your good soup and had a cookie. Now she's resting."

"Great. There's some ground beef in the refrigerator. Could you make a spaghetti casserole for dinner? The recipe's in my recipe box beside the cookbooks. I'll be home by 5:00, you'll have plenty of time to get to your class at the high school.

"Sure. Be glad to."

"Okay. See you at 5:00."

Am I glad to? I don't know. I still haven't decided if I'm going to take those classes. Della found the recipe box and searched for the spaghetti casserole recipe. *Just not sure I want to do it*. Without thinking, she began singing "I Fall to Pieces." When she realized what she was singing, the song died on her lips. She used to sing it with Mama.

CHAPTER 5

Della's Problem

"I drew you a map to the high school." Sister Bess handed Della a sheet of paper. "Look. It's only six blocks away. I bought you a notebook, and this little zip pouch holds pens and pencils."

"I don't want to do it." Della's stomach churned. Was it the spaghetti for dinner, nerves, or…?

"If you're staying with me, you're going to do it." Sister Bess looked at her hard. "Your choice."

"Bess? Can you come?" Mother Carrie yelled.

"When I come back into this room, I expect to see you gone." Sister Bess rose and headed for the bedroom.

Della snatched the notebook and pouch from the coffee table and slammed the door as she left. Her cheeks burned with anger and tears filled her eyes. "It's not fair," she mumbled as she plodded down the street. "I'm not a little child. I can make my own decisions."

But in Sister Bess's eyes I'm still a child. And what did I just do? Slam the door like a child taking a tantrum. She glanced at the map and turned right.

She passed a front porch where two teen couples were dancing to music from a radio. They looked up and waved, and she stopped and waved back, lingering to listen to the unfamiliar music, swaying to it. Looking away, she resumed her pace.

Looks like fun. She rounded the corner singing "500 Miles Away from Home" and spotted the high school a couple blocks down the street. With reluctant feet she climbed the steps. Pulling open the heavy front door, she entered, then went through a door marked *Office.*

"How can I help you?" a woman at the desk asked.

"I'm Della. I'm here for the GED school."

"Do you have a last name, Della?"

"Etter. I'm Della Etter."

"I believe I made you a folder when Mrs. Wagner called. And here you are," the woman said, extracting a manila folder from a drawer in the desk. "Please come with me." She bustled into the hallway, and Della followed her through an open classroom door.

"A new student," Mr. Huston. She handed him the folder, then turned and left.

Della looked around. About twenty students worked at desks. A few glanced up, then resumed their tasks.

"Pick a seat," Miss Etter.

Della sat down at a desk.

"I see you were a senior in high school before moving to Puttersville."

"Yes. But I had to quit."

"It's okay. We're going to help you get your high school diploma." He gave her a booklet of papers stapled at the top left corner. "This is a pretest to show us where you need to start. It doesn't count for a grade, but it's very important, so please do your best. Fill the entire circle of your answer choice with your pencil, making it entirely black inside. Any questions?"

The first section was reading short selections and answering questions about them. She breezed through most of them with no problems, then started a section on science. She struggled with interpreting some of the grafts, filling in one circle, then changing her mind. *Just keep going.* The social studies and history sections were next. *I always liked history. These aren't too bad.*

The next test was math, and she groaned. *My worst subject.* The first few problems were simple addition, subtraction, multiplication, and division, and she worked them carefully and checked her answers. Several word problems followed. A wave of nausea hit her stomach, and the words blurred. She raised her hand.

"Doing okay?" Mr. Huston asked, approaching her.

"I'm not feeling well."

He picked up her booklet and glanced through it. "You're supposed to stay until 9:00, and I'd rather you finish this in one setting."

"But my stomach hurts."

"I'll excuse you. I hope you feel better tomorrow."

"Thank you." She rose and left hurriedly, making a bee-line for Sister Bess's house. Entering, she saw Sister Bess sitting on the living room couch, watching a television show.

"I didn't expect you until after nine," Sister Bess said, raising her eyes.

"I didn't feel well, so he let me come home early."

"What's wrong?"

"My stomach. I feel like I'm going to throw up."

"Probably a case of test anxiety. Did you finish the entrance exam?"

"Most of it. The math is hard."

"You'll do okay. You can finish it tomorrow."

"I'd like to take a shower and get to bed if that's okay."

"Go ahead. See you in the morning."

After a quick shower, Della crawled into bed. *Tomorrow will be easier. My stomach won't hurt. I'll get through the day with Mother Carrie. I'll finish that test.* She closed her eyes and drifted into an uneasy sleep, dreaming of Mama, lying sick in her bed, and Daddy yelling at both of them.

A soft knock on her door wakened her.

"I have to leave early today," Sister Bess said. "There's more chicken soup in the refrigerator for lunch. Can you fry up a pork chop?"

"I think so."

"I took three out of the freezer. Wash three potatoes and stick them in the oven to bake about 4:30. Bye, now."

"Bess." Mother Carrie's cry came from the bedroom.

"Coming." Della scurried into Mother Carrie's room.

"I need to go to the bathroom."

Della helped her out of bed and helped her with her walker. When they returned, she asked, "What do you want for breakfast?"

"Eggs, sunny side up and coffee and toast."

"Coming right up." In the kitchen she cut an inch of butter off the cube and let it melt in the skillet, and then she broke a couple eggs into the butter and started the toast. The odor of the eggs cooking drifted up to her face as she shook salt and pepper onto them. Suddenly, she grabbed her stomach and ran to the bathroom, heaving acidic saliva into the toilet.

"You okay?" Mother Carrie yelled.

"I'm fine," Della replied, washing her hands and running to the kitchen to get the eggs and toast.

"You don't look okay," Mother Carrie said as Della brought the tray of food into the bedroom. "You didn't feel well yesterday, and today you're throwing up. Are you sick?"

"No, just feeling a little puny."

"If you're not sick, what's wrong with you?"

Della avoided Mother Carrie's eyes and set the food on the table. "I'll be fine." She smiled and tried to sound brave, but inside, she panicked. *Just like Mama when she found out she was expecting. I can't be! I'm only seventeen.* Her stomach lurched and she swallowed hard, but it did no good. She ran back into the bathroom.

"There's some saltine crackers in the cupboard," Mother Carrie said. "They can settle your stomach. And make yourself some tea and honey."

"Thanks." Della picked up the tray Mother Carrie pushed toward her. "I'll be right back." She carried the tray into the kitchen and scraped off the plate. The egg she cooked for herself was still warm in the skillet, and she put it on a plate, and taking the second piece of toast, dipped it into the yolk. Her stomach roiled, and she dumped the egg and toast into the trash.

Better check on Mother Carrie. She peeked into the bedroom. Mother Carrie sat propped halfway up against the headboard, her wrinkled hand grasping the *TV Guide,* her eyes closed.

"Are you asleep?"

"I was just waiting for you to turn on the television," she said, opening her eyes. "Channel 4."

Della reached up and turned the knobs. "If that's okay, I'm going to make me some tea." While the tea water heated, Della searched the cabinet and found a box of saltine crackers and the honey. She poured the hot water into a cup and dunked the tea bag until the water turned a rich brown, then stirred in a spoonful of honey. As she nibbled the crackers and sipped the tea, she forced herself to consider her problem.

She shuddered, the scene replaying in her mind. Daddy coming home smelling of whiskey. Being wakened in her dark bedroom as he groped for her and tore back the blankets, then his body on hers. She screamed in pain, and he put his hand over her mouth and whispered, "Don't scream again. Don't tell, or I'll kill you." Then he left.

She had lain awake the rest of that night, and as the darkness began to lift, she rose and bathed. Shortly thereafter, she heard Daddy get up and leave. When Mama called her, she washed Mama's face and cooked her breakfast, but her mind was numb. She couldn't talk, couldn't follow what Mama said, couldn't concentrate on what she was doing.

"Are you okay?" Mama asked, reaching up to stroke Della's hair.

She nodded, holding back the tears trying to plunge down her cheeks. She longed to tell Mama everything, but no, Mama was too fragile, and the warning hissed in her head, "Don't tell, or I'll kill you."

When Mama slept, she went and took another bath. Probably she would never feel clean no matter how many times she bathed.

More than a month later, she still felt filthy, worthless, and ashamed. Tears slid down her face as she washed the breakfast dishes. *My life is ruined. When Sister Bess finds out, she will tell me to leave. Where will I go? How can I raise a baby by myself? I can't hide it for very long.*

"Della, is it time for lunch?"

Della wiped the tears from her face and ran into Mother Carrie's bedroom. "It'll be eleven soon. Do you want to eat lunch early? More chicken soup?"

After lunch Mother Carrie slept, and Della did dishes again and washed three potatoes to bake in the oven. Worry gnawed at her. *Should I come clean and tell Sister Bess now, or should I wait until I can't hide it? But am I completely sure that's why my stomach is acting up? Not really. So I'll wait.*

CHAPTER 6

The Truth

Della trudged down the high school steps mumbling, "I hate math. I hate writing." She hadn't done well on the last two pretests, of that she was sure. *But then it's hard to concentrate when I'm fighting waves of nausea.*

By the time she arrived at Sister Bess's house, she had thought of a solution to her problem. If she were expecting, she wouldn't tell until she had to. Maybe by then Aunt Marie would be home, and she could go live with her. She opened the door and walked into the living room.

"Did you finish the test?" Sister Bess asked.

"Yes. The math was hard, but I finished."

"How do you feel tonight?"

"Okay, I guess."

"Look at me, Della. How do you feel?"

Della raised her eyes to Sister Bess's face, then looked down at the floor. "I don't know."

"Della, are you in the family way?"

"Am I what?"

"In the family way. To put it more bluntly, are you pregnant?"

"I hope not." Shame poured over her, burning her face. She stared at the floor.

"I get off at noon tomorrow. Mother has a doctor appointment at two. I'll call tomorrow morning and get you in to see the doctor, too."

"Yes, ma'am."

"Another thing. I went by your aunt's house this morning and peeked through the window. No furniture in the living room. Your Aunt Marie is not there. Not there, do you understand?"

"Yes, ma'am." Tears swam onto her eyelids. She turned and ran to her bedroom as they spilled out and ran down her cheeks.

It's not fair. Mama told me Aunt Marie would take me in. And she's not even there. Huge sobs shook her shoulders. *I have no place to go.*

The next morning she climbed out of bed feeling like a wet, cold blanket was wrapped around her shoulders. Only this time she couldn't take it off to hang it on the clothes line. Today she would find out if what she suspicioned was true. Tonight she might be out walking the streets, suitcase in hand, looking for a family to take her in.

"Della!" Sister Bess called from the kitchen.

"Yes?" she asked, running down the hall.

"Mother needs a bath today. Please help her with it." Sister Bess looked at Della's rumpled clothes and stringy hair. "And take one yourself and get some clean clothes. I'll see you a little after noon."

"Yes, ma'am."

"Bess! Bess!"

Sister Bess hurried to Mother's bedside. "I have to go to school, Mother. Della is going to help you get a bath and fix your breakfast. We have doctor appointments today."

Della followed, looking over Sister Bess's shoulder.

"Don't want no bath. Not going to the doctor," Mother Carrie said. A scowl crossed her face.

"Mother, you don't want me to come home and see you haven't had a bath. It's best you be ready to go."

"I'll go draw the water," Della said, glad to let Sister Bess persuade her mother. When she returned to Mother Carrie, Sister Bess was gone, but she had left a pile of clean clothes on the corner of the bed.

"Are you ready?" Della smiled as she pulled back the bedcovers and helped Mother get out of bed. Then she unfolded her walker and helped her guide it to the bathroom door.

"I can do it myself," Mother Carrie said, entering the bathroom and shutting the door in Della's face.

Della heaved a sigh and stood outside the door listening. *What if she falls? What would I do?* She breathed a sign when Mother Carrie came out and she could help her dress.

"Let's go into the kitchen and get breakfast," Mother Carrie said

Della nodded and pulled out a chair for her at the table. "How about some scrambled eggs this morning and some sausage?"

"No sausage, just the eggs and toast. And coffee."

By the time they ate breakfast and she propped Mother Carrie into her bed to watch television, Della had to hurry to do the dishes and get herself ready. Her hands shook and her legs trembled as she examined her abdomen. *What if it's true?* After dressing, she packed her suitcase, putting clean clothes on one side and dirty ones on the other side. *There. If Sister Bess kicks me out, my things are ready.*

Sister Bess walked through the door at 11:30. "They let us go early," she said. "Let's have some ham sandwiches before we go." She put a bag onto the table. "Even had time to run by the store."

Mother Carrie called, and Sister Bess went to help her. Della set the table and put two slices of bread on each plate, then put one back from her plate. "I'll be lucky to keep a half sandwich down the way my stomach feels," she muttered.

"Della, I was fortunate to get you in to see Dr. Haskins," Sister Bess said as she helped Mother into a chair.

Della nodded, focusing her attention on putting slices of ham and cheese on one piece of bread on each plate and spreading mayonnaise on the other slices. Her stomach revolted at the sight of the food, but after Sister Bess said the blessing, she tried to eat.

They arrived at the doctor's office and were barely in the waiting room when a nurse whisked her down the hall.

"Go into the bathroom here and get us a sample," she said, handing her a small paper cup. "The directions are on the cabinet."

When Della came out holding the cup, the nurse took it, then weighed her and took her to a little room and told her to wait for the doctor. A few minutes passed before the door opened and a woman dressed in white entered.

"I'm Dr. Haskins," she said. "And let me see. You are Della?"

"Yes."

"What's going on, Della?"

"My stomach hurts."

Dr. Haskins looked into her mouth, listened to her chest, and tapped her knees with a small hammer so that her feet flew upwards. "Everything seems to be in good working order. Lie down, and let me examine you," she said, easing Della back onto a pillow. Prodding Della's abdomen, she asked, "Does it hurt here? Here?"

"No. I'm sick to my stomach all the time."

"Nothing wrong with you, but from your symptoms, I believe you're going to be a mother. We'll know for sure in a couple days. I can tell you from experience I believe that's your problem."

Della stared at the floor as tears rolled down her cheeks. "Are you going to tell Sister Bess?"

"Well, that depends. Do you want me to?"

"No." Della took the tissue Dr. Haskins handed her and blew her nose.

"And why not?"

"I'm…I'm not married."

"I see. Well, it's not the first time I've heard that. You know you won't be able to hide it much longer. And since she's paying your bill, I think she needs to know."

"I suppose."

"So I'll tell her. Here, take one of these every day," Dr. Haskins said, handing her a bottle. "They're prenatal vitamins. Unless you hear from me that you are not pregnant, I want to see you again in six weeks, so make an appointment on your way out."

"Yes ma'am." Della stood and passed through the door into the waiting room. Remembering she needed an appointment, she stopped at the receptionist's window, then sat down to wait for Sister Bess and Mother Carrie.

She didn't have to wait long before they walked in. Sister Bess stopped at the receptionist window before turning to Della. "Let's go home."

Della rose and walked behind them to the car. She sat in the back and stared out the window, waiting for Sister Bess to say something, but she chatted with Mother Carrie as if nothing had happened.

Sister Bess turned up Grant Street and drove past Aunt Marie's house. The For Sale sign was topped by a banner in large letters that said SOLD!

Aunt Marie is really gone. She must have left and not told Mama. Why would she do that? Della felt tears well up in her eyes. *No, I won't cry. It won't help. I've got to be tough.*

Sister Bess turned the corner and pulled into her driveway. Della extracted Mother Carrie's walker from the other side of the back seat and gave it to her. Trailing behind them as they walked up the driveway, she made her plan.

They entered the house, and Sister Bess helped her mother walk to her bedroom. As soon as they were in the room, Della hurried to her bedroom and grabbed her suitcase. She would flee before Sister Bess told her to get out. She was in the living room headed for the front door when Sister Bess spoke behind her.

"And where do you think you're going?"

Startled, Della turned. "I'm leaving. I'm sure you don't want me here."

"I never said that." Sister Bess reached over and took the suitcase from her. "Sit down. We need to talk."

Della sat down like a zombie. Without looking up, she said, "Dr. Haskins told you."

"I already knew. Who's the daddy?"

"Daddy."

"No, who is the father of your child?"

"Daddy. Only he isn't my father. He's the man my mother married after my father died."

Anger furrowed Sister Bess's brow. "Then why were you running away without explaining?"

"I feel so dirty. I'll never be clean." Tears spilled from Della's eyes.

"It wasn't your fault." She handed Della a piece of paper. "Write down his name and address."

Della wrote and handed the paper to Sister Bess. "What are you going to do?"

"I'm going to report him to the sheriff." She picked up the receiver and dialed.

Della listened in horror as Sister Bess reported the details. *What have I done? Daddy will shoot anyone who comes to talk to him, especially a sheriff. But the sheriff will probably shoot him if he puts up a fight.*

Sister Bess put down the phone. "As a teacher, I care for children and feel a responsibility to report child abuse. The sheriff said he would investigate. Now you go put that suitcase up. You're not going anywhere."

"No, ma'am." Relieved, Della took the suitcase into her bedroom and opened it. With one hand she scooped out her dirty clothes and tossed them onto the floor.

She stared at the bottom of the suitcase. A flap closed with snaps lined it. She took her clean clothes and laid them on the bed, then unsnapped the flap and lifted it. A small gauze bag, yellow and wrinkled, lay flattened against the bottom. She pried it loose carefully and opened the top, then turned it upside down and shook it. A dull silver coin fell onto the bed.

Picking it up, she examined it. On one side was a rabbit standing on a platform, and under the platform were a large *3* with a small *d* beside it. A harp emblazed the middle of the other side of the coin. On the left side of the harp was the number *19*, and on the right side of the harp was the number *28*.

What kind of a coin is this? She turned it over in her fingers. *And what do these strange words on it mean?* Reaching into the bag, she felt a piece of paper, and she pulled it out. She couldn't make out the words, written in a tiny script in faded ink.

The soft sound of footsteps on the hallway carpet startled her. Cramming the coin and paper inside the small bag, she placed it under the flap and threw her clean clothes on top. A light knock, and the door opened.

"The sheriff may come talk to you tomorrow, so please don't make any plans to go out," Sister Bess said. "They want to know all the facts."

"Yes, ma'am. I mean no, I won't go anywhere."

"Good night. I'll see you tomorrow."

Della stared at her until the door closed. *Don't want to talk to no sheriff unless he can help me find Mama.*

CHAPTER 7

A New Skill

Two days later, when they were home from church, a sheriff knocked on Sister Bess's door. Della stood behind her, listening.

"Are you sure you gave us the correct address, Mrs. Huston?"

"You wrote down your step-father's address, didn't you?" she asked, turning to Della.

"Yes, ma'am. It was the correct address."

"The house is locked up. From what we could see, no one lives there. Seems no one knows where he went. We'll keep looking."

Della sank onto the sofa. "If no one's there, that means Mama died. Mama died, and I don't even know where they buried her." Tears slid down her face.

Sister Bess sat down beside her and wrapped her arm around her thin shoulders. "Don't let yourself think that. Maybe he took her and moved to a different city."

Della shook her head. "That would be just as bad. The way he treated her was awful. She died because he wouldn't take her to the doctor."

"Mother's taking a nap, so why don't you go rest? Tonight we'll tackle your math homework. I'll help you."

Della fell asleep as soon as she lay down. When she woke, she forced herself to take her math book, pencil, and paper to the dining room table. Opening the book, she stared at the first word problem. She read it three times, but she couldn't understand it.

She saw Sister Bess watching her out of the corner of her eye, but she was too embarrassed to ask for help. She reread the problem and then propped her chin on her hands and stared at it.

"Let me see that." Sister Bess bustled to her side and peered over her shoulder. "Tell me the problem in your own words," she said, reaching down and closing the book.

"It was about an airplane," Della said, looking up at her. "And how far and how fast it flew."

"Tell me about it."

"Let me think." Her brow furrowed. "Airplane A flew 1,200 miles in two hours. Airplane B flew 2,400 miles in three hours. Then it asks which airplane was faster and by how much. I think the answer is Airplane B."

"How do you know that?"

"Because it flew the farthest."

"How fast did it fly?"

"I don't know."

"Well, let's find out," Sister Bess said, picking up the pencil. "It flew 2,400 miles. How long did it take it?"

"Three hours."

"So how do you calculate miles per hour?"

"I don't know."

"You divide." She handed Della the pencil. "Put down the number of miles. What are you going to divide by?"

"Three?" Della drew the divide bracket over 2,400 and put 3 on the side, then looked up with doubt on her face.

"That's right. The number of miles divided by the number of hours give you your speed per hour. Go ahead and divide." Sister Bess watched as Della did the math.

"Eight hundred, right?"

"That's right. Now how do you find out how fast Airplane A was flying?"

"Oh, I get it. Divide 1,200 by two, right?"

"That's it. So how fast?"

"Six hundred." A smile spread across Della's face. "So Airplane B was flying 200 miles an hour faster than Airplane B, right?"

"Yes, that's right. Now let me see you do the next problem."

Della read the problem through. It was very much like the first, and she did it hurriedly and held up her answer.

"That's right. All you need is some self-confidence. You're very intelligent, and you can do this math."

A warm glow spread through Della. *No one ever told me I'm smart. But I am.* She finished the next eight problems and showed the page to Sister Bess.

"Let me see here," Sister Bess said, picking up the math book and reading. "Every problem is correct. Don't ever let me hear you say you can't do math again."

"Yes, ma'am. I won't." *I can do it, I know I can.*

"Come on, let's have some dinner. You set the table while I help Mother up."

"I'm feeling tuckered," Mother Carrie said as she shuffled into the room with the help of her walker. "Don't know when I been so tired."

"Going to church this morning wore you out," Sister Bess said, setting a bowl of steaming vegetable soup in front of her and handing her a roll. "This will fix you up."

Mother Carrie ate several spoons full of soup, then stared at Della. "So you went and got yourself pregnant."

"I…I" Della looked across the table at Sister Bess.

"Mother, it wasn't Della's fault," Sister Bess said.

"She must've done something. Things like that don't happen to nice girls."

Della dropped her spoon into her bowl and fled to her bedroom. She flung herself across the bed and buried her head in her arms, her eyes closed, trying to shut out the scene playing out in her head. *Wasn't my fault, Mama, it wasn't. I didn't do anything to cause it. It was Daddy's fault.* She tried to feel Mama's reassuring hand on her back, but it wasn't there. *It ain't fair, Mama. It ain't.*

A tap sounded on her door, and before she could answer, Sister Bess slipped in.

"I'm sorry, Della. Mother's from the old school. Please try to understand." She sat down on the side of the bed and stroked Della's back. "I know it wasn't your fault."

"No, it wasn't." Della forced herself to sit up, but she couldn't look at Sister Bess. "Daddy came into my room, and he—"

"Shh…say no more. I know how it happens."

"You do?" Della asked, looking into her eyes.

"Yes. I'm a school teacher, remember? Lots of girls have told me."

"It happens to other girls?"

"Yes."

"I don't want to be a mother." *There, I've said it, the truth. I don't want a baby to take care of.*

"You're going to have a baby."

"I'll get an abortion."

Sister Bess stared at her for some time. "I can't believe you said that. Abortion is murder. And it's illegal. Life is precious. A baby is a gift from God!"

"A gift from God?" Della stared at her in disbelief. "How am I going to take care of a baby?" She buried her face in her hands.

"God doesn't give you anything you can't do. You're going to go to school, get that graduation certificate, find a job, and support yourself and your baby."

"But how can I work if I have to take care of a baby?"

"You will have to find someone to help with your child. But trust in God's care. He'll work it out for you."

"I don't know about God. He's never helped me before."

"But He will. Come, finish your soup while I help Mother back to bed."

Della went, even though she didn't feel like eating, even though she would have to face Mother. Eyes fixed on the floor, she passed Mother, who rose from her chair and took the walker Sister Bess handed her. Della sat down and finished the lukewarm soup and roll. *How am I going to take care of Mother when she blames me? And how am I going to make it in this world?*

"I'm glad my week of teacher training is over," Sister Bess said, coming into the room and gathering the dirty dishes. "Mother's getting a bit cantankerous. Under the circumstances, she might be hard for you to deal with."

"Yes. But what am I going to do with my time?"

"You're going to need some new clothes. As the baby grows, you will too. Want to learn how to sew?"

"I've never sewn before, but…"

"You can learn. There's a sewing machine and cabinet in your bedroom. And I have some material that I think will work fine for a top." Her eyes smiled. "Maybe even a pattern. I made some maternity clothes for a granddaughter. Come."

Della followed her into the bedroom.

Help me get these boxes off the sewing machine," Sister Bess said, handing Della several boxes. "These hold all my patterns. Stack them in the corner there." She inserted her forefinger into a notch in what looked like a trap door on top the cabinet and lifted it up. Reaching under the door, she pulled up a sewing machine which swung on hinges. When it was all the way up, she replaced the trap door, making a solid base for the machine.

"Now what do I do?" Della asked.

"First you have to learn to thread the machine." She pulled a chair over. "Sit down."

Della watched as Sister Bess's nimble fingers guided the thread from the spool on top the machine through different parts of the machine and into the needle.

"Here, now you do it," Sister Bess said, pulling the thread from the needle and out of the nooks and holes where she had threaded it.

Della's eyes hadn't kept up with Sister Bess's fingers as they moved the thread through the different places. She picked the thread up and ran it through what she thought was the first slot, but Sister Bess stopped her.

"No, not there. Here. She slid the thread through a slot, then into a small hole, then around and down through the eye of the needle."

"Oh, now I see." Della unthreaded the machine and rethreaded it.

"Very good. Now look under the cabinet." She pointed to a pedal on the floor. "When you step on the pedal, the machine sews." She handed Della a four-inch by six-inch piece of material. "Make sure the needle is up by turning the wheel. Then raise the sewing foot." She raised a small lever near the needle. "Now put the material under the needle and lower the sewing foot."

Della did as she instructed.

"Now step on the pedal. Gently at first until it starts sewing."

Della put her foot on the pedal and pushed, and the needled jerked up and down as it flew across the material.

"Whoa, take your foot off the pedal."

Della lifted her foot and shifted the sewing foot upward.

"Now raise the needle with the wheel. When it's clear, you can cut the threads with these scissors."

"It sewed such a straight line," she said, examining the stitches. "I can sew!"

"You can do anything you put your mind to. No more excuses. Tomorrow I'll show you how to cut out the material. I need to check on Mother," Sister Bess said.

Della opened the sewing machine cabinet drawer and took out a box. Inside she found dozens of spools of thread of all colors, and she sat there dreaming of making blouses and dresses to sell. If she ever got good enough, that's what she'd do. She sat there, dreaming of sewing fabulous dresses and blouses and singing "Silver Threads and Golden Needles."

CHAPTER 8

Mr. Huston

"Is this right?" Della held up the piece of collar she had sewn to show Sister Bess.

"Perfect," she said as she held it in her hand and scrutinized the even line of sewn stitches. "Now turn it right side out and trim and notch the seam, just like the pattern shows you. I'll check on you later," she said as she left.

"Thanks." Della sat down at the sewing machine, and being careful not to cut too far, trimmed the seam and cut vee-shaped notches. *Wow! I can do this!* She smiled and pinned the collar onto the blouse.

"Della!" Sister Bess called.

"Yes?" She jumped from her chair and ran down the hall.

"The sheriff wants to talk to you," Sister Bess said, meeting her halfway to the living room. "It's about your stepfather."

Heart pounding, Della went to the door where the sheriff was waiting.

"Your father's car went over the hill on Bandy Ridge," the sheriff said when she reached the door. "He died in the accident. I'm sorry."

"How did it happen? How?"

"A hunter found him this morning. His body is at the county coroner's office. Looks like it happened a week or so ago."

Della's head spun. She wasn't overwhelmed by grief, nor was she glad. She felt nothing. A sort of numbness settled over her brain. "Thank you for letting me know," she mumbled. She sat down on the sofa and stared out the window as the sheriff's car pulled away.

"Are you okay?" Sister Bess asked.

"I don't know. He was probably drunk. Mama said it would happen someday. Mama was right." Tears filled her eyes. "I miss Mama. What happened to her?"

"I hope we find out." Sister Bess put her arm around her. "Should we plan a funeral for your father?"

"Never set foot in a church. Don't think he loved me. I don't want to."

"Then we won't."

"Won't *what*?" Mother Carrie stood at the end of the hallway, leaning on her walker.

"Della just learned her stepfather was killed in an accident. She doesn't want to have a funeral."

"Happens to most drunks," Mother Carrie said, turning her walker back down the hallway. "No big surprise."

A surge of anger washed over Della. The words *You have no right to judge* sprang up inside her, but she bit her tongue and said nothing. She couldn't defend him, couldn't think of one nice thing to say about him.

"Let's have some lunch," Sister Bess said. "Della, would you dip us all up a bowl of soup while I help Mother to the dining room?"

"Yes, ma'am." Della ladled hot vegetable beef soup into bowls and set them on the table, then put crackers and rolls out.

"I hope you're doing well in your classes," Mother Carrie said after Sister Bess gave thanks.

Della made a face, then regretted it. *Don't want to set her off on one of her speeches.*

"My grandson teaches there, you know," Mother Carrie said.

"Your grandson? What's his name?" Della asked.

"Reginald Huston. Ever see him?"

"Yes. He teaches math." Della recalled the tall, light-skinned Negro man who was her math teacher. *Funny I didn't connect the names.* "He knows a lot."

"Ought to. He worked hard delivering papers, sweeping up at the grocery store, anything he could do to earn money to put himself through college." Her voice swelled with pride. "Not many young men would do what he did to better themselves."

"So don't you go disappointing us by not succeeding," Sister Bess added.

"No ma'am, I won't. I'm trying."

"Trying's not good enough," Mother Carrie said. "I know you didn't come from very good beginnings, but if you work hard enough, you can change all that."

Della blushed. *Probably as good a beginnings as you had.*

All afternoon while she sewed, the words *You didn't come from very good beginnings* played in Della's mind. *I couldn't help what my family was. Daddy wasn't good, but I couldn't change him. And now I'm carrying his baby. Will that add more badness to our family? Will my baby be like Daddy? Does what he did to me make me a bad person?* She shook herself to make the thoughts go away.

As she walked to school after dinner, she glanced again at the young people dancing on the porch. "I don't have time for fun," she said, sighing. "And no friends to have fun with."

Inside the classroom she sat down and took out her math homework. When Mr. Huston came by to check it, she looked up at him and smiled. *Do I dare tell him I'm living with his grandmother? Maybe after class.*

He picked up her notebook and glanced over her problems. "Much, much better," he said. "You must have understood these."

"I had help."

"Get all the help you can get. The problems on this page are a little different. Read the instructions here and here," he said, pointing. Then do numbers one through five. When you've finished, hold up your hand, and I'll come check them."

Her eyes followed him as he walked to another student. *How can he be Mother Carrie's grandson? His skin is so light. Not quite white, but not so dark. His hair is darkish blond with a reddish tinge. And his eyes? I'll have to look.*

"Do you need some help, Della? I'll be right there."

"No, sorry. I was just..." She studied the page in front of her, but the words were not making sense.

"How can I help?" Mr. Huston asked as he moved to her desk.

"I don't understand this problem." She looked up into his soft brown eyes. "I don't get it."

He stared into her face for a few seconds, then focused on her book, but in those few moments, she saw into his soul and knew he was drawn to her. *Was he blushing?* She couldn't tell.

"Let me see. Yes. These problems are almost like the ones you did this morning, but instead of finding out how fast the car is going, you have to find out how many miles it gets per gallon. How many miles did the driver go in this car?"

"Three hundred miles."

"And how many gallons of fuel did he put in the tank before he started."

"Fifteen," she said, looking at the problem.

"So you take the number of miles and divide that by the number of gallons. That will tell you how many miles per gallon he got on his trip."

"Okay. Thanks." She looked up and smiled at him, but he had moved on to another student. Burying her head in her book, she worked three problems before daring to raise her eyes. He stood in front of the room speaking to her English teacher. She solved a couple more problems and looked up. He was gone.

After school she hurried home, eager to sew. Entering the house, she found Sister Bess sitting at the dining room table, her head in her hands and looking worried. "What's wrong?" she asked.

"Mother had a bad day, and that means we both did. She became upset at every little thing today."

"Like what?"

"Her favorite gown was in the laundry, her tv show wasn't on because of a special news broadcast, she wanted chili for lunch, not sandwiches. She was cranky and complaining all day. But she did something she's never done before."

"What?"

"She yelled at me, just like I was a little kid. And she threw her hair brush at me." She sighed. "I was so hurt and surprised I called the doctor."

"What did he say?"

"He said her behavior is indicative of having another small stroke, or maybe even a larger one, and he wants me to bring her in for more tests."

"I'm sorry. I hope she hasn't."

"I have to be back at school teaching in a couple more weeks. I can't afford to put her in a nursing home, and I can't afford someone to come in and take care of her."

"But that's why you have me," Della said, putting her hand on Sister Bess's shoulder.

"I don't know if you can handle her. You've been through so much that your emotions are already on edge."

"I took care of Mama. Only Daddy was the one yelling at me, not Mama. I can do it."

"We'll see how things go. How was school?"

"Remember when Mother Carrie said Mr. Huston was her grandson? I don't see how. He doesn't even look much colored."

"That's because his father, my brother Nat, married a white woman."

"He did? Really? I didn't know that was allowed."

"Oh, it's been happening for hundreds of years. But most people still don't look favorably on biracial marriages. It hasn't been easy for them."

"Oh." Della traced a line in the wood of the table top with her finger. "Do they live here in Puttersville? What do they do?"

"Nat works as a janitor at the elementary school. Winnie works out of her house as a seamstress, making wedding dresses for couples and doing alterations."

"I love to sew. Do you think I could meet them?"

"I'm sure you will in time. Did you have any problems with your math?"

"A little. But it was easy after Mr. Huston explained it, and I got all the homework done."

"I'm glad. I need you to help me take Mother to the doctor tomorrow."

"Okay. I'm going to go sew a little bit before bed. It helps me relax."

"Fine. But don't be too late. Think I'll turn in."

Della picked up her books and went to her room. Turning on the floor lamp beside the sewing machine, she studied the pattern directions. She picked up the piece of interfacing she had cut for the collar and stitched it to the piece.

The door squeaked as it opened. Startled, she turned around. Mother Carrie stood in the doorway, leaning on her walker. Her wizened eyes never left Della.

"I bought that sewing machine for Bess. I'm surprised she let you use it. I wouldn't." Mother Carrie pushed her stroller around, but it caught on the door. Reeling, she fell against the door frame.

Della leaped up and ran to her side, taking hold of her arm to steady her.

"I can get myself back to my room," Mother Carrie said, shaking her loose and shuffling down the hallway.

Stunned, Della debated following her. "Better not," she muttered. "Why is she so angry at me?"

CHAPTER 9

The Essay

"I'm not going. That's final." The next day after lunch Mother Carrie got into bed, pulled her blankets up to her chin, and stared at Sister Bess in defiance. "I'm tired of being pushed around. Nothing they can do. No more tests."

"But the doctor said you need one, Mother. Please let me help you get dressed."

"No. I'm your mother, not your child. You can't make me go."

Della stood in the hallway watching. "Can I help?" she asked, walking into the room.

"Go away. I'm not talking to that little brat." Mother Carrie glared at Della. "Get out of my room."

"Come on," Sister Bess said, taking hold of Della's shoulder. "No use in arguing with her. I'm going to call the doctor's office."

Della listened as Sister Bess explained the problem. "What did they say?" she asked as soon as Sister Bess hung up.

"They said don't force her." She turned and stared down the hallway. "You stood with me before, Heavenly Father. You have to help me now."

"Do you think God hears you?" Della asked. "You didn't even bow your head. But I've never prayed, so how would I know?"

"Praying is just talking to God, child. He listens whether we have our head bowed or not. All I know is I can't handle Mother alone, so I call on Him for help."

"I have to write an essay for English," Della said. "I'm going to work on it."

Inside her room, Della picked up her notebook and read the notes she had written about the assignment. *Write a two-page essay about a hard decision you had to make.* That was easy. Her thoughts drifted back to three weeks ago, when Mama told her to go, but her heart wanted to stay.

She wrote the first sentence. *Leaving Mama was the hardest thing I ever had to do.* She explained the pull and tug going on inside her, listening to Mama's pleas for her to escape, but realizing that she might never see Mama again. She had fought her own voice, those urgings coming from her own heart telling her she needed a better life, yet knowing that if she left, Mama would be all alone with no help from Daddy.

"Mama, Mama, why did you make me go? Where are you? Are you still alive?" The words blurred on her notebook paper as her tears fell on top of them. *Mama can't help me. No one can hear me. No one cares if I find Mama.*

Next she wrote about hiding behind the taxi parked in front of the bar. *Daddy's truck barreled down the street toward me. The front of the parked taxi hid me from his sight as he parked behind it. I crouched there, shaking, as he walked four feet from me around the truck and up the steps to the saloon door. He never once looked back.*

Mama realized I had to escape, but she didn't know it was already too late. She didn't know that Daddy ruined my life. No one will want to marry me. Not ever. I feel dirty all over. God will never forgive me. And I don't want no baby.

But how can I hate my own child? What did it ever do to deserve this? It won't have a daddy, no one to love it but me. How can I take care of a baby with no money? How can I have money when I can't work because I have a baby? Oh, Mama, Mama, why did this happen to me?

Mama wouldn't want me to give up. Maybe she's in heaven watching me and helping me. Did she send Sister Bess to take me in? But what about Mother Carrie? I think she hates me. But I know Mama will help me take care of her.

So Mama, I will do my best. I will go to school and get my diploma. I will help Sister Bess with Mother Carrie. But I don't know if I will love this baby.

A tap sounded on her door, and Sister Bess peeped in. "How is your essay coming?"

"Still working on it".

"Dinner will be ready in a bit."

"Okay. I'll be there soon." *I don't have anything else to write. But I don't want Sister Bess to know how scared I am. Especially the parts about hating my baby and what I think about Mother Carrie.*

After dinner Della put on her coat. "I'm going to school a bit early to finish my essay. I have to get the teacher to tell me what something means in her notes."

"You sure you don't want me to preview what you've written? Remember, I'm a teacher, and I can catch your mistakes."

"No thanks, I think it's okay." She nearly ran out the door to keep Sister Bess from seeing her essay.

The classroom was empty when she entered, and she sat down and took out her math. Only one problem remained, and she solved it in three minutes. *I can do this. Just like Sister Bess said.*

A new student came in and sat down in the seat across from her.

"I'm Chris," she said. She patted her extended abdomen. "And my little one."

"Della. When is your baby due?"

"In a couple months."

"I'm expecting, too. The middle of March."

"Morning sickness?"

"Only in the mornings now. I can't eat breakfast."

"No fun, right? But all we go through will be worth it."

Mr. Huston walked through the door. "Today we're going to review fractions." He stood at the blackboard and solved several problems. "I know most of you have studied these types of problems, so let's open your book and do some."

Della understood all the problems they worked together. As soon as class ended, she stood beside Chris's desk. "Do you live with your boyfriend?"

Chris's face clouded up in anger. "Boyfriend? What boyfriend? I live with my husband."

"I'm sorry. I meant to say *husband*."

"But you didn't. You said *boyfriend*." Chris picked up her books and her purse, and glaring at Della, headed for the door.

"I just thought…" Della said, but by the time the words were out of her mouth, Chris was out the door.

Mrs. Brown, the English teacher, came into the room. "Please bring your essays to my desk," she said.

Della tore hers from her notebook, walked up to Mrs. Brown, and handed her the two pages. Only two other students went forward.

"Is this all? Three out of twenty? What happened to the rest of you?"

Several shrugged, but no one spoke.

"Those of you who did not turn in your paper have this period to do it if you want a grade," Mrs. Brown said. "Those who did the assignment will get some special one-on-one tutoring from me. "Della, would you like to sit at the table with me so we can go over your essay?"

"No, ma'am. I mean I guess so." Her feet dragged as she made her way to the table and took a seat across from Mrs. Brown.

"Please sit here." Mrs. Brown pointed to the chair next to her own.

"Let me read it through first, then we'll talk about it."

Della nodded and glued her eyes to the top of the table. "I hope it's okay."

Mrs. Brown read the first page, then looked at Della. "Your father did this to you?"

"Yes," Della said, keeping her eyes on the table in front of her. "Only he wasn't my father. My stepfather."

"Then I should tell the sheriff," she whispered.

"Daddy's dead. Car accident."

"I'm sorry," Mrs. Brown said when she finished. "Can you stay after class to talk about your essay with me?"

"Yes, ma'am."

"Good. Why don't you go read the first story in your book? The class will discuss it next meeting."

"Yes, ma'am." Della returned to her seat and found the story, but she couldn't keep her mind on what she was reading. *Have I done something wrong in writing about leavin' Mama? It was the assignment.*

When class was over, Della watched as the last student left the room.

"Come, Della. Let's talk about your essay, about you." Mrs. Brown sat down at the table.

Della took a seat across from her. "I'm sorry if I shouldn't have written about Daddy," she mumbled, not looking up. "But it was so hard to leave Mama."

"Where are you living?" Mrs. Brown asked.

"With Sister Bess Wagner. She's a school teacher."

"I know Bess. She's a fine woman. Did you show her this?"

"No. She wanted to read it, but I didn't let her. She knows everything anyway. She even called the sheriff on Daddy, but they found his car gone over the bank and him dead in it."

"You're not sure you want this baby, are you?"

"No. It'll look just like Daddy, and that will bring back all those bad memories, and besides, I can't give it the things it needs like a good mama. I feel like I'm in a stream, a muddy, swirling stream right after it rained hard, and I swum and I swum, but I ain't makin' no headway. And then all of a sudden the water came over my head, and I feel myself goin' under and bein' washed downstream, but there ain't no way I can get out."

"Do you have someone you can talk to? A pastor or a friend?"

"No friends. I go to church with Sister Bess, but I don't know the preacher, and he don't know me."

"We have a counselor at this school. He's here during the day, but you're welcome to come talk to him anytime. Just call and ask for an appointment with Mr. Handly. I think you need to, Della. What do you think?"

"Maybe. But I don't want to talk to no stranger."

"You will like Mr. Handly. I know he can help you. Will you promise me you'll at least give him a try?"

"Okay." Della put her elbows on the table, balled up her fists, and lowered her head on them to hide the tears starting down her cheeks. Wiping her face with her hands, she raised her head. "I'll have to talk to Sister Bess first. She might need me to help with Mother."

Della left the classroom with tears still forming in her eyes, but somehow, she felt better. It was good to tell someone about her problem, someone who might see her from a different viewpoint and get her some help. It wouldn't hurt to talk to Mr. Handly just once.

CHAPTER 10

A Chance Meeting

"You want to make an appointment with the school counselor?" Sister Bess asked the next morning as she helped Mother into her chair at the dining table. "What's the counselor's name?"

"Mr. Handly. I think that's what Mrs. Brown said."

"Mother and I are staying home, so why don't you try to get in today?" Sister Bess turned to her mother. "You haven't eaten since yesterday noon. How about some orange juice? I bought it especially for you."

"Don't want orange juice." Mother placed her hands on the table and pushed herself to a standing position. "I don't want breakfast. Help me back to bed."

"Mother, you didn't eat last night. You need to eat. I made you the omelet you like."

"No omelet. I'm going back to bed." She reached over to get her walker and swayed.

"Mother!" Sister Bess reached out and grabbed her, then gently guided her into her chair. "Help me get her back to bed, Della."

Della wrapped an arm around one side of Mother, and together she and Sister Bess lifted her from the chair and supported her weight as they made their way into the bedroom. They eased her into the bed.

"How about a sip of water?" Sister Bess brought the glass to Mother and supported her head as she guided the straw to her lips.

"No water," Mother said, turning her head to the side. "I need to rest."

Della glanced at Sister Bess, who shook her head and sighed.

"If she doesn't eat something for lunch, I will take her to the hospital." She motioned for Della to follow her from the room. "Let's look up the school's number and make you an appointment."

Della took the telephone directory and found and dialed the number.

"My name is Della Etter. I need to make an appointment with Mr. Handly,"

"Just a minute, let me look and see what's available. Can you be here by two o'clock?"

"Yes, I believe so."

"I have an appointment at two," she said as she hung up the receiver. Is that okay?"

"Wonderful. I'm glad they could get you in so quickly."

Mother Carrie ate very little for lunch, and after helping Sister Bess get her back into bed, Della finished her math homework. Then she brushed her teeth and fixed her hair, and taking her notebook with the essay in it, headed downstairs.

"Bye," she told Sister Bess. "I think the appointment is for half an hour, so I won't be gone long." Her head filled with thoughts of Mr. Huston. He was so nice. By the time she reached school, she imagined herself dating him.

Loud talking, laughing, and the clanging of locker doors greeted her as she walked through the front school doors. Students swarmed everywhere. *Sure is different during the day*. For a moment she stood watching what seemed to be pure bedlam, but almost instantly the crowded hallway emptied.

She entered the office. "I'm Della Etter, and I'm here to see Mr. Handly," she told the secretary.

"Della? Yes, he's expecting you. His office is the third door on the right."

"Thanks." She walked until she spotted his name on a door. Stopping, she held her stomach with her arms, trying to still the butterflies inside. Slowly she raised her arm and gave the door a timid rap.

"Come in, come in." The door swung open, and a tall, thin Negro man stood in front of her, a smile on his face. His hand reached out to her. "I'm Tim Handly. You're Miss Etter?"

"Yes, sir. Mrs. Brown said I should come see you."

"Come right in and have a seat." He pulled a chair out for her, then sat down on the other side of his desk. "What's troubling you?"

"Mrs. Brown didn't tell you?"

"No. That's your job."

Della handed him her essay and waited as his eyes traveled down the page.

"So, you don't want your baby," he said, handing her back her paper.

"No. I want an abortion."

"Abortions aren't legal." His face clouded. "Besides, in God's eyes, abortion is murder."

Sister Bess had said that, so it must be true. "Then I'll put it up for adoption," Tears of shame pooled in her eyes. "I can't keep this baby. Can't get a job and take care of a baby. Ain't got no money. And no place to live that is mine."

"Where do you live?"

"With Sister Bess Wagner."

"I know her," he said, smiling. "A wonderful woman. You're lucky she took you in."

"I miss Mama. My mama."

"I understand. I hope you find her."

"I don't want to be a mama." Della sighed. "Not now. Maybe not ever."

"Adoptions aren't easy." He laid his hand on her essay and tapped it with his fingers. "Not for you. Not always for the adoptive parents. Catholic Charities, Florence Crittenton, and I believe the Methodist Church have children's homes and adoptive agencies. But no guarantee they'd accept you. And nothing here. You'd have to go to Wheeling or maybe Charleston."

"Wheeling and Charleston are a long way from here, aren't they?"

"About a three-hour drive."

"I'd better go." Della rose. "Thank you for seein' me."

"Why don't you stop in the office and make another appointment with me. I'd like to see you in a week."

"Okay." Della closed the door behind her, and taking deep breaths to clear her mind, walked into the office and made the appointment. *He didn't do anything to help me. So I made the appointment. Not that I plan to keep it, but just in case.*

Her mind was spinning as she walked out the school door and down the street. *Have to go clear to Wheeling or Charleston. No money to take the bus. Sister Bess don't have no time to take me. How am I gonna get there?*

She entered Sister Bess's house and heard her voice, louder than usual.

"Talk to me, Mother. Come on, wake up." She was putting socks on Mother Carrie, and without looking up, she said to Della. "I just called for Nat to come and help. She can't stand. When I can get her to say something, she's incoherent. Grab that small suitcase under the bed and put her hairbrush and comb, her toothbrush, and some clean underwear in it."

By the time Della packed Mother Carrie's things, Nat was there. Della ran to open the door as he and Sister Bess carried Mother Carrie out the door.

"Thanks. Come with me to the hospital," Sister Bess said. "Winnie's meeting us there."

"What happened?" Della asked as she got into the car.

"She wanted to use the bathroom, but she couldn't stand. She wet the bed. Then she started mumbling. I couldn't make sense of anything she said. She seemed very confused. So I called Nat."

"I'm sorry."

"She's never been like this before. Her health is fragile, and I won't risk not getting her the proper care." She glanced at Della. "How did your appointment with Mr. Handly go?"

"Okay."

"Just okay? Did he give you some good advice?"

"Not much. I don't know."

"Don't know what?"

"What to do about the baby."

Sister Bess gave her a long, hard look. "You're going to have that baby, that's what."

"I'm gonna give it up for adoption."

"Takes money and a lawyer for the adoptive parents unless you can get to an agency certified by the state."

"Mr. Handly said there's places that do it for free in Wheeling and Charleston."

"And how do you propose to get yourself to one of those places?"

Had some small hope she would take me. Looks like that won't happen. I'll have to find a way.

Sister Bess pulled into the hospital parking lot. "Go tell them we have an emergency here."

Della got out of the car and ran inside. "Mother Carrie's sick and can't stand," she told the nurse at the desk. "Please help us."

The nurse made a call, and a young man pushed a gurney into the room. "Where is the patient?" he asked.

"Outside in our car. Come quick," Della said as she ran back out to the parking lot.

Nat helped him load Mother Carrie onto the gurney and take her into the Emergency Room.

"As soon as the doctor checks her out, he'll let you know," the nurse told them. "You can wait here."

"Thank you" Sister Bess said. She chose a chair against the wall and motioned for Della and Nat to sit beside her. "Winnie should be here soon."

"I'll go meet her," Nat said.

Sister Bess turned to Della. "Now about your baby."

"I think I'm startin' to pooch out," Della put her hand on her stomach.

"That baby's part of you. How can you be thinking about giving it up?"

"It's part of Daddy, too. I don't want that part."

"You'll soon be needing that maternity blouse. Better get it finished so you can start another."

Della stared out the window. *Sister Bess is right, but she's wrong about one thing. One more maternity blouse won't help. Need more clothes than just a couple blouses. And no matter how many clothes I get, it ain't gonna make me want this baby.*

The door opened, and Nat held it as a white woman passed into the waiting room.

Sister Bess rose. "Della, meet my brother Nat"s wife Winnie. And this is Della, the young woman staying with me and Mother."

Nat shook her hand, and Winnie smiled. "We've been hearin' about you," she said.

"Sister Bess told me about you, too."

"How's Mother?" Nat asked.

"We're waiting on the doctor to come tell us."

"Miss Della."

Recognizing the voice, Della whirled around. "Mr. Huston!"

"Out of class you can call me Reggie." He smiled and hugged Sister Bess. "How are you, Aunt Bess?"

"Things could be better. I just don't know what I'm going to do with Mother."

A nurse walked up to them. "Mrs. Wagner, you can see your mother now. She's in Room 121."

Della followed them down the hall and into the room. A short, spectacled man put down a clipboard and reached out to shake Sister Bess's and Nat's hands.

"I'm Dr. Fortney." He turned to Sister Bess. "Your mother hasn't been getting enough fluids. Her electrolytes are low, and that unbalances her metabolism, which upsets her whole system. She'll be much better once we get some fluids into her. Probably can go home tomorrow."

"Thank the good Lord," Sister Bess said as the doctor left. She took her mother's hand. "We'll get you back up and running in a bit, Mother." Mother Carrie's eyes closed, but a slight smile crossed her lips.

"Well, that's a relief," Reggie said. "I have a class to teach, so better go. Miss Della, do you have class this evening?"

"Science and history."

"Come on, I'll give you a lift to school if that's okay with Aunt Bess."

"Can we stop at the house and get my things?" Della asked.

"Back door's unlocked," Sister Bess said. "I'll see you later."

"Let's go then," Reggie said, heading for the door.

Della glanced around, but everyone's attention was on Mother Carrie. She hurried to catch up with Reggie, already halfway down the hall.

CHAPTER 11

A Cause

Reggie held the car door open, and Della climbed in. *Strange. He's my teacher, Mr. Huston, and now he's taking me someplace like he's my friend. Ain't never had no teacher who was a friend.*

"What are you thinking?" he asked, looking down at her.

"Just things."

"What kind of things?"

"Just how I ain't never been in no teacher's car."

"I want to be your friend as well as your teacher. So starting with the teacher part of me, don't say *ain't.* Say *I've never been in a teacher's car*. Go ahead, say it."

"I've never been in a teacher's car," Della said, feeling a blush cross her cheeks.

"What is it you want from life, Miss Della?"

"I don't know, but I don't want no baby."

"Say *I don't want a baby.*"

"I don't want a baby."

"Better. So you're expecting a baby? And you don't want it? Why not?"

"Because…because I just don't."

"So what are you going to do?"

"Don't know. But nobody's gonna tell me what t'do."

"Let me know when you figure it out. Whatever you do, remember to rely on God and do His will."

"Rely on God? God don't help girls like me who've been ruined."

"Ruined? What do you mean?"

"You know. By Daddy."

"God doesn't look at people like that. Not anyone, and certainly not you. I want you to remember that."

"Maybe." She was anxious to be away from Reggie and his lectures, but he kept hammering.

What do you think people are wanting and striving for these days?"

"What?"

"Freedom. Freedom's the most important thing we can work for. All kinds of people are crying for freedom. White people, black people, women, people all over the world."

"Maybe."

"No maybe's. Your baby deserves freedom, too. Freedom to be born, to grow up and have a life, to make his own decisions. Think about that."

"Guess so. But what about my freedom?"

"You have the freedom to make a choice, to do what's right or what's wrong. And if you are a child of God, He will give you freedom from your past. He is a forgiving God." His eyes fixed on her as he came to a stop. "Well, here we are at Aunt Bess's house. Run and get your things."

Della hurried through the back yard gate and into the house. She grabbed her purse and her notebook and returned to the car. Opening the door, she leaned in. "Thanks for the ride. I want to walk to school. I have time."

"Okay, have it your way. Please think about the things we talked about, especially the part about God. I'll see you in class tomorrow."

"Bye." She closed the car door and turned her face down the familiar street toward school. No teenagers danced on the neighbor's porch. The heat reflected from the sidewalk in dizzying waves, stifling her, and she gasped for breath. *Heat's just like this baby inside me, keeping me down, not lettin' me fulfill my dreams.*

She climbed the school steps and went through the doors. Chris stood on the other side of the door, holding her abdomen and bent over in pain.

"Are you okay?" Della asked.

"No. I think the baby's coming. It's way too early!"

"I'll get help." Della raced into the office. "Call Chris's husband at the mine. She thinks her baby's coming!"

"Where is she?" the receptionist asked.

"Right inside the front door. Hurry!"

"I'm calling the police to take her. Mr. Baker might not make it in time.

The receptionist dialed, and Della ran back to Chris. "Your husband's coming. And the police. It's going to be okay."

"Oh, it hurts!" Chris slid to the floor, tears running down her face. "I don't want to lose this baby."

A police care pulled in front of the school. Two officers rushed in, and each took one of Chris's arms as they helped her out the door and into the police car. They drove from the parking lot, sirens blaring.

A man burst through the door. "Where's my wife?" he shouted.

"The police just took her to the hospital," Della said.

"Thanks." He ran out the door, and Della held it open and watched as his car sped onto the street.

She heaved a sigh as she entered the classroom and sat down. Science was almost as bad as math, but she found it more interesting. The teacher stood in the front of the class explaining magnetism, but her mind kept wandering to Chris. *Was her baby going to be okay? Would they keep her in the hospital?*

Social Studies Class came after Science. Of all her classes, she had the hardest time sitting through the boring lectures. This evening was different.

"Is our country perfect?" Mrs. Mason asked.

"Could be more freedoms," a student from the back shouted.

"Explain what you mean."

"There are a lot of inequalities in our land. Things that aren't fair."

"Like?"

"Discrimination based on color and race. We want more freedoms."

"What kind of freedoms?" Mrs. Mason asked.

"Freedom to go into restaurants and hotels that are only for whites," a young black man shouted.

"Equality in hiring practices," another student said.

"You're so right. All of you. The Civil Rights Act is a law that is long overdue. I confess that my great, great grandparents owned slaves, but they gave them their freedom after President Lincoln signed the Emancipation Proclamation."

After class Della hurried out the door. *I've always focused on my life, my problems. Daddy and Mama. I've seen those signs sayin' No Blacks Allowed in business windows downtown, but I never thought about 'em.*

As she was going down the high school steps, one of the young men from the class came up beside her.

"A group of us is going downtown to McDevitt's Restaurant," he said. "We're going to do a sit-in in front of his doorway. Want to come? Mr. Huston is taking us in his van."

"A sit-in? Why?"

"He has a sign in his window. *White patrons only.*"

"I better not, Jim," she said, remembering his name. "Too much homework."

"Okay. Next time."

A Volkswagen van pulled up in front of the school. White and pink stripes around its blue body complimented the pink hubcaps and white rims and nuts adorning the wheels. In the driver's seat sat Reggie Huston.

A gasp caught in a laugh escaped Della as ten or more students piled in. If this had been the car he offered her a ride in earlier, she wouldn't have ridden with him. She headed toward Sister Bess's house and was still laughing as she walked into the house.

"How is Mother Carrie?" she asked.

"Much better. Sleeping for now, and she's coming home tomorrow." She sighed. "Just don't know what we'll do with her when I start back to school. She can be so stubborn."

"I know." Della sat down on the couch beside her. "I saw something so funny. At least I think it's funny." She described Reggie's van.

"His father gave him that van. Reggie added the decorations." She smiled. "That boy has a sense of humor."

"He was taking a bunch of students down to McDevitt's Restaurant to protest the sign."

"The white patrons only sign?"

"Yes."

"It wouldn't surprise me if he went into politics someday. He not only participates in those rallies, but he sets them up. I'm afraid he's going to get hurt."

"I hope not. Why does he do it?"

"He fights for what he believes in. Freedoms for our people. You whites don't know what it's like to be denied everything you have a right to as a human being."

"Maybe I do know. I lived with Daddy, and I saw how he treated Mama. He did what he wanted to us."

"You understand our fight then," Sister Bess said, her voice softening. "But it's not over. Probably won't be for years."

"I'm still a captive."

"Why do you say that?"

"Look at me," Della said, patting her slightly protruding abdomen. "I don't want no baby, and I don't have no husband to help me."

"God will help you. He'll see you through this. You just have to trust Him."

"I'm going to work on an essay for English. It's about what I think freedom is."

"Good night, then. Tomorrow morning we'll go bring Mother home." She stood to leave, but the phone rang, and she picked up the receiver. "What? When? What are you going to do?"

"What happened, Sister Bess?"

Sister Bess put her finger to her lips and cupped her hand around the receiver. "I see. I expected something like this to happen. I'll keep him in my prayers."

"What happened? Keep who in your prayers?"

"Reggie. The Puttersville police showed up and took him and the other students who were sitting in front of McDevitt's Restaurant, preventing customers from entering, to the police station."

"Mr. Huston's in jail?"

"He would be if Nat and Winnie hadn't gone to sign for him." She sighed. "No, it's not over."

Della sat down at the dining room table and opened her notebook. *What does freedom mean to you?* She read the words and jotted down her ideas.

Freedom is not being Mama and having to lie in bed sick and listen to Daddy who won't buy you medicine. Not having someone tell me how to live my life. Not having to have a baby I can't take care of and don't want.

"These are the things freedom isn't. I need to think about what freedom is," she told herself. Her thoughts returned to what Mr. Huston said that morning, and she started a new list.

Freedom is thinking about my own life and doing what I want to do. Freedom is having a job and enough money to buy what I want, including a house. Freedom is being allowed to be me. Freedom is standing up for what I believe in even though others don't agree with me. Even though it gets me into trouble, she wrote, thinking of Reggie.

The door slammed, and she heard loud voices as Reggie and Nat came up the steps. *Sounds like quite an argument. If I dared, I'd go out there and tell Nat how brave his son is and how much I admire him.*

CHAPTER 12

Counting The Cost

The next morning Della awakened to a tapping on her bedroom door.

"Can you be ready for breakfast soon? The hospital called to say the doctor would be in at nine to release Mother."

Della looked at the clock on her nightstand. Seven o'clock. "Be there soon," she yelled, gathering clean clothes and heading to the bathroom. By seven-thirty she was spreading grape jelly on toast and eating scrambled eggs.

"Will we have time for me to visit someone at the hospital?" she asked.

"Who do you know there?"

"A classmate. Chris. When I got to school last night, she thought her baby was coming, but it's not due until September."

"I'm sure you'll have time while I get Mother ready."

Della picked up the dirty dishes, took them to the sink, and rinsed them, then followed Bess to the car.

"Winnie called while you were in the shower," Sister Bess said. "She is so relieved that Reggie didn't end up in jail."

"Does he have to go to court?"

"No. But the police warned him about disturbing the peace. They said next time it happened, he would spend time incarcerated. He would have a record."

They pulled into the hospital parking lot and found a space. Della opened the hospital door for Sister Bess, then stopped at the front desk. "What room is Chris Baker in?"

"One twenty-two," the receptionist said.

Della ran to catch up with Sister Bess. "I won't be long," she promised.

She peeked into the room. Chris was sitting up in bed reading a book, so Della knocked on the door frame.

"Come in," Chris said, putting the book down. "Thank you for helping me last night."

"Are you okay? The baby?"

"We're fine for now, but the doctor has confined me to bedrest for the rest of my pregnancy. If I had lost this baby..."

"Did the doctor say what happened? Was the baby coming?"

"I was in labor, but it stopped. My husband Dale will be here to get me at noon."

"I'm glad it stopped."

"Dale and I lost our first baby. A little boy. He came at four months, and he was not developed enough to survive."

"I'm sorry."

"I want this baby so, so much. I just *can't* lose it."

"Well, I told Sister Bess I wouldn't be long. May I call you and see how you're doing?"

"Yes, please do. We just moved, so we won't be at the same address in the phone book. We're at 136 Grant."

Aunt Marie's house! Della stifled a gasp and said, "Okay, I'll be seeing you." She left and crossed the hall to Room 121.

Sister Bess and Dr. Fortney stood in the doorway, talking in low voices, and Della couldn't go in, so she stood there listening.

"Don't know how I'm going to manage Mother. I have to go back to work in a little over a week."

"Have you checked with Pleasant Oaks Nursing Home to see if they have a room?"

"I don't want to put her there. She wouldn't go anyway."

"Let me know when you can't cope any longer. I'll help you find a place."

Della glanced at Sister Bess's face, set like a steel trap. *Sister Bess isn't putting Mother Carrie anywhere. I'm going to be stuck with her forever.* She followed her into the room where Mother sat in a wheelchair, her feet tucked into slippers. Della walked on one side of the wheelchair as a nurse pushed Mother Carrie down the hallway. When they reached the door to the outside, she ran ahead to hold the door open, then took the car keys from Sister Bess unlocked the car.

"Sure is nice to be going home," Mother said as they helped her into the front seat.

"I'm going to make sure you can stay at home," Sister Bess said. "Don't you worry."

"How's your friend? What'd you say her name is?" Sister Bess asked as soon as they pulled out of the parking lot.

"Chris. She has to stay in bed until her baby comes."

"That's too bad. I hope everything goes well with her."

"Me too. I don't see how she's gonna keep up with her classes."

"Right now, that baby's the most important thing, I'm sure.'

"It is." *Will I ever feel that way?*

They pulled into Sister Bess's driveway, and Della retrieved Mother's walker from the trunk and unfolded it. After helping Mother out of the car, they walked on each side of her as she made her way into the house.

"I'm hungry," Mother said.

"We can have an early lunch. How about some ham sandwiches?"

"No sandwiches," Mother said.

"Some chicken soup then?"

Mother sat at the table like a stone, staring at the wall in front of her. "No."

"Let's have a half sandwich and a cup of soup. Della, will you make the sandwiches?"

"Not eating any sandwich she makes."

"I'll make the sandwiches," Sister Bess said, a look of exasperation crossing her face.

Della rose and got the soup out of the refrigerator, put it in a pan, and put the pan on the stove to heat. When the soup was hot, she ladled it into bowls and took them to the table.

"Thanks," Sister Bess said.

Della nodded and listened to Sister Bess say grace. Mother's remark gnawed at her. *How can I take care of her? She hates me.* After eating, she washed the breakfast and lunch dishes while Sister Bess helped Mother into bed and read to her.

"I know you're hurt when she says things like that," Sister Bess said as she returned to the kitchen. "I'm sorry. I know it's hard, but don't dwell on it. She says things like that to me, too."

"Thanks. I have some math do to, and then I want to sew the buttons on my blouse. Then it'll be done."

Della finished the math homework.

"Sure you did those correctly?" Sister Bess asked.

She handed her notebook to Sister Bess and held her breath while she scanned the problems.

"All of these are correct," Sister Bess said. "I'm so proud of you. Do you mind if I look at your blouse?"

"Come see it." Della went into the bedroom and turned on the pole lamp beside the sewing machine. "I think it turned out well," she said, handing the blouse to Sister Bess.

"Hmm…seams are straight and even. You did a fantastic job on the collar and front facings. The hems on the bottom and on the sleeves look professional. This is great work for your first try."

"I like the buttons you gave me," Della said. "Never saw no buttons in the shape of flowers."

"I thought you would." Sister Bess smiled. "Try it on for me after you sew the buttons on."

"I will." Della found a needle and threaded it, doubling the thread and tying a knot at the end. It took her a little over an hour of painstaking work, pulling the thread first in one button hole then through another. Snipping the thread for the last time, she wiggled out of the blouse she was wearing and slipped her arms through the new one. Its delicate blue flowers flowed down her front. Running into the bathroom, she stood in front of the mirror hanging on the door and admired herself.

"Looks perfect," Sister Bess said when Della went into the living room and showed her. "You're quite the seamstress."

"I think I'll wear it to school," she said later while they ate dinner. "I haven't had anything new for a long time."

"Well, you can make yourself lots of new things now that you can sew. Della did a great job, Mother. Just like you'd taught her yourself," Sister Bess said loudly enough for her mother to hear. A warm feeling coursed through Della.

"After helping dry the dishes, Della said goodbye and left for school. *If only I knew where Mama is. If only I didn't have this baby. Then I'd be happy.*

She entered the school, still thinking about the way things had turned out. "God will be with you," Sister Bess had said. Maybe He was. She took her seat in the classroom and opened her notebook to her homework.

"My name is Mrs. Peterson, and I'll be your math teacher."

Della stared at the woman in the front of the classroom. She was stocky, had white hair, and a you-better-not-mess-with-me face. *Where was Reggie Huston?* She worried about that question all through math and English class. As soon as classes were over, she hurried out the door, eager to find out.

He stood in the hallway outside the classroom. When all the students had left, he entered, smiled at Mrs. Peterson, and said, "Just picking up my things."

Della waited. When he came out, she stepped in front of him. "Why aren't you our teacher, Mr. Huston?"

"Just Reggie," he said. "They let me go."

"Because you protested at the restaurant last night?"

"Could be. The powers that be don't like disturbances."

"What will you do?"

"Pappy said I had to find something. Maybe finish out the summer stocking shelves at the grocery store. Give you a lift to Aunt Bess's?"

"Sure, thanks." She walked beside him to his car and heaved a sigh of relief. It wasn't the van.

"You going to do any more protestin'?" she asked as they neared the house.

"There's a hotel over in Martinsburg that won't let us in. Might go over there with some friends this weekend."

Della didn't know what to say. *Does he want to be thrown in jail? Is he crazy?*

"Well, here you are. Tell Aunt Bess hi for me. I'd come in, but I have things to do."

"Thanks." She got out of the car and walked into the house.

"Sit down a minute," Sister Bess said from the couch. "We need to talk."

"Yes, ma'am. What about?"

"I'm sorry, really sorry, but you're going to have to move."

CHAPTER 13

Moving

"Move? Why? I thought I was doin' good." Tears stung Della's eyes. "Where will I go?"

"I have a younger sister in Charleston. Chloe never married. She has a slight disability, and she lost her job last week. Her landlord increased her rent. She has no place to go."

"What kind of disability?"

"When she was about a year old, she fell off a high porch. It damaged her left leg, broke the bone in several places. It didn't heal correctly, and she walks with a bad limp."

"Oh. So she couldn't work fast enough."

"I don't know if that was why she lost her job. Maybe. But Mother always loved Chloe and listened to her. She will be able to take care of her, and you know Mother won't listen to you."

"I understand. But I need a place to live."

"How would you like to live with Nat and Winnie?"

"With Nat and Winnie?"

"Yes. I called Winnie while you were at school and told her how well you did on your blouse. She has a stack of clothes that people have left for her to fix and alter. You can help her. You'd be great at hemming pants and dresses."

"But how would I get to school?"

"They live near the school, maybe closer than I do. It's not far from where your Aunt Marie lived."

"When will I move?"

"Let's see, this is Wednesday. Chloe is coming Saturday. You don't have school on Fridays, so how about this Friday?"

"Okay. I went to math class, and we have a new teacher. The school let Mr. Huston…I mean Reggie…"

"I know. Winnie told me. She and Nat have talked to him about getting a job. They're worried he'll fool around and not have any money for school this year. He wants to get his Master's Degree."

"Mama always said some guys have to sow their wild oats before they become a man. Aunt Marie's son Bill got into all sorts of trouble. Only he's doin' good now, workin' in the coal mine. Supposed to get married soon."

"Good. I don't believe Reggie is sowing wild oats. He's very serious about standing up for our peoples' rights."

"What if he gets put in jail again?"

"We'll deal with it. He's doing what he thinks he needs to do for our people."

The next day Della avoided Mother as much as she could. She ate her meals before Mother came to the kitchen, and from the living room she listened as Sister Bess coaxed her to eat.

"Just one more bite, Mother."

"No more. Take me back to bed."

"One more bite so I can tell Chloe how well you're doing when she comes."

Sister Bess is right. I don't have the patience to work with Mother. She probably won't let me help her. She was glad when dinner was over and she could do the dishes and escape to school.

Mrs. Brown asked for the students to turn in their essays on freedom. Della had written it twice, but she wasn't happy with it. Was it because she hadn't decided what freedom meant to her? Or was it that she felt guilty and ashamed at what she had written? She didn't know.

The class discussed Walt Whitman's poem "O Captain! My Captain!" Della had read it that day, but she hadn't connected it with the struggle for freedom. The words *fallen cold and dead* stuck in her mind. Would someone kill Reggie when he protested? Would that be his fate for leading his people? She slipped from the classroom as soon as Mrs. Brown dismissed the class.

Sister Bess was watching a television show when she arrived at the house. "Finally got Mother to sleep," she said. "She thought Chloe was coming tonight and wanted to wait up on her."

Della laid her things down on the couch. "I'm sorry. Can I get you something? Some coffee?"

"No, thanks. I'm beat, and I'm going to bed. Winnie will come pick you up around ten tomorrow morning. Can you be ready by then?"

"I think so. I have an appointment with Mr. Handly at one-thirty, so that should be fine."

"Good night, then."

Della headed for her bedroom, stepped inside, and pulled her worn suitcase out from under the bed. She sighed as she picked it up and set it on the bed. "Mama, you told me to go, and now Sister Bess told me to go, and I don't have no place to call home," she whispered. "Are you in heaven lookin' down and helpin' me?" Keeping an outfit for Friday, she put her clean clothes in the suitcase and tossed her dirty clothes in a bag.

After brushing her teeth and washing her face, she crawled into bed. She fell asleep and dreamed of Mama reaching out to her and beckoning her. "It'll be okay, Della," she whispered over and over.

Della woke with a start. Six-thirty. Opening the door, she heard singing coming from the kitchen, and she padded down the hallway and down the stairs.

"Hurry up and get ready for breakfast. Bess is cooking bacon and eggs," Mother said, a smile spreading across her face. "We're having a feast."

Well! For the first time in two months, Della felt hungry for breakfast. After taking a quick shower and dressing, she walked into the kitchen as Sister Bess placed the food on the table.

"Good morning, Della. Hungry?"

"I am." She helped herself to the eggs and bacon.

"Chloe's coming tomorrow," Mother said, eating one bite after another. She drank half her orange juice. "She'll be here soon."

"Yes, Mother," Sister Bess said. "And Winnie will be here this morning to get Della. Della's going to live with Nat and Winnie."

"And Chloe's coming to live with us," Mother said. "Oh, I'm so happy."

Della did the dishes while Sister Bess helped Mother with her bath, then finished her packing.

Sister Bess came into her bedroom. "Mother's watching her television show. Why don't you go through this box of material with me? You might see some material you want."

Della picked out a piece with a red, blue, and white patchwork pattern and another with orange and yellow flowers on a brown background. "Thanks for everything you've done for me," she said. "You've been like my mother, and I don't know how to repay you."

"Help someone else when you can," she said, not looking up. "Besides, it's not like you're leaving. You'll be living with family. We'll see you often at church and when we visit."

Della hugged her. "Still, you took a big risk on me."

"Don't forget your pattern." Sister Bess tucked it into the bag of material. "I know you'll be busy, but I expect to see you wearing these in the next month or so."

"You will. Thanks."

"Bess!" Mother yelled. "Winnie's here!"

"Well, guess it's time." Sister Bess picked up the bag of material. "Don't forget that God loves you."

"I won't." Della grabbed her suitcase and followed Sister Bess into the living room. Winnie stood in the middle of the living room, her black hair cut just to the bottom of her ears with kinky curls that bushed outward. She wore blue jeans rolled halfway up to her knees and a worn tee shirt.

"Hi Della, how are you?" Winnie asked, putting her arms around her.

"Fine, Winnie. Thanks for havin' me."

"Can you cook?"

"Yes."

"Clean house and do laundry?"

"Yes."

"Then you'll fit right in." She laughed, a long and loud cackle.

Startled, Della looked at Sister Bess, who handed her the bag of material. "I'll do my best," she said. She followed Winnie out the door.

"Put your things in the back seat. You can sit up front."

Della slid her suitcase onto the back seat and laid the bag on top of it, then climbed into the front seat.

"Be nice havin' some help around the house," Winnie said.

"I can help. Can you show me the way to the school? I have an appointment this afternoon, and I take classes Monday through Thursday evenings to get my GED."

"Bess told me. Always good for a woman to have an education. You'll need a job so you can raise your kid. Only one thing you have to remember."

"What?"

"No hanky-panky between you and Reggie. You don't go in his room, and he won't be comin' in yours. You can be friends, and that's all. Understand what I mean?"

Della blushed. "Yes, ma'am. Does Reggie have any brothers or sisters?"

"Not really." Winnie's lips pursed, and she turned away from Della. "Let's get home."

"Not really?" What kind of an answer is that? Della didn't dare ask. She looked out the window as they passed the school, rounded the corner, drove four blocks, and turned onto Grant Street. "That house used to belong to my Aunt Marie." She pointed. "My friend Chris and her husband bought it. I want to visit them sometime."

"Okay." Winnie's face was still flustered.

They turned right onto Maple Avenue and stopped at a two-story brick house. Gathering her suitcase and bag, Della got out and climbed eight steps leading to the porch.

Winnie opened the door, and they entered into a small foyer with stairs on the other side.

"Your bedroom is upstairs," Winnie said, starting up the steps. "You'll have to share a bathroom with Reggie, but he probably won't be here much."

"That's okay."

"Here's your room," Winnie said, opening a door.

Della walked into the room. A single bed topped by a patchwork quilt sat in one corner of the room, and a highboy dresser stood against the opposite wall. On the wall across from the door was a small closet and an open window, its blue gingham curtain billowing into the room. She put her things in the closet.

"This room gets a good breeze in the summer," Winnie said. "Come on down, and I'll show you the rest of the house. That's Reggie's room," she said as they passed a door. "When he's home. And our bedroom and bath are at the end of the hall."

"Where do you sew?" Della asked as she followed her down the stairs, through the living room, and into a combined dining room with a kitchen.

"Nat turned the garage into a sewing room for me," she said, opening a door on the far side of the kitchen. "Go ahead, turn on the light and look in."

"How nice," Della said as she peeked in at the tan carpet and oak paneled walls. Oak shelves filled with boxes covered one side of the room, and on the other side, two large sewing machine cabinets separated a table piled with what looked like various mending projects. A washer and dryer sat on the end where the garage door would have been.

"I hope I get a chance to help with some of that," Della said.

"Don't worry. You'll get your turn."

"Mom! Mom, where are you?"

Reggie bounded through the kitchen. "Where's my new blue jeans? And my tan shirt?"

"When did you last do your laundry?" Winnie asked, turning around to her son. "And where are you goin'?"

"To Martinsburg. Junior and I are leaving tomorrow morning."

"Why?"

"Lead a sit-in. There's a hotel there won't let black people stay."

"You'll pay your own expenses. And remember what we told you. Don't expect me and your dad to come bail you out of jail."

CHAPTER 14

Much To Learn

That Friday evening Della took her place at the dinner table as Nat pushed himself up from his chair in the living room and limped in to sit at the end of the table. She kept her eyes on him while he thanked God for the food. He paused only a second to reach into his worn jean pocket for his handkerchief to wipe the sweat from his brow before he said, "Amen."

"Reggie, how'd your job hunt go today?" He ladled his plate full of beans and ham from the large dish in front of him and crumbled up a piece of corn bread into them. "Where did you apply?" he asked, raising his eyes to his son.

"Stopped in at Dobbs's Food Market. They don't have any openings. At least not for me."

"And what does that mean?"

"Just that. I told them I'd do anything. They said no openings."

"Did you check in with the school?"

"Yes. They gave me an application. Said they might have an opening once school starts. I need a job now, not when school starts."

"You be sure and get the completed application back to them early Monday just in case. Jobs don't stay open for long."

"I know that. I'll get it turned in. Tomorrow Junior and I are driving to Martinsburg, leaving early. Should be back Sunday afternoon. I'll work on it then."

Nat laid down his fork and stared at his son in silence. "Stay out of trouble," he said, then turned to Della. "And how are your classes goin'?"

"Me?" Della looked down at her plate.

"You the only one takin' classes, right?" His voice was stern, but a half smile lingered on his lips.

"Fine, Mr. Huston. Except for math." She glanced at Reggie, wishing she hadn't said it. "I mean the new teacher don't explain it the way you did, Mr. Huston."

"Please, Della, call me Reggie. Or Reginald. Or even Reg. Anything but Mr. Huston. I'll help you with it when I get back, okay?"

"Thanks."

"I hear Aunt Chloe's coming tomorrow," Reggie said. "Haven't seen her for a while."

"How about let's havin' them over for a chicken barbeque tomorrow evening, Hon?" Nat smiled at Winnie. "We can roast some potatoes, have a salad, and well, you might make one of your famous tubs of strawberry ice cream."

"Sounds good. 'Specially now that Della's here to help wash up all those dishes," she said, winking at him. "Well, I got work to do. Della, would you mind cleanin' up?" She stood and disappeared into the sewing room.

"I have to finish packing." Reggie said, following her into the sewing room. He returned with an arm load of clothes and headed up the stairs.

"I'm going to work in the yard," Nat said. "Thank you for helpin' Winnie."

Della rummaged through cabinet drawers looking for containers for the leftovers. *Just got used to Sister Bess's kitchen, and now I got to hunt for things here.* She found bowls and lids and put the food in the refrigerator, then filled the sink up with water for the dishes. After washing the dishes, she wiped the table and stove and counter tops. When she finished, she sat down in the living room and picked up the newspaper.

"Della."

All she wanted to do was rest a few minutes, but she got up and made her way to the sewing room and opened the door. "Yes, Winnie?"

"Finished with the dishes?"

"Yes."

"Good. Come over here and have a seat so I can show you somethin'." She pulled a box from one of the shelves and opened it. "Look here."

Della sat down and watched as Winnie took out packages wrapped in pink and blue tissue paper.

She handed a pink package to Della. "Open it."

Untying the thin white ribbon and pushing the paper back, Della gasped at a tiny pink dress. Dainty red flowers danced on the material. Thin white lace adorned the collar, sleeves, and hem. "It's beautiful, just beautiful," she said. "Where did you get it?"

"I made it. Open the next one."

Della lifted a blue package from the box and undid the wrapping. Inside were a tiny blue gingham shirt and a matching blue pair of shorts. The shirt collar and a pocket on the shorts sported embroidered stars. "Oh, so cute. Who are they for?"

"I'm starting a line of baby clothes. So far I've made five dresses and four outfits for boys. After we get caught up on the mendin', I'll let you help me."

"I'd love to help."

"Speaking of mendin', Mrs. Morris brought over five pairs of her husband's dress pants to hem. She pinned them up to the proper length. Would you like to do them?"

"You trust me?"

"Sure. Bess showed me your blouse. I get fifty cents for each. I'll give you twenty cents a pair. That okay?"

"I can do it."

"I know you can. Just be careful and don't let the stitchin' show through on the outside of the material."

"When do I start?"

"No time like the present. The iron and ironing board are over there. I stand the board up there and plug it in at that outlet," she said, pointing.

"My first job to earn money," Della said, putting the board up. Picking up the top pair of pants, she laid it out on the ironing board and studied the hems. "I need to undo these hems, right?"

"Just clip the thread and pull it out. I think you can cut the length off here where the old hem is folded up. You'll have to fold it under, press it down, then fold and press down again to make the hem. Here's the scissors and a ruler. Be sure to measure each fold."

"I see." After Della finished each step, she showed her work to Winnie. Once the pant legs were cut to the proper length and the hem pressed in, she sewed them with tiny stitches that did not show through on the front side of the pants leg. She gave them a final pressing and unplugged the iron.

"Are you finished? May I see?" Winnie asked. Della gave her the trousers, and she held the hem up to the light and studied it. "Couldn't have done it any better myself."

"Took me over an hour."

"That's okay. Take your time and do it right."

"I'll pay you tomorrow," Winnie said. "I need to finish this dress this weekend."

"I'd like to go to my room and work on some homework, it that's okay with you."

"Sure, go ahead.'

Della passed Reggie's room on the way to hers. Was he in there? She didn't hear him. Had he gone out while she was in the sewing room? She sat down on her bed and opened her math book to the page with five word problems and scowled. After reading the first problem, she read it again, then made a stab at solving it. Her answer had to be wrong. *I should go knock on Reggie's door and ask him. No, I can't do that. He said he would help me Sunday*. Sighing, she closed her notebook.

Strange how she missed Sister Bess's house and the pattern of daily living she had fallen into while there. Sister Bess would have helped her with the math, and she wouldn't have piled housework on her. But then, Sister Bess didn't pay her for doing anything. Not that she expected her to. Here she could earn money and save it.

The next morning, Winnie made no mention of the twenty cents she owed her. Reggie didn't eat breakfast with them. Winnie disappeared into the sewing room, and Della did the breakfast dishes without being asked.

"Have to get this dress done before Bess, Chloe, and Mother get here," Winnie said when Della joined her. "I'm making it for Chloe. She doesn't have much."

"When will they be here?"

"I told Bess six o'clock. Nat went to the store for chicken and potatoes. I'm glad I have you to help with dinner."

"I'm a great potato peeler."

"Good. In the meantime, why don't you hem another pair of pants? We can work on dinner this afternoon."

"Okay." Della set up the ironing board and repeated the steps she had taken the night before. By the time she finished, it was nearing lunch time. Nat returned with the groceries, they ate a quick sandwich, and Winnie again buried herself in her sewing.

"You ever cut up a chicken?" Nat asked.

"No."

"What? Your mammy never showed you how?"

"No." *Didn't have enough money for buyin' chicken.*

"I'll show you how."

Della watched as he unwrapped the large brown package holding three whole chickens. His large hands skillfully severed the wings, cut off the legs where they attached to the bodies of the birds, cut lengthwise between the ribs to separate the back from the breast, and bent the breast to cut between the wishbone and the neck.

"Here," he said, handing her the knife. "Let's see you do one."

"Me? I can't."

"I'll do them this time, and you just watch. Next time it'll be your turn. You learn by doin'."

Della stood there, glad she didn't have to touch the bumpy chicken skin and the bones oozing blood where they were cut. *Mama didn't teach me this. But she couldn't.*

"I'm goin' out and start up the grill. Chicken needs to be cooked long and low." He swung a sack of potatoes onto the counter. "Why don't you give these a good scrubbin'? No need to peel them. I'll cook 'em on the grill."

"What else are we havin' for dinner?" she asked Winnie as she stepped into the sewing room.

"Bess is bringin' a peach cobbler. I made a bean salad last night. Iced tea. And potatoes and chicken. That should do." She held the blue flowered dress up. "What do you think?"

"If Chloe doesn't like it, I'll wear it. I love these tiny buttons down the front." She traced the lace on the bodice. "It's beautiful."

"Winnie! Winnie!" Nat's voice boomed through the house. He threw open the sewing room door. "Reggie's hurt! Come quick!"

CHAPTER 15

Beat Up

"What happened?" Winnie burst through the sewing room door as Nat and Junior half carried, half dragged Reggie up the steps leading to the house. She held the front door open, eyes filled with terror at the sight of her son.

Della stepped out of the way so they could lie Reggie on the sofa. She barely recognized him. His face was bruised and puffy, and a two-inch vertical cut split his forehead. Another gash streaked across one cheek, and his eyes were swollen shut.

"We got there 'bout eleven," Junior said. "Some of our friends met us. We stopped for something to eat at the restaurant down the street and heard talk about some trouble last night at the hotel. We didn't want no trouble, so after we ate, we took it real easy, just sorta sauntered over. They were waiting."

"Who?" Nat demanded.

"A gang of white thugs. The redneck type. Hotel must've hired 'em to stand guard. They lit into us before we got there. Probably ten or twelve of 'em. We didn't stand a chance."

"Weren't there any police around?" Nat asked.

"Nope. We yelled for help, but no one came. Reg got the worst of it. We fought 'em as hard as we could, but they had us outnumbered two to one. I managed to get Reg in the van, and we all hightailed it outta there."

Della watched as Winnie dabbed at Reggie's face with a wet wash cloth while Nat felt his body. Reggie groaned when he touched his ribs.

"Think he has a broken rib or two," Nat said. "I'm going to wrap him. Let's get some ice for his face."

Della ran to the kitchen, grabbed a dish towel, and emptied an ice cube tray into it. Tying it shut by gathering the edges and twisting a rubber band around them, she took the ice bag to Nat.

"Where'd you learn how to do that?" Junior asked.

"Just life," she said, shrugging. *Daddy's beatings, that's how.* She shivered, remembering.

"We'll have to cancel our barbeque," Nat said. "I have to take care of Reggie."

"I know how to barbeque," Junior said. "Just show me what you want me to cook."

"Thanks," Nat said. "I got the fire going."

"The chicken's in here," Della said, leading him into the kitchen and handing him the pan of cut-up pieces. "I'll bring the potatoes."

They passed through the back door into the yard. Della watched as Junior arranged the chicken onto the homemade grill and put the potatoes around the meat.

"I'm Della," she said when he closed the lid.

"I know. Reg told me 'bout you."

"He did? What'd he say?"

"Just that you were staying with them and helping his mom. We had other things to talk 'bout." He got up and adjusted the grill fire. "Got to keep it low so the chicken don't burn."

"How long you and Reggie been friends?"

"Since we were little. I live down the street. We went to the same church and schools from grade school through high school."

She studied him. *So different from Reggie. So black. So sure of himself. At ease with me.* "I think I'll go in and check on Reggie."

"Sure, go ahead."

Della walked into the living room as Winnie hung up the phone.

"Mother Carrie wants to come," she said, "but Bess thinks we should cancel and take Reggie to the doctor."

"I took medical emergency classes as part of my job training, remember?" Nat said. "Ain't nothin' a doctor would do that I can't. Besides, you know Mother gets what Mother wants." Reggie groaned as Nat slipped his hand under his back and pulled the strip of sheet to the other side. Every time he went under Reggie, pain filled the young man's face.

"My poor baby, what'd they do to you?" Winnie moved the ice bag to the other cheek. "Still think these cuts need some stitches."

"You're probably right, but I don't want to move him anymore 'n I have to."

"I'm callin' Dr. Bob and see if he'll come over." She picked up the phone and dialed. "He'll be here in a bit."

Della lingered in the dining room when Dr. Bob came, but when Reggie screamed, she ran into the back yard with her hands over her ears. "They're hurtin' him. Can't stand to hear it."

"How're they hurtin' him?" Junior stopped turning the chicken pieces over. "What're they doin'?"

"Sewin' up his forehead." Della shuddered. "Oh, I can't stand it!"

"Go back in so you can tell me what the doctor says."

"Don't want to watch."

"Then you take care of this chicken. I'll go."

What if I burn the chicken? "I'm goin."

"Good job wrapping him," Dr. Bob said. "I'll give him a penicillin shot to ward off infection." He pulled Reggie's eyelids up and shined a small flashlight into his eyes. "I think he suffered a concussion. Watch him tonight."

"What're we watchin' for?" Nat followed him out the door.

Della went back outside and told Junior what the doctor said. "I'm gonna help take care of him so Winnie can sew.

"He's tough. Can take care of himself," Junior said, not looking up from the grill.

"Della! Della, where are you?"

"Right here, Winnie." She hurried into the kitchen.

"Let's get the rest of the food prepared and set the table. Can you help me get this leaf into the table?"

"Mother Carrie, Bess, and Chloe are here," Nat announced from the living room. He opened the door. "Come in."

Della watched as Mother Carrie stopped inside the door. "Is that Reggie? What happened to Reggie?"

"Some thugs in Martinsburg beat him up." Nat took the ice bag from Reggie's face and tossed it to Della. "More ice."

"In Martinsburg?" Chloe asked. "What was he doin' over there?"

"Something about doin' a sit-in at a hotel not lettin' our people stay there," Nat said. "He and his friends never had a chance."

"They treat us bad no matter what we do," Chloe said. "Lost my job because they wanted to hire some young white thing."

"Might've been 'cause she was young and not crippled," Nat said, eyeing Chloe. He turned toward Della. "You gonna get that ice or not?"

Startled, Della jumped and ran to the kitchen as Junior carried a heaping platter of steaming chicken through the back door.

"You're staying for dinner," Winnie said. "Sit down here at the table."

"Yes, ma'am." A smile flashed across Junior's face as he took his place on the back side of the table.

Della took her place beside him, and the others gathered around and reached for each other's hands. She held out her hand toward Junior, but he had his eyes closed and his head bowed.

"God knows how this old world turns," Nat declared after giving thanks. "He sees what goes on. I don't understand why there's so much hate when we all have the same Father." He looked up as Winnie rose from her chair. "Where you goin'?"

"See if Reggie can eat a few bites." She went into the living room and returned. "He's asleep. We'll save him some for later."

"Della, what do you think about all this? Do you think it's right for people to treat others like they treat us?" Chloe asked.

"What?" Della put her chicken leg down and stared at Chloe, whose right eye squinted shut, then opened, then shut. "Were you talkin' to me?"

"I say you think it's right for people to treat us like they do?" Chloe asked.

"There's lots of things not fair," Della said. "Don't have to be black to get the short end of the stick."

"Della's suffered her share," Sister Bess said. "She ain't had it easy."

"Who wants some of Bess's peach cobbler?" Winnie asked, rising and gathering plates.

Della picked up hers, Junior's, and Nat's and followed her to the sink. She filled it with hot soapy water and slid the dishes and eating utensils in. "Why'd Chloe ask me that?" she whispered.

"Don't pay no mind to Chloe. She means well, but sometimes she don't think before she says things."

Della returned to the table and tasted the cobbler in her bowl. Savoring its richness, she glanced around at the others and smiled.

"Pretty good stuff, right?" Nat asked.

"Mama never made nothin' this good," Della said. "Course Mama never had no peaches."

"Chloe helped make it," Sister Bess said.

"Thanks," Della said, smiling at Chloe. "It's delicious."

"Ain't nothin' workin' ten years in a restaurant didn't teach me," Chloe said. "I think—"

A loud knocking sounded at the front door, and Nat rose to answer it.

"We're looking for Reginald Huston and Junior Johnson," Della heard. "We're sheriffs from Berkeley County."

"What's the problem, officers?"

Junior rose from the table and slipped out the back door.

"Seems like them niggers went to Martinsburg and made a lot of trouble. Do you know where they are?"

"Don't know where Junior is, but my son Reginald is inside."

"We need to talk to him." One officer opened the door and shoved Nat out of his way, and the other officer followed him inside.

"Reginald's right there," Nat said, pointing to the sofa. "He ain't in any way for you to talk to. Wasn't doin' anything, and a bunch of thugs beat him up. They're the ones you need to talk to."

Reggie turned his head and moaned, but his eyes never opened.

"You can go talk to Dr. Bob if you want to. He said my son suffered a concussion. I've a good mind to hire a lawyer and go after the whole Martinsburg Police Department for lettin' them do this." Nat glared at them. "You too. You had no right pushin' your way into my house. Get out, both of you!"

One of the officers scowled at Nat and started to say something, but the other jerked his head toward the door. "Let's go."

Nat slammed the door shut. "They better stay in Martinsburg if they know what's good for 'em," he muttered. He looked down at Reggie and sighed. "And they better leave Junior be."

CHAPTER 16

No Goodbye

"This is the second Sunday you've not gone to church." Winnie stood in the dining room, hands on her hips, and glared at Della. "I won't have no heathens in this house."

"Reggie might need some help. I'll go next Sunday."

"I'll be okay for a couple hours. Go on, church is important." Reggie sipped his coffee and winced.

"See, even raisin' your arm hurts. What if you fall?" Della asked.

"I'm not going to fall. But some company would be nice."

"All right, have it your way. But I'll turn you both out if you're not in church next Sunday. Della, since you're stayin' home, make some meatloaf for lunch and peal those potatoes and put them on to boil." Winnie stalked to the bottom of the stairs. "Nat, get your body down here before I go off and leave you!"

"Yes, I'm comin'." He appeared at the top of the stairs, tie in hand.

"Let me help with that tie."

"Here I am." He handed her the tie and waited while she put it around his neck and knotted it.

"Let's go. Remember you two. Next week you're goin' to church," Winnie said as Nat opened the door for her.

"You really should have gone," Reggie said. He limped into the living room and sat down on the sofa. "I'm hurting, but I can take care of myself."

"Church don't mean so much to me as bein' here with you. Besides, there's somethin' I need to talk to you about."

"What's that?"

"I done hemmed five pairs of pants for your mama and five skirts. She promised me twenty cents each, and she ain't paid me a cent."

"I wouldn't bring it up."

"Why not? Ain't she gonna keep her promises or not?"

"Della." Reggie's brow furrowed. "If you don't learn to quit saying *ain't,* I'm not going to talk to you."

"Okay. But is she gonna pay me?"

Reggie stared out the window for what seemed to Della forever. "Well? Is she gonna pay me?" she demanded.

"I don't know. Maybe she figures you live and eat here. Maybe she'll pay your doctor bills instead. I wouldn't mention it to her if I were you."

He makes sense. "But I need the money. How am I gonna care for a baby without no money?"

"Without any money. Say it."

"Without any money," she muttered.

"Sounds like you should be in church learning how to trust in God's care." He leaned forward and laughed. "That's what Mammy would say. And don't argue with her. Won't do you a bit of good."

"I don't care what she'd say." Della held back the tears gathering in her eyes. *He's just as stubborn as his mama. And I ain't stayin' here to listen to him.* She rose to go to her room and was at the bottom of the stairs when the door burst open.

"Junior Johnson, what are you doing here?" Reggie asked. "What will the preacher think if his son is not in the audience?"

"Don't matter." Panting, Junior plopped into the nearest chair. "I..I...been drafted," he said between breaths. "I have to report next week."

"I'm sorry," Reggie said. "Get out of it. There's ways."

"How? What am I supposed to do, say I won't go?"

"I heard about a guy who paid a doctor lots of money to say he was disabled."

"I don't believe in lyin'. And I don't believe in war." He rose and paced back and forth. "I'm a conscientious objector. God called us for peace, not killin' people."

"Get married. Married people don't have to go."

"Don't even have a girlfriend."

"Register to go to college. They don't draft people in school. But guess it's too late for that."

"Don't have the money. Can you loan me some?"

"Junior, I have a little saved. But I need it for school myself."

"Come on, man. I need it to get me to Canada."

"Canada? You going to Canada?"

"Yeah. My pappy's got a preacher friend there, said he'd take me in."

"Where is *there*? What will you do?"

Junior sat down and placed his hands on his knees. "British Columbia. Pappy's friend lives in Victoria. I talked to him on the phone Friday, and he said he'd be glad to let me stay with him and his wife until I can get on my feet. He works part-time cuttin' timber, and he said they're needin' help. I'm strong. I can do it."

"I don't want you to go."

"Don't have a choice. I go to Canada, or they send me to Viet Nam, and I get hurt or killed. Or have to shoot someone. I can't do it, no matter what they do to me."

"When will you go?"

"Today. Car's outside, packed with my things."

"What does your pappy think?"

"He don't know."

"You can't just go off without telling your mammy and pappy."

"You tell them."

"That's not right. You should be the one to tell them. They'd want to hear it from you."

"It'd just make leavin' harder. You're my best friend. You have to tell them for me."

"If I have to, I have to. But they won't be happy. And I don't think they'll understand."

"Maybe not. But I got to go, need to be out of Puttersville before church is over. You goin' to loan me some money or not?"

Reggie reached into his pocket and pulled out his wallet. "Just got my last pay from teaching. Here's fifty dollars. That's all I have."

"Thanks, man. I'll pay it back soon as I can. Hopefully, by the time you start school in September."

"When will you come home?"

"Don't know."

Reggie pushed his body to a standing position with his hands and wrapped his arms around Junior. "Write me, brother. I'll keep you in my prayers."

"I'll write. Bye, now. You too, Della." He waved and hurried through the door.

Reggie pushed back the curtain and watched Junior get into his car. "Hope that old jalopy makes it to Canada." He stood, gazing out the window long after Junior's car was out of sight.

Della hadn't moved since she reached the bottom of the staircase. *How quickly five minutes can change our lives. Like the time Mama told me to go. Like when I saw Sister Bess and she took me in. Like when I learned I'm gonna be a mama.* She glanced at Reggie, sitting on the couch again, his head bowed, his face filled with pain.

He looked up at her. "Would you like to hear some music?"

She nodded.

"Okay, I'll put some on." He rose and walked to the record player in its case, which he opened, then rummaged through a stack of records. Choosing one, he laid it on the turntable.

"Who's that?" Della asked.

"Do you like Ray Charles? Listen to his song 'You Don't Know Me' and tell me what you think."

"Never heard of him."

Reggie lowered the arm of the record player, and a soulful tune filled the room.

Della listened intently at the sad tale of a lover trying to be understood. The man watched and cried as his lover walked away.

Then another song, "Georgia on My Mind," about a man remembering his true love, his arms reaching out to her, as he worked his way back to her in Georgia.

Reggie sat on the sofa, his head leaning back against the cushions, tears streaming down his cheeks. "Don't know when I'll see him again," he whispered. "Maybe never."

"He'll be back," she said. "This is home."

"If he can come home. He's now a fugitive, hiding from the United States government. If he comes home and gets caught, they'll probably lock him up."

"I can never go home. No home to go back to. Home is where Mama is, and she's probably dead."

"I think we'll find her. Don't give up hope."

Della sat down beside Reggie and leaned her head back against the cushions. "I can't believe Junior didn't even tell his mama and daddy goodbye."

"I know. They'll be heart broken. I don't want to do it."

The music stopped. Reggie walked to the record player and lifted the record off the turn table. As he slid it into its case, the door opened, and Winnie walked in.

"Junior wasn't at church today," she announced. "His parents didn't know why, but he never showed."

"I know," Reggie said. "He was here."

"He was here?" Nat asked as he walked through the door. "Why was he here?"

"To tell me he's going to Canada to live. He got drafted."

Winnie's jaw dropped. "Without tellin' his parents? He can't do that."

"I guess he can." Nat sat down beside Della and stared at the floor. "He did."

"We've got to tell them." Winnie ran to the phone and picked up the receiver.

"Don't call," Reggie said. "He asked me to tell them."

"Come on. Let's go tell'em." Nat headed out the door.

Reggie and Winnie walked to the door. As Reggie reached for the doorknob, he turned to Della. "Come with us. Maybe you can remember what he said better than I can."

"Wish I'd been here," Nat said. "I would have stopped him. I wouldn't have let him out that door until he told his parents."

"I don't think so, Pappy. I tried to get him to stay, but he was determined. I hope he makes it okay."

"I hope he doesn't make it at all." Nat stepped on the clutch as he shifted into third gear, then gunned the engine. "If we get there in time, maybe Brother Johnson can catch up to his car and stop him."

They pulled into the Johnson's driveway. Nat and Winnie were knocking on their door by the time Della and Reggie were out of the car.

"We know where Junior is," Della heard Nat say. "On his way to Canada. He stopped and told Reggie this morning before leavin'."

Sister Johnson joined her husband outside their door. "Hurry, Ted! Maybe we can catch him if we go right now."

"What time did he leave?" Ted asked.

"Must have been around ten-thirty. I doubt you can catch him by now."

Sister Johnson covered her face with her hands and wailed, and Brother Johnson wrapped his arm around her shoulders.

"It'll be okay, Thea. God will take care of him. I'm sure he'll write us."

"He didn't even tell us," sobbed Sister Johnson. "He never said goodbye."

CHAPTER 17

Dreams

"I hate math." Della threw her books on the table and sat down. "I studied so hard for that test." She put her elbows on the table and rested her head in her hands.

"What test?"

She jumped. "I didn't know you were here, Reggie."

"Show me the test." He straddled the chair next to hers.

"I didn't do well on it. And I really studied. I was sure I could pass it." She opened her math book and found the folded paper. "See, a sixty-five percent."

"Well, it could have been worse. You almost passed."

"I wouldn't have been happy with a seventy, either. That's barely passing. That new teacher just don't explain it like you did."

"These problems are about percentages," he said, scanning the test. "How come you understood fractions and percentages when I was there, but you don't now?"

"Don't know. Numbers just seem different on paper."

"If I gave you half a cookie, what percent of that cookie would half be?"

"Half."

"How do you write one-half with numbers?"

She looked at the paper and shrugged.

"Well, if I give you half a cookie, how many parts does it take to make a whole cookie?"

"Two."

"So here's how you write just one of them." He wrote the number 1 on her paper and drew a line under it and wrote a 2. "We write a 1 on the top because that's how many parts we're talking about. Then we write a 2 on the bottom because that's how many parts there are in all. We can read this 1 out of 2 equal parts. That's half. Get it?"

"Yes."

"So what percent is half?"

She looked up at him. "Fifty?"

"Yes. So if I broke the cookie into four parts and gave you one part, how would you write that?"

"One over four."

"And how would you say that?"

"One out of four."

"Yes. But usually, we say one-fourth. Let's go over the basic fractions." He wrote them on her paper with the percentages after them and had her explain each one. When they reached 9/10, he said. "You got way more of that cookie than I did."

"I can't believe I couldn't do this," she said, laughing. Her blue eyes met his brown eyes, and for an instant, she held his gaze before looking away. *He's so nice. I wish we could be more than friends.*

"Okay, Miss Della, I want you to correct every problem you missed. I'll be back to check your answers."

He left, and she picked up her pencil and started working. The numbers were larger, but it didn't matter. *I understand what they mean, and that makes all the difference.* As she finished, Reggie walked into the room.

"Did you solve them?" He picked up her paper and perused it. "Every problem correct. You just lack self-confidence."

"And some good teachin'," she said, blushing.

"Look what I found." He sat down and laid a newspaper page in front of her. "Look here." He pointed to a two by three inch square on the page.

Puttersville School District is looking for a math teacher for middle school students. Must be certified and have experience teaching basic math skills. Apply by Wednesday. Interviews will be Thursday and Friday.

"That's my job. I'm going down there right now and get an application. Just as soon as I get some decent clothes on."

"You're so smart. You'll get it," she said as he disappeared up the stairs.

Winnie stuck her head out the sewing room door. "Della, can you come hem a skirt for me? I've got to finish a dress, and Sister Johnson will be here tonight to get her skirt."

"Be right there." *Will I ever get paid?*

"After lunch, I need you to help with dinner," Winnie said when Della handed her the finished skirt. "Make the meatloaf and potatoes you didn't make yesterday."

"Yes, ma'am. I can do that. I want to go see my friend Chris right after lunch. I'll be back in time to do dinner."

"That's okay, but remember it has to be ready at six."

"It will be. I promise."

"I'd love to see you," Chris said when Della called after lunch. "It gets lonely when my hubby's at work."

Twenty minutes after doing the few dishes from lunch Della made her way up the walk to what used to be Aunt Marie's front porch and rang the doorbell.

"Come in, the door's open."

Inside, Chris stretched out on a reclining chair. Della took her hand. "It's great seein' you," she said. "How are you feelin'?"

"Pretty well. Except my doctor is worried about my baby's health. He's keeping a close eye on things."

"When is your baby comin'?"

"In two to three weeks, if I can hold out that long. Other than that, I'm bored. I have the television, but there's nothing on during the day. I have books to read. It's hard to lie here and let Dale do all the work. We eat a lot of beans and wieners."

"I wish I could help you more, maybe cook for you. I've been livin' with Reggie Huston's family and workin' for his mother, Winnie, hemmin' skirts and pants. She promised me twenty cents for each one I did. She owes me two dollars and twenty cents, but she ain't paid me a cent. Nothin' I can do about it."

"I'm sorry. But you do get to sleep and eat there."

"That's what Reggie, I mean Mr. Huston, said. But I do a lot of work too, like wash dishes, clean house, cook, help with the laundry. Plus I'm still goin' to school and have to study."

"So how are your studies going? When will you get your GED?"

"I start a new semester in September, but all I have to take is math and English. That is, if I pass the courses I'm taking now. Math is hard."

"But you're living with the math teacher. You should get some help."

"He's not the math teacher now. But he does help me. He's really good…and so kind and sweet."

Chris studied her for a moment. "You like him, don't you?"

Della's neck and face tingled. "It's hard not to," she said, bowing her head. "But if I let one squeak out about what I think or feel, me and my suitcase would be thrown out of that house faster than lightening. So please let this be our little secret."

"I won't say a word. Not even to Dale. But keep me updated."

"I will. I better get back. Have to cook dinner."

"Come back when you can."

"Let me know when your baby comes."

"I will. Bye."

As soon as she got home, Della washed her hands and started the meatloaf. Making it was almost a rote task, and she let her mind wander as she mixed in chopped onions, salt, pepper, bread crumbs, two eggs, and a half cup of catsup.

So Chris noticed. Am I that obvious? Does Reggie feel anything for me? After a week of changin' his bandages, waitin' on him, and talkin' to him while he recuperated, he should. But now that he's feelin' better, he mostly ignores me. Just like a man.

She turned on the oven and started peeling the potatoes. *Where is Reggie? I haven't seen him since he went to pick up the application. He didn't even eat lunch.* She cut up a large potato and plopped the pieces into a pan of cold water. *Maybe he's up in his room completin' the application and I'll see him at dinner.*

"You should be gettin' that meatloaf in the oven." Winnie stepped into the kitchen, bringing her back to reality.

"Yes, ma'am, just a few more minutes for the oven to heat."

"Good." She peered into the pan. Cut those potatoes into smaller chunks. When they're about halfway done, fry them in some bacon drippin's. Be sure to salt them."

"Yes, ma'am."

"Cut the last of the spinach in the garden and make a salad. Be sure and wash it well. Nat said there's a few tomatoes out there."

"I can do that."

"I'm almost done with the dress. Let me know when dinner's ready."

"Yes, ma'am, I will."

Della watched as Winnie disappeared into the sewing room. *Do this, do that. Yes, ma'am, yes ma'am. Mama at least said thank-you. When am I gonna get to look for her?*

By dinner time Della's feet and legs ached. She set the table, put the food on it, and told Winnie it was time. Nat came in, but Reggie was nowhere in sight.

"Where's Reggie?" Winnie looked around the table, then yelled, "Reggie, if you don't get down here, you're not eatin'!"

A door slammed, and Reggie, a smile on his face, bounded down the stairs and took his place.

"What you been up to, Son?" Nat asked.

"A project." He scooped up a mouthful of meatloaf. "Something special."

"I'll tell you something special," Nat said. "Heard there was an opening for a math teacher at the middle school. You should get down there and get an application."

"And that," Reggie said, a wide grin on his face, "is just what I've been doing. Got it completed, and I'll take it in first thing tomorrow." He clicked his fingers. "That job has my name on it."

"I'm so proud of you," Winnie said. "Whoever thought one of my children would have a college degree and be a teacher?" She cast her eyes on Nat. "Better than a janitor."

Nat looked down. After swallowing, he said. "Winnie, I have a good job I enjoy. It pays our bills. I'm not ashamed of bein' the janitor."

"But it could be so much better. For you and for us." She turned to Della. "How're your classes comin'? Did you pass that math test?"

"I'll take it tonight, and I'm sure I'll pass." She sneaked a peek at Reggie, but he was eating, his eyes on his plate.

"I'm goin' out to work in the garden," Nat said, rising from his chair and slipping out the door.

"Don't know what's left out there to do," Winnie said. "Della, you'll have to do the dishes. I have customers comin' over."

"Yes, ma'am."

Winnie left without looking back.

Reggie stood up with his plate in his hand. "Let me help you with the dishes. You have school, and I want you to pass that math test." He winked at her.

"Thanks. I'll wash, and you dry." She washed plates, rinsed them, and put them in the drainer.

"You're fast. Can't keep up with you," Reggie said. He studied her. "My parents' fussing bothers you, doesn't it?"

"Arguin' bothers me. Daddy was always yellin' at Mama."

"Way it's always been. Don't worry about it."

"I visited my friend Chris. We had a good talk."

"How is Chris?"

"Worried about her baby. Only a couple more weeks before it's due."

"Can't blame her. Little ones are so precious. Maybe one of these days I'll have children." He hung the wet dish towel on the oven handle. "I want to look over that application, make sure everything's just right."

"Thanks for your help," Della said with a smile. *He likes and wants children. Maybe my being pregnant won't be too big a turnoff. Maybe someday he'll look at me differently.*

CHAPTER 18

No Rights

"I have an interview for that teaching job this morning at ten," Reggie told Nat and Winnie at the breakfast table Thursday. "Have my dress pants and coat cleaned. Della sewed the button back on my dress shirt."

Della smiled as his eyes met hers. "Glad to," she said.

"Well, you've finally grown up," Winnie said. "I sure didn't have time to help. Been too busy." She stood. "Della, I'm going to have to talk to you about becomin' a full partner."

Della started to reply, but Winnie hurried into the sewing room.

"You've been a big help to her," Nat said, patting her hand. "She told me last night she doesn't know what she'd do without you."

Especially when I work for free. Della gathered dishes to take to the sink. Nat left for work, and Reggie ascended the stairs. She was almost finished with the dishes when he came down. "You look very nice," she said, hoping her eyes didn't give away her thoughts.

"Wish me luck. No, say a prayer for me. I need this job."

"Della!" rang Winnie's voice.

Della had planned to work on an English essay, but she turned her steps toward the sewing room. "Comin'."

"I've been thinkin'," Winnie said as Della entered. "Labor Day will be here in a little over a week. Ten days, to be exact. Yesterday at church Bess suggested we gather at her house for hamburgers. She wants us to bring some potato salad and a dessert. Have you ever made brownies?"

"No, but I can follow a recipe if you have one."

"I do. Let's plan on puttin' black walnuts in them. They're in a bucket in the cellar, and you'll have to shell them. It takes a while, so why don't you start today?"

"I have an essay to write for English class tonight. I'll try to do some after I finish."

"Well, this afternoon I need you to hem some pants, so don't be too long. You better get started on that essay."

"Yes, ma'am."

Della opened her notebook on the table and looked up the assignment. *Write an essay on what you believe are basic human rights.* She thought for a few minutes, trying to separate her beliefs from the anger building up inside. She picked up her pen and wrote:

A basic human right that I strongly believe in is being able to determine one's goals and how he is going to accomplish them. However, it seems that most people in our society are kept from reaching their goals because of a lack of money and opportunities.

What are my goals? To get my GED and find a job where I can make lots of money. To marry someone who will help support me and my child and love me. But it ain't easy. She erased 'ain't' and replaced with 'isn't'. *I'm stuck living here with the Hustons. I feel like a slave working for nothing. I'm expecting a baby I don't want. I don't have no clothes, and I don't have no money to buy new ones or to get material to sew.* She erased the two 'no's' and wrote 'any'. *It wouldn't matter, though, since I work so much I don't have time to sew.*

How can I find someone to love me? Who wants a wife who is carrying someone else's baby? Who wants a wife who isn't pretty and has no decent clothes? No one is ever going to look at me twice. No one.

She read what she had written. Three short paragraphs. It wasn't much of an essay. But she was too upset to write more, so she closed her notebook and went down to the cellar to find the walnuts. Opening the door, she peered into the darkness. A wave of cool, musty air hit her in the face, and she reached inside to hunt for a light switch.

"You have to reach up here and pull on this string to turn on the light," Winnie said from behind her.

"Oh! You startled me." Della placed her hand over her pounding heart as Winnie yanked on the string.

"I heard you open the cellar door, and I knew you wouldn't find the light switch." She pushed past Della. "You'll probably be back down here to get things, so let me show you around."

Della followed her around the room as she pointed to bins of potatoes, onions, and turnips and showed her the shelves full of canned berry jams, tomatoes, and green beans.

"Nat does most of the cannin'. I don't have time. Oh, here are the walnuts. They're last year's harvest. Hope you can find some good ones."

Della picked one out of the bucket. "What's this around it?"

"Some of the hull. But it should be dried and come off easily. Here's a hammer you can use. Go out in the back yard and find a flat stone to crack them on. Don't forget to take a bowl to put the nuts in. And don't hit your fingers with the hammer."

"I'll try not to." She picked up the bucket and hammer and headed for the kitchen to get a plastic bowl, which she set on top of the walnuts. Outside she found a flat stone and took it to the edge of the patio, where she sat down. After a few minutes, her hands were beginning to stain rusty brown from the shells, and she had cut her finger on a sharp shell. "Well, I can see why Winnie assigned me this job," she muttered. Pursing her lips, she brought the hammer down with a smashing blow, and the walnut shell crumbled, leaving nothing but dust.

"That one was rotten," said a voice behind her. She whirled around. Reggie stood two feet from her, dressed in his everyday clothes.

"How did your interview go, Reggie?"

"I believe it went pretty well. But there were two other guys waiting their turn, and I heard they had more coming this afternoon and tomorrow morning."

"When will you know?"

"They said they'd tell us by five tomorrow afternoon." His brow furrowed. "Didn't seem like they spent much time with me. Maybe they already have someone they want to hire and this was just a formality."

"Maybe they're gonna interview today only and discuss it tomorrow," she said, glancing up at his intense face.

"Maybe. Anyway, I'm feeling lucky. Want to go with me to the store to get some milk, cream, and strawberries? I'm going to make ice cream for dinner."

"I'd love to." She jumped to her feet and looked at the walnut pieces covering the bottom of the bowl. "Not many, but I can work on them later." She followed Reggie through the back door into the kitchen.

The sewing machine room door swung open, and Winnie stuck her head out. "Did you shell those walnuts?"

"Some. I'll finish them later."

"Let me see." She stepped into the kitchen and looked in the bowl on the counter. "Better do more than that. We're goin' to need at least a cup for those brownies."

Della's heart sank. "But you said I could work on them later."

"Later might never come. Let's do them now. And Reggie, if you're goin' to the store, bring home some cheese for sandwiches."

"Yes, Mammy." His face fell, and as he passed Della on the way to the door, he whispered, "Sorry."

Della picked up the bowl and headed out to the back yard. Tears streamed down her face, and blindly, she felt for the edge of the patio and lowered her behind onto the cement. All the anger and frustration from the morning burst forth in a flood of sobs. "It's not fair," she said between gasps. "I don't have any friends, no one to talk to. I hate this place!"

She pounded away at the walnuts and threw pieces into the bowl. After a half hour, her anger was spent, and the walnuts were two inches deep in the bowl. *That has to be more than a cup.* Picking up the bowl, she carried it to Winnie.

"Is this enough?"

"That looks like plenty. Put the lid on the bowl and put them in the freezer so they won't spoil."

"Yes, ma'am."

"Oh, I might as well go with you," Winnie said, rising. "We'll make some sandwiches and eat lunch. Then I need you to hem these pants."

After lunch Della cleaned up and set up the iron and ironing board in the sewing room.

"Here are the pants," Winnie said. "You need to cut the old hem off plus another inch. Then hem them the usual way. I'm goin' to run down to the fabric store to get some hemmin' lace. I won't be gone long."

Wonder if she even thought of takin' me. No, that ain't gonna happen. And here I am, gettin' bigger and bigger, and still only one blouse made. What's Sister Bess gonna say?

She finished the pants just as Winnie came back in, followed by Reggie.

"They're havin' a Labor Day sale," Winnie said. "Good buys." She pulled a folded piece of material from a bag. "Got this to make Chloe a church dress. What do you think?"

Della glanced at the black calico full of tiny blue flowers, and a lump filled her throat. "Should make a pretty dress."

"We're going to whip up some ice cream for dessert," Reggie said. "Come on, Della, come help me."

She slipped out the door behind Reggie before Winnie stopped her. "Thanks, I needed to get out of there," she said, swallowing.

Reggie reached into a high cabinet and extracted the ice cream maker. "I'll let you help me turn the crank." He filled the inner container with strawberries, cream, and sugar, and then he emptied all the ice cube trays into the outer part. "Fill these up for me, will you?" He handed the empty trays to her.

After she filled them and put them back in the freezer, he picked up the ice cream maker and said, "Let's take this outside. I want to talk to you. Will you bring that dish towel? This thing gets cold."

Della grabbed the towel and held the door open for him. He sat in a chair and began turning the crank.

"I hope this won't upset you," he said after a few minutes, "but I read your essay. I want to tell you how pleased I am that it contained no *aint's*. Your writing is improving."

Anger flashed through her. "You had no right."

"True." He churned more cranks. "But I know you're unhappy. I can see it in your eyes."

"Wouldn't you be?"

"First tell me why."

"I can't." *I'm goin' to cry just thinking about it.*

"You have to. I can't help you if you don't."

"You read my essay. You should know."

"But I don't think that's all of it. So try."

The tears slid down her face no matter how hard she tried to keep them back. "I'm a nobody, that's why. No clothes. No friends. All I hear is 'Do this. Do that.' Not even a thank you. She never thinks of me."

"What do you mean?"

"She bought material to make Chloe a dress for church. What do I have to wear to church? Nothing! Nothing, I tell you! But she expects me to go. Sister Bess was like a mama to me, but your mama? She treats me like a slave!"

"She told me she wishes you were her daughter. She said you're a big help."

"If that's how she treats her daughter, I don't want to be her daughter. I want my mama. I don't even know where to look for her."

"I know." He rose and put his arm around her. "Don't give up. Have faith in Mammy and in yourself. Promise me."

She looked up into his face. "Why should I?"

"Because faith is the assurance of things hoped for. Believe, and it will happen."

CHAPTER 19

Labor Day At Bess's

On Labor Day they gathered at Sister Bess' house.

"Reggie didn't work his way through college to be a janitor." Sister Bess glared at Nat across the dining room table. "He can't find a good job if he's workin' at a menial task."

"I been doin' it for twenty-five years, and it's never been too lowly." Nat glanced at his son, sitting beside Della and staring at his food. "He'll do whatever it takes, won't you, Reggie?"

"They said they'd call by Friday evening, but all I got was a mimeographed form letter in the mail," Reggie blurted, his eyes sparking with anger. "Said *Thank you for your interest in teaching at Puttersville Middle School. We have chosen another candidate.*"

"How'd your interview go?" Sister Bess asked.

"Okay, I guess," Reggie said, shrugging. "I answered every question. Wasn't quite sure of a few, but I made a stab at them."

"You could have started applying earlier instead of going places to protest," Winnie said. "I wonder if that hurt your chances."

"I'm going to the school to find out who they hired instead of me. If it's a white, I'm going to protest at the school board office."

"As if that'll do you any good. All you'll do is get yourself in trouble." Winnie shook her head. "Better not do it."

"Better not do it," Chloe echoed. "Right, Grandma?"

"I think we should eat," Mother Carrie said. "I don't plan on being here next Labor Day."

Della's stomach revolted at the sight of the hamburger on her plate, and she glanced at Reggie. He picked up his fork and pushed it through his baked beans, but said nothing. *He's really down in the dumps.* She reached over and squeezed his hand, and a tiny smile flickered across his lips.

"What'd you go do that for?" Chloe shouted, her eyes fixed on Della.

"Do what?" Della asked.

"I saw you. You think you're Reggie's special friend, don't you? Well, you ain't."

"Let's hurry and eat," Winnie said. "I have a special surprise for you, Chloe. Just for you."

"For me? Really?"

Della ate most of her hamburger but was going to turn down the blackberry pie and ice cream when Reggie nudged her.

"Come on, have some. You'll miss a piece of heaven if you don't. Nothing like Aunt Bess's blackberry pie."

"Okay," she said taking the proffered bowl. *That sounds more like Reggie.* She brought a spoonful up to her mouth. *Chloe's staring at me with her hateful eyes, especially the one that bats up and down all the time.* She took a couple more bites of pie, then rose from her chair and went to scrape the rest into the trash can.

"Della, I hope you don't mind clearing the table and doing the dishes while I show Chloe her surprise," Winnie said. "It would be a great help as my legs are swelling."

"No, ma'am." She almost choked on the words. She turned on the faucet, and the steam rose and joined the sweat trickling down her neck. She waited until the family moved into the living room, then put the leftovers in the refrigerator and wiped the plates with soiled paper napkins before putting them into the hot, soapy water.

"Oh, it's so beautiful! You made this dress just for me? I love it. Thank you, Winnie, thank you," came Chloe's voice from the living room.

"I'm glad you like it," Della heard Winnie say.

"It's wonderful. How can I ever pay you?"

"You could go help Della with those dishes," Sister Bess said.

"As soon as I try on my new dress so everyone can see how it looks."

Thank you, Sister Bess. Someone is thinking about me. Della heard uneven steps ascending the stairs. *No use waiting on her.* She washed the last plate and grabbed the dish towel to dry what was in the drainer so she could finish washing. She was drying the last drainer full when she heard Chloe's labored descent.

"You look beautiful in your new dress, just like a princess," Della heard Mother Carrie say. "Turn around so we can see the back."

"Winnie is quite the seamstress," Sister Bess said. "No one does better stitching."

"Except the sewing machine," Della said under her breath, a smile twisting her mouth. "Too bad Sister Bess hasn't bought one of those new-fangled dishwashers." *But it doesn't matter. I'd rather be in here and not have to say how pretty Chloe looks.*

"Well, Nat, we better get towards home," Winnie said as Della joined them in the living room.

"So soon?" asked Sister Bess.

"Yep. Me and Della got lots of pants to hem, don't we, girl?

"And I gotta work tomorrow," Nat said. "And Reggie here, he's goin' to apply for that janitor job. Right, Reggie?" He reached over and clapped Reggie on the shoulder as he walked toward the door.

As soon as they arrived at the house and Nat opened the door, Della went to her room, closed the door, and pulled her suitcase out from under the bed. Opening it and unsnapping the flap on its bottom, she pulled out the little bag with the coin in it.

"You're my good luck charm," she said, turning the bag upside down and letting the coin slip into her palm. "A link to Mama's family and my ancestors." She stuck two fingers into the bag. How strange. On one side, the material rubbed the top of her fingers like fuzz, while the bottom side was slick.

She turned the bag wrong side out and discovered a yellowed piece of paper with two lines of strange words sprawled across it. Squinting to see it better, she held it up to the light. The letters looked English, but the words were not.

The sound of footsteps coming up the stairs made her jump, and she shoved the coin back inside the bag without turning it right side out, hid it under the flap, and closed the suitcase as someone tapped on her door.

"Who is it?"

"Me. Reggie."

"Oh, come in."

The door opened a crack. "Can't. Come here."

"Yes?" She opened the door.

"Junior just called. Said he made it to Canada okay and that he'd write later."

"Thanks for letting me know."

"Also want you to know that I appreciate everything you did tonight. You know, cleaning up, washing dishes, and…and." His eyes met hers. "And not fussing at Chloe. You know, when she said…"

"About us being special friends? What could I say? I don't even know if we're friends at all."

"Really? Don't I help you with your math? Talk to you about your problems? Sure we're friends."

"Thanks. I want to be your friend." Her cheeks burned, and she lowered her head.

Nat called, "Reggie, come down here. I want to talk to you about that janitor job at the school."

"Good night," he said with a sigh. "See you tomorrow."

Della locked her suitcase and scooted it under the bed. She had left her door open, and her ears caught the sound of Reggie's voice.

"Pappy, I don't want to work as a janitor. I studied hard at college so I could get a good job. Please don't make me apply for that job."

"Then what you goin' to do?"

"I'll work in the mine."

"No son of mine is goin' to work in that filthy, dangerous mine!" Winnie yelled. "Over my dead body!"

Shaking, Della closed the door, crawled into bed, and threw the covers over her head. *Just like when Daddy used to scream at Mama. I hate it.* She reached for her pillow and pulled it over the covers, but the angry confrontation still reached her ears.

The next morning she awoke to hear Reggie whistling "Dixie" as he passed by her door on his way to the bathroom. She lay there, waiting for him to finish his shower and thinking about last night. *How can he be so happy? Is he going to apply for the janitor job? Or at the mine?*

She heard him leave the bathroom. Getting up, she grabbed clean clothes and went to take her shower. Fifteen minutes later she was in the kitchen pouring herself a cup of coffee. Dirty dishes filled the sink. She would tackle them later. She sat down at the table, relishing the peace and quiet, and opened her math book to do the homework for class that evening.

After finishing her math, she did dishes. As she put the last cup up, Reggie walked in. He sat down and leaned his head on his hands.

"Did you apply for the janitor job at the school?"

"No. They said they had no jobs." He smacked his fist on the table. "No jobs my foot! A white man came in as I was leaving, and they handed him an application." He stood, anger written on his face. "I don't know what to do. Seems like there's a big sign hanging over Puttersville. *DON'T HIRE REGGIE HUSTON*!"

"Maybe that man was applyin' for something else. You tried, Reggie."

"Trying isn't going to give me money to get my Master's Degree. Trying doesn't give me experience. Don't know what I'm going to do."

"It ain't…isn't fair," she said.

"The whole world's not fair." He reached across the table to pick up her math book. Opening it, he flipped to the sheet that had her homework on it and studied it. "Hey, not bad. Only one little miscalculation. See here, where you subtracted, you forgot that you borrowed."

Della grabbed a pencil, erased the number and fixed it. "There. Better?"

"Perfect." He stood. "Think I'll mosey down to the coal company headquarters and put my application in there. Have to make some dough."

"Your Mammy won't be happy."

"Don't tell her. Or Pappy either. I'm a twenty-two-year-old man and can decide what I'll do," he said, heading out the door.

"Della, you done with those dishes?" Winnie stuck her head out the sewing room door. "You have time to hem a couple pairs of pants before lunch if you start now."

"Comin'." Entering the sewing room, she set up the ironing board and iron.

"Do your best," Winnie said. "You remember Sister Morrow at church? The woman in the wheel chair?"

Della nodded. She couldn't think of anyone in a wheelchair at church, but then she never paid any attention to most of the older women.

"Her daughter is having these pants hemmed for her birthday."

"Oh, okay." Her fingers flew as she snipped the old hem and ironed in the new folded seam at the mark, but her mind took flight in another direction. *What if Winnie finds out Reggie applied at the coal mine? I don't want to hear all that yellin'. Wish she would pay me.*

The phone rang, and Winnie pulled the receiver out from under a pile of clothes.

"Yes? Yes? Really? Oh, no! I'll tell Della," she said, hanging up. "Nat was in the break room at the school, and he overheard some of the teachers talkin'. One of them knows your friend Chris and her mother. Chris had her baby this morning."

"Was it a boy or a girl?"

"A little girl. But it was stillborn."

A wave of grief struck Della, and she sank down on a box of material and burst into sobs. "Oh, no! Poor Chris," she cried, tears streaming down her face. "She wanted this baby so much. Poor Chris. What can I do?"

"Nothing you can do," Winnie said. "Terrible things happen. God don't tell us why."

Della sat there crying until Winnie handed her a roll of toilet paper. "Might as well get back to work."

Della blew her nose. As she rose, she felt a tiny movement inside her. *I know what I'll do. There's only one thing I can do.*

CHAPTER 20

Blessings

A week later, the sound of Reggie whistling "Dixie" woke her. She got out of bed and pushed the window open to let in the breeze. A red and yellow maple leaf floated onto the still green grass in the back yard. Nat worked in the garden, pulling yellowed corn stalks from the hardened soil and stacking them in a pile.

She waited until she heard Reggie go back into his room, and she headed for the bathroom. After getting dressed, she went down to the kitchen. Reggie sat at the table, his face beaming.

"You look happy today," she said, pouring a cup of coffee and sticking a piece of bread into the toaster.

"As of right now, you're looking at a man with a job."

"Where?"

"Coal mine. Only I'm not going to be a miner. I'll be keeping their books."

"For real?"

"Yep. I won't be the top bookkeeper, but all that means is that there's room for promotion."

"I'm so proud of you." Without thinking, she threw her arms around him.

"Whoa, what's goin' on in here?" Nat burst through the door, his eyes passing from Reggie to Della, who jumped to the other side of the table.

"She was congratulating me on my new job, Pappy. I was just coming out to tell you."

"Don't tell me you applied at the coal mine."

"I did." An impish grin spread across Reggie's face. "Only I'll be one of their bookkeepers, not a miner."

"Well, don't that beat all," Nat said, slapping Reggie on the back. "Did you tell your Mammy?"

"No, just found out. You can tell her if you want."

"Oh, no. That's your job. You go tell her. But I'll go with you."

Winnie's scream of joy pierced Della's ears as she rose to start the dishes. *She's in a good mood. I'm going to ask her for the pay she owes me.* She glanced at her growing abdomen. *I need some maternity clothes.*

She finished the dishes, then went into the sewing room, knowing that Winnie would want her to work on the pile of pants that needed hemmed. After completing two pairs of men's trousers, she showed them to Winnie.

"You do good work," Winnie said after examining them.

"Thanks. Do you think…maybe you can pay me for the fifteen pieces I've done? It'd be three dollars."

Winnie stood and reached for a notebook on the top of a pile of boxes. Opening it, she pointed to a list of figures. Each item recorded the date, the piece of clothing she had hemmed, and the growing total. At the bottom she added the pairs of pants Della had just finished.

"See, I am keeping track of all your work," she said. She flipped to the next page in the notebook. "And your expenses."

"My expenses?"

"Yes. Last week I took you to the doctor for your monthly checkup. Three dollars. So we're even." She placed the notebook on top the boxes.

Della's heart sank. "But how about all the other work I've been doin'? Dishes, cookin', laundry, cleanin'? That has to count for something."

"Oh, it does. Let's see. You eat here. You sleep here. So a dollar a week for room and board. How long have you been with us? Six weeks?"

"I think so," Della said, tears filling her eyes.

"So you see, your being here works well for both of us. You have a place to stay, and Nat and I have the help we need. Am I correct?"

"Yes, ma'am."

"Good. Let's go have some lunch."

Della did the lunch dishes. The tears in her eyes had disappeared, replaced by anger and frustration. Everything Winnie said was true. The work she did earned her keep, but it didn't make her feel good about herself. *I am Winnie's slave. No one cares for me. I don't have no clothes. My birthday's next week, and no one knows.*

Reggie, his arms full of dirty clothes, hurried through the kitchen on his way to do laundry. Several of his socks and a pair of boxer shorts escaped his clutch and hit the floor.

Della laughed out loud, and he turned and made a face at her.

"Pick them up and give them to me, will you?"

"No, I ain't touchin' your dirty things." She made a face of mock horror and drew back as if they were the plague. "I ain't...am not your slave, Reggie."

"You'll need something sooner or later, and just wait and see all the help you won't get from me," he said, stomping to the sewing room. Returning shortly, he picked up the dropped laundry. "I was going to take you out for a milkshake at the drug store to celebrate my job, but..."

"Ah, come on, Reggie. I was dryin' dishes. Can't pick up your dirty clothes when I'm doin' dishes."

"I'll think about it." He stuck his head through the sewing room door. "Mammy, Della and I are going to the drug store," he yelled, then shut the door. "Come on, let's get out of here."

Is this a date? Sure would be nice to fix my hair. Reggie neared the door, and she caught up with him.

"Have you gone to see your friend Chris?" he asked as he opened the car door for her.

"I'm tryin' to get up my courage. Maybe she won't want to see me pregnant and everything and her with no baby."

"I understand. But I think you need to see her."

Should I tell him my plan? What would he think if he knew? "I'll go after she's had more time to grieve."

"That might be better." He turned to her with a hint of mischief in his brown eyes. "What flavor of ice cream are you having?"

"Strawberry. You?"

"Chocolate. After all…"

"I should have known," she said, laughing, "but you're half and half, so you could have had vanilla."

He gazed at her, a half smile curling his lips. "You never told me when your birthday is."

"Next week. Friday after next."

"And you'll be how old?"

"Eighteen."

He parked, opened the door for her, and took her hand as they walked up the steps.

What will people think? Part of her wanted to pull her hand away, but her heart leaped with the thought that someone cared for her, maybe even loved her. *Oh, if only…but I can't let him know how much I need him, want him.*

"Two shakes, chocolate and strawberry," Reggie said, propping himself on a tall stool in front of the bar.

"Okay," the man behind the counter said. "What you two up to?"

"Della, meet my friend Rand," Reggie said. "His dad owns the place."

"Glad to meet you," she said, struggling to wriggle her body up onto the stool.

"Reggie, I didn't know you were with someone," he said, eyeing her slightly bulging tummy.

"Oh, I'm not. Just friends." He glanced at Della. "And no, I'm not."

Not the father. Della's face prickled as heat crept up her cheeks.

"Sorry," Rand said to Reggie. "What's new?" He handed them tall glasses topped with whipped cream and a cherry.

"Got me a job doing books for the mine." Reggie's voice was smooth as the contents of his glass.

"Surprises me," Rand said. "Being as you're…you know."

"Black. Go ahead and say it, man. But I got a good education. Know how to figure the numbers and keep them straight."

"Guess so." The phone rang, and Rand went to answer it.

Della studied Reggie, staring out the window into the street. *He called Rand his friend. Some friend.*

"You alright?" she asked in a whisper.

"Sure, sure. Let's drink this stuff and get out of here." He didn't say much more until they finished and were walking back to the car. As he opened her car door, he said, "Seems like being half and half is worse."

"Seems like everywhere you turn, people put you down for bein' black," Della said as she got into the car.

"Sometimes, I say I'm used to it and go on like it doesn't bother me. Other times, it hurts."

"Especially from your friends."

"Yes, especially from people like Rand. But I know I'm smart. I can do anything. I'll show them."

Back home, Della hurried to make spaghetti and a salad for dinner. As they sat down to eat, Winnie handed Reggie an envelope.

"From Junior," she said. "Read it to us."

Della could tell by the look on Reggie's face that he would have rather read it in private, but he opened the letter.

Dear Reggie,

As I told you, I made it to Preacher Del's house just fine. Ain't no country prettier than here. Sister Tucker's really good to me. Loggin's hard work, but when I come in after my shift, she always has dinner waitin' for me. And I can tell you, ain't nothin' prettier around here than their daughter, Betty. Just between you and me, I got my eye on her.

I need to write Pappy and Mammy. I think Mammy's forgivin' me for runnin' off, but Reggie, you know wasn't anything else I could do. Don't believe in fightin' someone else's war. If our country be in danger, I'd be right there in the lineup, but in Asia, no sir. I hope you don't get drafted. Stay in school so you won't. Or get married. That's what I plan to do. Then maybe I can come back home.

I'm tired, so will get this ready to mail so Preacher Del can take it into the post office tomorrow. Say Hi to your family and Della for me and write me. Your friend, Junior

"Nice letter," Winnie said. "Sounds like he's goin' to be okay."

"What would you do if you got drafted?" Nat eyed Reggie.

"Don't know," Reggie said, shrugging. "That's why I need money to get back to school. Guys in school don't get called."

"Doesn't seem fair," Della said. "They should have some kind of lottery system or something."

"Hear they're talking about it," Nat said. "Just hope Reggie here don't get drafted. Glad you got that job." He put his hand on Reggie's shoulder.

"I'm thinkin' about getting' a job," Della said. "Need maternity clothes. Lots of things I want. New shoes. Makeup. Don't even have any lipstick. So I need a job."

"You have a job, girl." Winnie got up and put her plate in the sink. "As I told you, it pays for doctor visits and a nice house to stay in. Count your blessin's, and do these dishes so I can sew."

CHAPTER 21

Decisions

Two Fridays later, Della was finishing the dinner dishes when Reggie came home from work.

"Anything to eat?" he asked, sinking into a chair at the table.

"I saved you a plate," Della said, grabbing a mitt and getting the plate from the oven. "Fried chicken. I couldn't believe Winnie would buy chicken just for my birthday. And guess what…cake and ice cream, and they sang 'Happy Birthday' to me."

"Thanks. Sorry I had to miss your birthday."

"But how did she know it was my birthday?"

"Someone must have told her." He didn't look at her.

"I cut up the chicken and fried it by myself. I hope you like it."

"It's great. You've learned a lot."

"Well, I had to get your pappy to show me again, and it took me a longer time than it would have taken him, and…" She looked at Reggie, his head drooping, his eyes closed. "Reggie…Reggie, are you hearing me?"

"Sorry," he said, jerking his head up and opening his eyes. "I'm so tired. I never dreamed this job would be so hard."

"But you can do it, right?" she asked, putting her hand on his arm. "It isn't too much to learn, is it?"

"Not hard. Just seems like I get most of the work."

"Why's that?"

"I'm the newbie. The two other guys in the office think I can do it all."

"Oh. What do they do?"

"Go out for long lunches," he said, shrugging. "Gather in the back room and play cards. I'm not sure."

"Isn't there someone you can tell? Something you can do?"

"Probably not. I'm going to bed, too tired for cake and ice cream."

"No, not before Della opens her present, you're not," Winnie said as she came from the sewing room holding a wrapped package. "Open it, Della."

"For me? You got me a present?" She took the package wrapped in red tissue paper and pulled the white yarn bow, letting the outside of the wrapping fall open. "Oh, it's so pretty!" She lifted up a dress of soft peach material sprinkled with little pink flowers. Delicate white lace edged the neck and sleeves, and three tiny white flower buttons adorned the front center.

"I hope you like it," Winnie said. "I had to make it when you weren't in the sewing room so it'd be a surprise."

"I love it, just love it." She looked up at Winnie, and her eyes filled with tears. "I didn't know...didn't know you cared."

"I think a lot of you, Della, just don't know how to show it."

Della stood and hugged her. "Thank you for making my birthday so special."

"It's just for church. Soon as you finish the dishes, you can go try it on."

Della washed Reggie's plate and utensils. "Wait. I'll be back in a few," she told Reggie. She picked up the dress and climbed the stairs to her room. Getting out of her grungy jeans, she slipped the dress over her head, ran into the bathroom, and stood in front of the full-length mirror. The full bodice flowed beneath the tucks under her breasts. "I hardly look pregnant," she said as she ran smoothed her hands down the waves of the skirt. Running down the stairs, she stood before Reggie. "What do you think?"

He breathed out, and a loud snore echoed through the room.

She shook him. "Reggie, what do you think?" No response. "Reggie! Wake up!" she yelled, shaking his shoulder.

"Huh? I'm going to bed." He rose and stumbled up the stairs, never looking back.

"Well, you look very pretty," Nat said as he came through the back door. "Doesn't she?"

"It fits perfectly. Just like I knew it would," Winnie said as she slipped through the door behind him.

"Thanks again," Della said. "This has been the best birthday ever." *Unless it was my fourth birthday when my real daddy was still alive. He bought me a doll that drank from a bottle. I wish I could remember him better.*

She ascended the stairs to her room and changed clothes. Her pants were too tight around her waist, and she had to tug to get them up. "I'm going to tell Winnie I don't have any pants that fit," she said. "Soon no blouses, except the one I made."

Now would be a good time to talk to her about my clothes. She stepped outside of her room. Low voices murmured in the living room—Nat and Winnie talking to each other. *Not* a *good time.* Reentering her room, she looked at the clock. *Seven o'clock. Nothing to do, nowhere to go. I feel like a prisoner in this house.*

She picked up her purse, went down the stairs as quietly as she could, and went out the back door and around the house to the street. *I'll be gone only a short while. No use to tell anyone.*

Her steps turned toward Chris and Dale's house. For weeks she had centered her thoughts on this visit, about what she would ask and what she would tell them. *Is this something I really want to do? What would Mama think? Will Nat and Winnie be so angry when they find out that they will kick me out? Will Reggie think I'm terrible? That's what matters most to me, what Mama and Reggie think.*

Turning onto their street, she forced herself to put one foot in front of the other until she reached the front door. *Yes, this is something I have to do.* She rang the doorbell and waited, her heart pounding.

"Della, come in. I wasn't expecting you," Chris said, opening the door.

Della stepped inside. Chris smiled, but dark circles hung under her eyes. Della wrapped her arms around her. "I'm so sorry, so sorry," she whispered.

"I'm going to be okay. Please sit down."

"What happened?" The minute the words came out of her mouth, Della wished they hadn't.

"I…I can't talk about it now. Someday maybe, but not today. How are you feeling?" Chris's eyes rested on Della's protrusion. "When did you say your baby is due?"

"The middle of March."

"So you're doing alright?"

"I saw the doctor last week. She seems to think so."

"Good." Chris hesitated, then asked, "And Reggie? How's Reggie doing?"

"Working too hard. He says the other two men who are in the office give him all the work."

"I could have guessed that would happen. Dale knows them. Says they're good-for-nothings. One's the boss's son, the other his nephew."

"I don't know what Reggie is going to do. He's trying so hard to get everything done. I think he's goin' in tomorrow."

"Tell him he better not do anything to antagonize them. Dale says they're mean. I hope he can hang in there." She smiled. "And how is it with you and Reggie?"

"About the same. He says we're friends."

"And you want to be more than friends."

"Yes. This may sound strange, but he's the only man I know who will even look at me. I need someone to love me and take care of me.

Because of this," Della said, pointing at her stomach, "no man isn't ever gonna look at me twice."

"I'm sorry you feel that way. You should be happy. You're…how I wish I was you."

"Chris, this is a terrible thing to say, but I…I don't want this baby. I can't take care of it. Would you want to adopt it?" *There, the words are out of my mouth.*

Chris's mouth flew open, but she said nothing. Then, in a mere squeak, she said, "Adopt your baby? Really? How could you let him go?" Tears spilled down her cheeks, and she buried her face in her hands and sobbed. "Oh, Della, how could you give up your baby? How could you?"

"I'm sorry I said anything. Guess I'll go." She walked to the door and opened it.

"Wait!" Chris ran to her side. "I don't understand," she said, taking Della's hand. "I don't understand how you feel and how you can do this, but if you really mean it, I'll talk it over with Dale. He drove to the store for a few things. I'll talk to him when he gets home."

"Okay." Della let go of her hand and turned to go out the door.

"But Della, please think this through hard. If you give your baby away, I think you might regret it. I'll call you next week to tell you what Dale said, but I want you to really think about it."

"I have been thinking about it," Della said. "Ever since I got this way. One more week isn't gonna hurt."

"Just a minute." Chris ran down the hall and returned with a large bag. "The doctor says I shouldn't get pregnant again. Would you like to have my maternity clothes? I think we're about the same size."

Della took the bag from Chris's arms. "You're such a good friend. I do need them. Thank you."

"You're welcome. Talk to you next week, but please, please, think about what you're doing."

"I will, I promise." Della waved goodbye and shut the door. Carrying her precious load, she made her way back to Nat's and Winnie's and entered through the back door.

"Della, where you been?" Winnie asked. "I didn't even know you were gone. You should have told me."

"Sorry. My friend Chris told me I could have her maternity clothes, and I went to get them. That's all."

"Well, next time you decide to go gallivantin' off, you need to let me know."

"Yes, ma'am." She headed up the stairs and slammed the door as she went into her room. *I am eighteen, after all. I can take care of myself.* She dumped the clothes on her bed and looked at each piece. Five blouses, five pairs of long pants, and two dresses. *Almost brand new, all of them. With all these clothes, I can get a job and look respectable.*

She went down to the living room. From the back porch came the low voices of Nat and Winnie talking. The Sunday newspaper rested on top the magazine rack, and she picked it up and went back to her room, where she spread the *Help Wanted* pages out on her bed.

What can I do with no experience? She ran her finger down the column and saw General Store Help Wanted. Stock shelves, clean, make deliveries. *Well, the 'make deliveries' part leaves me out. No driver's license and no car.* Another ad caught her eye. Live-in house keeper and baby sitter. Clean, cook, and care for two young boys and two young girls while parents work. Must be good with children and know how to clean house and cook healthy meals. $20 a week plus room and board. Call to make an appointment for an interview. A phone number followed the ad, and she wrote it down. *Wow! That's eighty dollars a month. I'll call tomorrow.*

She went to bed, her head buzzing with excitement. *I won't have to listen to Winnie's "Do this. Do that." I won't have to wait on her hand and foot. I won't have to hem pants for free. I can cook what I want to eat. When the parents come home, I can do what I want to do and go where I want to go. I'll be a free woman.*

Then reality hit. *What if I don't like the parents? What if they give me a horrible room or I have to sleep with the children? What if they tell me what to cook? Of course they would. I'd have to cook whatever they buy. What if those kids won't mind me? What if they go around making big messes that I have to clean up? What if I never get any time off, not even the evenings when the parents are home or weekends? Worse yet, what if I never see Reggie again?* Tossing and turning, she drifted into an uneasy sleep.

CHAPTER 22

A Dream

The next Friday the phone rang just as they were sitting down for dinner. Winnie answered it, then handed the receiver to Della. "Your friend Chris wants to talk to you."

"I can come over at seven? Okay, I'll come as soon as I get the dishes done. See you." Her heart stuck in her throat as she returned to the table. "I'm going to visit with Chris after dinner," she said, trying to keep her voice calm.

"That's okay. She's a nice girl, and I'm glad she's your friend," Winnie said.

"Wish Reggie didn't have to work so late," Della said, glancing at his empty chair. "He's too tired to help me with my math when he comes in.'

"Told me this morning he'll have to go in Saturday again," Nat said.

"Just as long as they don't make him work on Sunday," Winnie stated. "I'll put my foot down good if he can't go to church."

"Oh, they'll probably let him off so he can sleep in church." Nat stabbed another meatball from the spaghetti bowl. "Couldn't keep his eyes open last Sunday."

The door opened, and Reggie came in and put his lunch pail on the counter. "Did you save me some food? Be there soon as I wash up."

"How'd your day go?" Nat asked as soon as Reggie sat down. "Any better?"

"I told them I wasn't coming in tomorrow. If they want it all done, they can help." Reggie scooped spaghetti and meatballs onto his plate. "I can do this job, but I can't do it all."

Della gazed into his face. It was hard, set, and weary, not at all like the Reggie she knew. "I'm glad you're standin' up for your rights. Don't let them run over you."

"Owner's going to have to do something about those two boys," Reggie said. "That's what they act like. Just little boys."

"Some kids never grow up," Winnie said.

"One of these days I'm going to be their boss," Reggie said, a smile on his face. "The way they're messing around, won't be long."

"Chris's husband Dale said they were the owner's son and nephew, so you must be kiddin'," Della said.

"I don't want to be their boss, not ever, but it's fun thinking about it. I aspire to higher callings."

"Be careful, son. Tread lightly," Nat said. "That's how you get along in the work place."

"I have a dream. Just like Martin Luther King, Jr. That dream doesn't mean working under white men and being mistreated by them. I'm going to be over white men. Men of all races are going to look up to me." Reggie put his fork down and looked around the table. "Going to make a difference in the world, just like King. Did you hear he's been nominated for the Nobel Peace Prize? I should have been down there in Selma and Washington, D.C., helping and supporting him."

"King didn't have no easy road," Nat reminded him. "Got put in jail lots because he protested. Got beat up, too. I don't want you goin' through that."

"King stood for something. Made a difference." Reggie sighed. "Look at me. What do I stand for? Just sitting here, letting others doing what I should be out there accomplishing." He turned his eyes to Della. "What's your dream?"

"My dream? Am I supposed to have a dream?"

"You better. A dream to do something with your life. Better yourself. Help others. Don't think God put us here to do nothing but consume. Jesus said to be a light."

"Guess I don't have no dream," Della said. "Maybe I need to find out who I am, who I want to be. Don't even know much about my family. My real family. Mama's family."

"That's a place to start," Winnie said, standing. "I better get back to my sewin'. Customer comin' tomorrow."

Della took her own plate and Winnie's to the sink. After Nat excused himself, she returned to the table and sat down next to Reggie.

"Would you like to listen to some records with me?" he asked.

"Thanks, I can't. Goin' to Chris's house soon as I get the dishes done." She headed back to the sink. After drying the last dish, she brushed her hair and stopped by her room for her purse.

"Am I sure this is what I want to do?" she asked as she walked down the street. "Yes, I've been sure ever since I found out I was carryin' Daddy's baby. It would be different if I was like Chris, married and had a husband to support me, and we had planned for this baby. But I don't want no baby." She knocked on the door.

Chris opened it. "Come in," she said. "Dale is here. Have a seat."

"Hi, I'm Dale," he said, rising to shake her hand. "Chris tells me you are willing to give up your baby for us to adopt."

"Yes. I can't have no baby. I can't provide for no baby. And..." she paused before adding in a whisper, "I don't want this baby. I need someone to give it a good home and love and care for it. Things I can't do."

"And you're one hundred percent sure of this?" Chris asked.

"A hundred percent. Do you want me to sign something?"

"We drew up a contract," Dale said. He handed her a sheet of paper. "Here it is."

Her hands trembled and her heart pounded as she took it and read:

I, Della Etter, do on this day, Friday, October 9, 1964, declare that I will relinquish the child I am now carrying to Dale and Chris Baker when it is born. I therefore terminate all rights to be the baby's parent. The baby will be their child to rear as their own, to wear their last name, and to be a part of their family. I hereby renounce all claims to this child and promise to let them have it as soon as it is born.

Signature Date

We, Dale and Chris Baker, promise to adopt Della Etter's baby to be our own son or daughter. We will love it and provide for its physical and emotional needs as if it were born from our bodies.

Signature Date

"It is legal?" Della asked.

"As legal as we can make it. Course we're not lawyers, but we think it will stand up in court."

"Okay," Della said, "Give me a pen, and I'll sign and date it."

"Do you want us to add anything? Like maybe we could send you pictures or updates?"

"No. It will be your baby to raise. When it leaves me, I'm done with it."

"Do you want a copy?"

"No. Don't need no copy for people to find."

Chris handed her a pen. "You're doing something for us that we can never repay."

Della laid the contract on their coffee table and wrote her name and the date. "And you're helpin' me out a lot, more than you can know." She passed the contract and pen to Dale.

"Can you feel the baby moving?" Chris asked after she signed. She put her hand on Della's abdomen. "I think I feel our baby move, honey. Here, put your hand here."

"No thanks. I'll hold him when we have him. It's going to be a boy, you know."

"Maybe. I really don't care. Boy or girl, I will love it. I can't wait."

Della rose. "I found out the baby is due March 15."

"I hope it comes sooner. Thank you so much." Chris picked up the contract. "I'm going to put this in a safe place."

"Does it need to be filed at court?" Della asked. "I heard once about a coupe adoptin' a baby, and they had to do that."

"The book I used from the library didn't say anything about that," Dale said. "I'll go to the courthouse and check."

"How's it going with Reggie?" Chris asked.

"He's so busy with his new job. No time to be with me, not even help me with my math. Thanks for askin'. I'd better go. I'll let you know what happens when I have my checkups."

She left. *Strange. I've just given away my baby, and I don't feel anything. Not sad. Not even numb. Nothing. If Mama were here, it'd be different.*

Opening the door, she found Ted and Thea Johnson sitting in the living room with Nat and Winnie.

"Come join us," Winnie said, scooting over to make a place for her on the sofa. "Have some fun. Tomorrow we have a lot of hemmin' to do, and I need your help.'

"Is Reggie here?"

"Here? No, he's down at the church building with the young people," Nat said. "I'll run you down there if you want to go."

Della shifted here weight to her other foot, then back. "Who's gonna be there?"

"Why, everybody," Thea said. "Our daughter Janice is here for the weekend, and all the other young people you know."

"I'm tired. Think I'll go to bed," Della said. She climbed the stairs, and inside her room, sat on the bed. *Never heard no announcement about a meetin' at church. Don't know any of those people anyway.* She picked up the copy of *The Great Gatsby* sitting on top of her school notebook and opened the page to her book marker. Sitting on the bed with her legs curled under her, she yawned as she scanned the pages. "Rich people party, party, party. They have one awful love affair after another," she muttered. She tried to settle down, but the antics of Nick, Daisy, Jordan, Tom, and Gatsby couldn't hold her attention. *Wish I'd gone to the party at church. At least I wouldn't be lonely.*

She tossed the book to the other side of the bed, got off the bed, and walked to the window. Throwing back the curtain, she stared at the moon, then down in the yard. It was almost dark, but the porch light lit up the yard enough so she could see two figures standing and looking up at the sky. Reggie and a woman!

That must be Janice. Why are they here instead of at church? Wish I could open the window and hear what they're sayin', but they'd know I'm watchin'. She closed the curtain until the opening was a mere slit, and unable to tear her eyes away, peered out through the space.

He put his arm around the woman's shoulder as they turned and walked to the porch.

Della watched until they made their way into the house, and then she sat down on the bed. *Reggie has a girlfriend!* The reality hit her like a slap in the face. She folded her arms across her abdomen and rocked back and forth. *I have no one. Not even Reggie!*

CHAPTER 23

Family Secret

Saturday morning when Della came downstairs, the dining room was empty and dirty dishes filled the sink. The clock in the kitchen said 9:15. She poured a cup of coffee and sank into a chair, her head pounding. *Where is everyone? Oh, now I remember.* Images of Reggie walking into the house with his arm around a woman, her tossing and turning for hours and wondering how she could have imagined that he would love her, and the feelings of emptiness and aloneness that drowned her.

She took a sip of coffee. *I'll never let him know how I feel. Not even a clue. That'll show him.* The sound of Reggie's whistling floated down the stairs, but she didn't look up.

"I've been thinking about doing something fun," he announced. "Pappy and Mammy went into town shopping. Want to go with me?" He walked over to her and touched her arm. "Della, I said you want to go with me?"

"Who, me?" She smiled. It was a fake smile, she knew, but then she meant it to be. "Go with you where?"

"Oh, go see some friends, maybe grab a hamburger and an ice cream. We've been working too hard."

"I don't have the money."

"I do. Just got paid."

"I've got dishes to do."

"They won't run away if you leave them in the sink."

"Winnie will kill me."

"Okay, then, I'll help you. We'll have them done in no time." He grabbed a dish towel, twirled it around, and snapped it in the air so it made a cracking noise. "Let's get hopping."

Della smiled, but every time she looked at him, she saw him walking with that woman, and she grew sullen. *Here he is dryin' dishes, wantin' to take me out, and I'm poutin'. Doesn't he have the right to see someone? After all, we're not goin' steady or anything.*

"Sorry you missed the church party last night," he said after several minutes of silence. "It was a lot of fun."

"I bet."

He stopped drying a dish and stared at her. "What's that supposed to mean?"

"Was that Janice Johnson you were with last night?" She turned away, not wanting him to see the hurt look on her face.

"Oh, I see. You think..." He bent over laughing. "You think Janice is my girlfriend?"

"Well, it looked like it to me."

"Janice is engaged. Besides, she's my cousin. We grew up together like brother and sister."

"Your cousin? How?"

"Thea Johnson is Aunt Bess's cousin. So guess that makes Janice my second cousin. She stayed with us a lot when I was young."

"Oh. I didn't realize. I...I feel so silly."

He lay the dish towel down and placed his hands on her shoulders. "You were jealous, weren't you?" His hand slipped under her chin as he lifted her face and looked into her eyes. "I know you were."

"Maybe." She pushed his hand off her chin and headed for the stairs.

"Where you going? You don't want to go out with me?"

She stopped, one foot on the step above her. "You think I'm goin' out I like this? No makeup? Without my purse?" She turned and took the steps two at a time. *As if I have makeup to wear.* "I'll be down in a minute," she said, closing her bedroom door behind her. Joy rippled through her as she changed into the blouse she made at Sister Bess's. She pulled a pair of maternity jeans from the bag Chris gave her and put them on. After stopping in the bathroom briefly to brush her hair, she joined Reggie in the living room.

"You look nice, Della. Don't let anyone ever tell you you're not pretty."

Tears sprang to her eyes and rolled down her cheeks, and she wipe them away with her hand.

"Why are you crying?"

"No one ever told me I was pretty."

"You are pretty." He smiled and took her arm. "Let's get going."

"Where'd you say we're goin'?"

"To meet with some friends. Don't worry. You're safe with me." He held the door of his Volkswagen van as she climbed in.

She looked out the window as they turned onto a street, then onto another. "I know where. To church."

"You're right. Since you didn't go last night, I figured you might enjoy helping us finish our project."

"Project?"

"You really don't listen at church, do you?" He pulled into the parking lot at the grocery store. "The young people are painting the classrooms. We did all except two last night. Let's go get some food."

"How could you be doing that or anything else when you were at home with Janice?"

"We came here to get some supplies out of the shed. You know, paint brushes."

"You're like the leader of the young people, aren't you?" she asked as they picked up bread, bologna, cookies, and soda.

"Janice is the instigator. This was her suggestion."

"I see." A pang of envy swept through her as she sensed the belonging and friendships he had experienced. "Who's goin' to be there?"

"Not sure everyone can make it today, but we'll see." He paid and carried the groceries to the van, where he put them in the middle seat.

In a few minutes they were at the church building, and Della picked up a bag and handed Reggie the other. She followed him into the back part of the building where the classrooms and the fellowship room and kitchen were. "I'm not paintin' in my good clothes," she told him. "You should have told me what we were doin'."

"That's okay. You and Janice can get the food ready. Here she comes now."

"Hi, all," Janice said as she walked into the kitchen carrying two more bags. "This morning I got up early and made oatmeal raisin cookies and egg salad sandwiches. Hope you like them." Her eyes lit on Della as she put the bags on the kitchen counter. "And you must be Della. So nice to meet you," she said, taking Della's hands in hers.

"You too. Janice, right? Reggie told me about you."

"Did he tell you I have to work constantly to keep him out of trouble?" She laughed and gave him a gentle poke on the shoulder.

"Yes, she knows me pretty well," Reggie said, a wide grin on his face. "Oh, here comes Brenda. And behind her is Bobby. You know them from church. Junior's sister and brother."

"Hi. Nice to see you both."

"You, too," Brenda said. "Where we paintin' today?" she asked Reggie.

"Middle school classroom. It'll be nice not having to look at those ugly blue walls anymore." He handed her a bucket of paint. "It's already stirred, and the brushes are over there." He pointed to a tray."

"Danny said he has football practice this morning," Brenda said. "I know he'd be here if he could."

"What can I do?" Della asked Janice when the others had gone to paint.

"Let's get drinks ready. I'll write names on these cups. Here, you put some ice in each cup from the ice bucket, and I'll set the iced tea and soda out. That way, they'll have a choice."

"I can do that," Della said, scooping out the ice with a large spoon.

"Have you picked out a name for your baby?"

"No. Nothing' for a boy or a girl."

"How far along are you?"

"A little over four months. It's due the middle of March."

"Bet you're excited, aren't you?"

"Excited? Well, yeah. Be more excited when it's all over. What do you do?"

"I'm a high school English teacher. Right now my classes are reading *Great Expectations* by Charles Dickens. Ever read it?"

"No. You know, I done told Reggie he's like the youth leader here."

"Reggie's always been like that. A leader, no matter where he goes or what he does. Guess he's been a leader of the young people ever since Nat and Winnie moved here when he was six."

"They didn't always live here? Where'd they live before comin' here?"

"Dallas. But they didn't like the heat. Didn't like the way people looked at them when they were together, either. Since Carrie, Nat, and Bess were here, they came home. Hometown people seem kinder."

"What happened to them? I mean, in Dallas?"

"To hear my mother tell..." She stopped, as if pondering how to say what she thought. "My mother said lots of people didn't like that they were biracial. They received threatening notes in the mail. Ugly graffiti painted on their house. Things like that."

"It must have been hard for them."

"Yes. Nat told my mother once that they both would've had better lives if they'd married someone of their own race."

"Why did they get married?"

"Family secret. Promise you'll never tell anyone?"

"Yes."

"Before Winnie married Nat—"

"Hey, anything to drink?" Reggie came around the corner, the others trailing behind him. "We finished the walls of one room. Figure we can do the baseboards before lunch."

"Drinks are here, and we put your names on the cups," Janice said. "Help yourselves."

Della could have shot Reggie, but as she found no more opportunity to continue their conversation with the crew in the kitchen, she sidled up to Brenda. "Heard from Junior lately?"

"Yeah, he called last night. Said he's happy. We miss him."

"Glad he's okay," Della said. "What he did took courage."

"Maybe not as much as the guys who go to Nam and fight," Janice remarked. "We worry about what others will think about him."

Winnie ran into the room. "Della, I need you to help with the hemmin'. Hurry! We have only this afternoon to finish everything for Mrs. Brown."

"Reggie will bring me home after lunch, won't you?" Della asked, looking his way.

Reggie's eyes traveled from his mom to Della to everyone in the room. "Would you all like to eat now?"

"It's a little early," Janice said, glancing at her watch. "Only about eleven."

"I'm sorry, Della, but I need you now. You promised." Winnie took hold of Della's blouse and tugged her toward the door.

I don't remember promisin' I'd help hem today. Della's throat closed in a knot, and she choked back anger. "Thanks, Reggie, but I better go," she said, waving, "See you all later." She had to run to catch up to

Winnie, already getting into the car. She slid into the seat and stared out the window as Winnie sang "What A Friend We Have in Jesus".

"Sorry to drag you away from fun, but my business depends on havin' things done on time," Winnie said. "You can do fun things later." She continued singing.

"I was just tryin' to get to know the others, but it doesn't matter." She gripped the side of the seat. "Nobody wants to be my friend anyway."

Della stared out the window all the way home. *How am I goin' to find out what happened with Nat and Winnie? And how can I make friends if I never have a chance to be around them? Every time I feel like I'm makin' headway, here comes Winnie with 'Do this! Do that! I can't stand her, and I hate her constantly singin' church songs. Just like she's doin' now. I wish she'd shut up.*

Winnie parked the car, and Della followed her into the sewing room. *I'll go hem her dumb pants, but I don't have to talk to her.* She set up the ironing board and picked up the first pair of pants in the pile.

"You know, Della, you can say you don't have any friends," Winnie said. "You can pout and act like a child all you want to, but it's not goin' to help. If you want something out of life, you have to get out there and work for it. And that starts with puttin' a smile on your face so people will like you. Do you understand?"

CHAPTER 24

Tragedy Strikes

"I hear rumors around the office that Steve Hyers, the owner, is thinking about hiring someone part time just to keep track of the men's work hours," Reggie said at the dinner table Monday. "But not until after Thanksgiving."

"What's the pay?" Nat asked. "Maybe Winnie should apply."

"No, not me. I got my sewin'. Can't do any more."

"I was thinking of Della," Reggie said. "Be good experience for her."

Della's heart leaped just thinking about having a paying job. "I know I can do it. Especially since I almost have my GED."

"Then who'll help me around the house? Help me keep up with my hemmin'?" Winnie stopped eating and glared at Reggie. "I think Della has enough to do."

"It's part time, Mammy. Eight until noon is what I hear. I'd like you to give Della a chance."

"I can hem pants after dinner. Please, please let me try," Della pleaded. "I'll keep up with my work here, I promise."

"I'll pick you up an application." Reggie grinned. "It's due back at the office in a week. I'd get it in as soon as you can. I'll help you with it."

"How much does it pay?" Della couldn't sit any longer. "How much does it pay?" she asked again when Reggie didn't answer.

"Probably minimum wage, a dollar twenty an hour. But everyone has to start somewhere."

Della glanced at Winnie, who pursed her lips and picked up her plate. "Don't know how you young whippersnappers think you can do two jobs at once. I never could." She took her plate to the sink, and without looking back, flounced into the sewing room. As she opened the door, she said, "If you think you can do so much, come help me after you do the dishes."

At least she didn't put her foot down and say no. Della made a face at Winnie as she disappeared through the door.

Reggie burst out laughing. "I was hoping you could listen to some records with me."

"I'd love to, but..."

"It's okay. Another time. I'll help you with the dishes."

She filled the sink with dirty dishes and hot, soapy water, and Reggie stood ready, dish towel in hand. "I like your records. We never had no record player."

"We never had a record player," he corrected her. "Did you have a radio?"

"Yes, till Daddy broke it. Couldn't afford another."

"I'm sorry."

"But Mama sang. 'Specially when Daddy wasn't there. I can sing like Mama."

"You never told me. What do you sing?"

"Mama really liked Patsy Cline. So do I. Sometimes we sang 'I Fall to Pieces' together.'"

"Sing it for me."

"Can't."

"Why not?"

"Don't have Mama to help me."

"Teach it to me. Then we'll sing it together."

Della gathered her courage and belted out the first few lines of the song.

"Say, not bad." He looked at her, head bent down, tears streaming down her face. "Della, why are you crying?"

"Because," she said, wiping her face with her sleeve. "Because the person in this song falls to pieces because they love someone, but maybe the other person doesn't want them around. And they can't be just their friend."

"So? That's sad, but not sad enough to cry about."

"It's sad 'cause Mama and I changed the words 'cause of Daddy. We sang 'I never want to be your friend.'"

"I'm so sorry." He wrapped his arms around her.

Della burrowed her head into his shirt and melted as he stroked her back. She could have stayed there for a long time, but he let loose.

"What other songs can you sing?"

"'Crazy' by Patsy Cline. Mama always said her songs made her feel like she wasn't the only one. The only crazy one, that is. Here's how it goes."

The door to the sewing room opened, and Winnie's head popped through it. "Della, you done with the dishes?"

"Will be soon." She drained the sink and wiped off the stove top. "Thanks for your help." She sighed and turned toward the sewing room.

"Hey, I think you have a good singing voice. Some real talent," Reggie said.

"Thanks." She turned to smile at him, but he was halfway up the stairs.

"Heard you singing," Winnie said as Della set up the ironing board. "Did Reggie tell you he was in the high school band? Played the violin, the trombone, and the clarinet. That boy loves music."

"He didn't tell me." She gazed at the wall as if she were trying to see through it. *What else can he do I don't know about?*

"Della, set the iron up. It's burnin' the ironing board pad!"

"Oh, sorry." Grayish smoke wafted up toward her, and she grabbed the iron. "Only a little brown spot on the pad," she said.

"That little brown spot will wear faster than the rest. Pay attention."

"Yes, ma'am." She picked up a skirt. The hem was already turned up, and she finished it in fifteen minutes.

"Biracial marriages are no fun," Winnie said as Della picked up a pair of pants. "People shun you, pull mean pranks on you, and then when you have little ones, they don't get to play with the blacks or the whites."

Della nodded and kept ironing.

"What I'm sayin' is this. You and Reggie can be friends, but don't get no ideas about fallin' in love with him. It won't work."

"No, ma'am. I mean yes, ma'am." *I figured that was comin'. But her sayin' it can't change the way I feel. And I'm not lettin' it.*

"So what's this baby's name goin' to be if it's a girl?" Winnie asked.

"Don't know."

"How about if it's a boy?"

"Haven't thought about it."

"No? Why not?"

What to say? "Seems so far away, that's all."

"Well, it'll get here before you know it. Better be thinkin.'"

"I need to go do some math homework," Della said, folding the finished pants and laying them on Winnie's sewing table.

"Okay, you can do a couple more hems tomorrow."

Reggie passed her at the bottom of the stairs, his face filled with happy anticipation. "Hey, I'm going out," he said, poking his head into the sewing room.

"With who?" came Winnie's voice.

"Meeting some of the kids to paint the classroom we didn't get finished. You want to come, Della?"

"Can't. Have to do math." Her feet felt like they had bricks tied to them as she dragged them up the last six stairs. Inside her bedroom, she sat down on the side of her bed, then lay back. A cool breeze lifted the window curtain and passed over her face, and she closed her eyes. *Just a minute. I'll lie here just a minute, and then I'll work on math.*

Loud screams and cries from downstairs awakened her. Jumping up, she ran down to the living room. Nat and Winnie were sitting on the couch, sobbing. Reggie stood at the open doorway, his shoulders shaking.

Della went to him and laid her hand on his shoulder. "What's wrong?"

"Junior's dead." He turned to her, and she wrapped her arms around him. He lowered his head and let it rest on her shoulder as sobs wrenched his body. "Can't be. Not Junior. No, no. Dear God, please say it's not so."

"How'd it happen?" she whispered.

"I went down to church. Just as we got started painting, Ted and Thea came running in, crying for Brenda and Bobby. Said a load of logs rolled off a truck trailer and crushed him."

"He was so sure of himself. So capable at everything he did. How could that happen?" Della asked.

"Wasn't his fault. Ted said the truck driver was drinking. Couldn't control the trailer. They arrested him."

"Won't bring Junior back," Nat said, wiping his eyes with the back of his hand. "Think we should go over to Ted's. Least we can do is pray with 'em. Be there for 'em."

"May I go?" Della asked.

"Thea would be hurt if you didn't," Winnie said. "Let's go."

Della crawled into the back seat of the car beside Reggie. He sat hunched over, his elbows on his knees, his face in his hands. "He was my best friend. Always has been," he said. He lifted his face and looked into Della's eyes. "No man could ever have a better friend. Now I don't..." He stopped and shook his head. "No friend."

"You have me." Della reached over and laid her hand on his arm. "I'm here for you."

"Thanks. Not quite the same, but thanks." He took her hand and held it like it was his safety rope.

She said nothing. He held onto her as Nat parked in front of Ted's house.

"We're here," she said.

"Okay." He let loose and got out of the car, and she followed him up the walk to the Johnson's front door. Ted hugged Nat and Winnie.

"Come in," Ted said. Della noticed the defeated look in his eyes.

"So sorry," she said, taking Ted's left hand as Reggie took his right.

"Don't know what to say," Reggie told him. "Don't know what I'll do without Junior."

"Life will go on," Ted said. "I don't know how, that's all. Don't know." He sighed. "Kids are taking it real hard. So's Thea."

"And how're you doin,' brother?" Nat laid his hand on Ted's shoulder. "What can we do to help?"

"Del in Canada said the coroner needs to keep Junior's body until they complete the investigation. They'll send it back here when they're done, but, Nat…" He took Nat's hand and pressed it. "It'll cost a powerful bunch of money." He pulled Nat to his side, and they walked away arm in arm, heads bent together.

"Let's go see the others." Reggie opened the door for Della. "I heard Thea say they were in the dining room."

They passed through the living room and through a doorway. Janice, Bobby, and Brenda sat at the dining table, their faces stained by tears.

"I'm so sorry," Reggie said.

"Junior's in heaven," Bobby said. "We ain't never gonna see him again."

Brenda started crying, and Della sat down beside her and hugged her close. She tried to hold her tears back, to be brave for the children, but they slipped down her cheeks. "We'll have to wait and see him in heaven," was all she could think to say.

"Wanna see him right now, not in heaven!" Brenda jumped out of her chair and ran out of the room. Thea, who had been talking with Winnie in the living room, ran after her.

"How are you doing?" Della asked Janice.

"It's so hard. I'm trying to be brave for them," she said, tipping her head toward Brenda and Bobby. "And Mammy and Pappy." She lowered her voice to a whisper. "He didn't even tell them goodbye."

"I know," Reggie said, wrapping his arm around her shoulders. "I know. I tried to get him to go back and tell them. He didn't listen."

CHAPTER 25

Sad Music

The middle of November Della wakened and felt the baby moving inside her. A soft glow came through the closed curtains, and she rose from bed and tiptoed to the window. Pulling back the curtain exposed a world of white. A two-inch blanket covered the trees, the ground, and the garden plot. Flying flakes filled the air, obscuring her view across the backyard.

She went downstairs. Reggie sat at the table eating breakfast, and she poured herself a cup of coffee and sat down beside him. "Today's Saturday. Do you have to go to work?"

"Told them I'm not coming in on Saturday anymore. I'm going to look for a different job."

"Oh?" She tried to say it like she didn't care, but inside, panic swept through her. "How come?" *If I get the job at the mine, who's going to take me to work and bring me home?*

"You know when you're not appreciated. When they don't want you around. Tom Hyers, the owner's son, would kick me out if he thought no one was looking. Dick Hyers, the nephew, calls me names like 'Blackie, Boy, even uses the 'N' word. It's hard to keep my mind on my work when I'm thinking about punching one or both of them in the face."

"That'd probably get you thrown into jail."

"And that is the only reason I don't do it." He rose and poured the rest of his coffee down the sink. "Going down to the grocery to see if they have any openings."

"Never heard from the mine 'bout that job," she said. "Two weeks since I sent in my application, and not a word."

"There's still time. Don't get impatient. They might wait until the last minute."

"Della, can you come in here a minute?" Winnie's voice came from the sewing room.

"Comin'." She grabbed her coffee and made her way into the room, where she sat on a box of material.

"Talked to Bess about Thanksgiving last night," Winnie said. "It'll be here in ten days. They're comin' here to eat with us."

"Okay. What're we having?"

"Turkey, of course. Ever cooked one?"

"No. Mama never could afford one. Then after she got sick..."

"Well, we'll do it together. Know how to make dressin' and pumpkin pies?"

Della shook her head. "Mama never taught me 'cause we didn't have no pumpkin. But I can make pretty good pie crust."

"Good. We'll have to do a lot of cookin'. Bess and Chloe so busy takin' care of Mother Carrie, don't know what they'll be bringin'."

"Mother Carrie needs a lot of care." *Strange how Mother Carrie's always causin' problems and everyone still does everything for her.*

"She does, but she's done so much for this family, and we all love her. That's what it means bein' a family. Lovin' each other and takin' care of each other no matter what." She picked up a light blue piece of gingham checked material. "Had this left over from a dress I made someone last year. Think it's enough for makin' you a blouse?"

"Maybe." Della put it on her lap and smoothed out the fold marks. "Chris gave me mostly pants. I could use another blouse."

"You can have it then. Don't need to hem more pants right now, and I'm pretty caught up. Think you can have it made by Thanksgiving?"

"Thanks. I'll start on it right now." She got out the iron and ironing board, ironed the material, and laid it on the cutting table. Working without stopping, she had it cut out and the back and front sewn together at the shoulders before Winnie called her for lunch.

Reggie came in for lunch while Della was doing dishes. After tossing his jacket onto the sofa, he flopped into his chair at the table. Scowling, he ran his fingers through his hair.

"Any luck?" Della asked.

"None," he growled. "I thought they might need holiday help at the store, but they said they didn't. Didn't need anyone at the hardware store. Even tried at the restaurant." A half-smile crept onto his face. "They laughed. Don't blame them."

"I can't imagine you cookin'." Della put her hands on his shoulders and kneaded. "Your muscles are tied in knots. Why don't you keep the job you have?"

"Don't think I'll have it for long. Tom and Dick are doing everything they can to get rid of me. If I had enough money, I'd move to a bigger town."

"What's this I hear about movin'?" Nat said as he came through the door. "Ain't no one in this house goin' nowhere."

"Might have to. I want a decent job."

"Stick with the one you have," Nat said, setting a bag of groceries onto the table. "You haven't been there long enough to put it on your resume."

"Anything to eat?" Reggie asked Della.

"Some chicken soup left over. I can heat it up for you."

"Thanks, sounds good."

She reheated the soup and handed him the bowl, and he devoured it. She rubbed his neck.

He set down the bowl and stood, shaking her hands off. "Don't do that."

"Sorry." She backed up. "What'd I do wrong?"

"Nothing. Just don't want bothered." He stepped into the living room, picked up his jacket, and headed up the steps. As Della finished the dishes, he came down and bypassed her like she was invisible. Saying nothing, he left.

She began singing "Am I That Easy to Forget." *Funny how a song seems to come into my mind for every occasion.* After singing for a bit, she stopped. The words only made her sadder. *Reggie likes me sometimes. When he needs comfort, he runs to someone else.*

Della tried to dismiss his actions. *Guess he's in a bad mood. Can't expect him to be nice when he's goin' through so much. I'll work on my blouse since Winnie went to visit Mother Carrie.* She sewed and listened for him to come through the front door, but heard nothing.

"Did Reggie say where he was goin'?" Nat asked at the dinner table. "Not like him to miss a meal."

"He didn't tell me," Della said.

They were finishing the meal when Reggie walked in, sat down, and ate.

"Mind tellin' me where you been?" Winnie asked.

"Just out." He helped himself to more potatoes. "Had to go clear my head."

Later Della sat on her bed, working on an essay for her English class. From Reggie's room came the unmistakable sound of a violin playing a low, melancholy tune that carried her back to the holler where she used to hang out when she was twelve. Mama and her real daddy were happy. They had enough food and clothes. Then her father's illness, and her whole life changed.

The music came faster, whirling through the air like a vast thunderstorm crashing around her, spiraling higher and higher until it ended in a victorious crescendo. *Reggie's telling me that life is gonna be okay for both of us. Strange that he's never played his violin. I didn't even know he could until Winnie told me. He sure is good.* She started to go knock on his door, but decided against it. *Don't want to be too nosey.* She finished her essay and went to bed.

Sunday, after going to church, having lunch, and doing the dishes, Della made the collar for her blouse and sewed it on. She had started the front facings when Winnie stuck her head through the door.

"You have company, Della. Someone to see you."

"Me? Who?"

"Come see."

Entering the living room, she saw Chris sitting on the sofa.

"Della, how are you?" Chris rose and hugged her. "Have you been feeling okay? How's the wee one coming?" Chris placed her hand on Della's abdomen. "You're really pooching out there."

"Can we go up to my room to talk? I want to show you something." When they were inside Della's room, she turned to Chris and whispered, "They don't know I'm giving you the baby. No one knows."

"Oh." Chris's face clouded. "You're going to have to tell them sometime, you know. I would feel happier if they knew."

"I'll tell them, I promise. Soon."

"Can I tell my parents? My relatives and friends? I've been dying to let everyone know."

"Soon. I'll let you know when. I think maybe by Christmas. Wouldn't the news make a wonderful Christmas present?"

"Great! By Christmas is fine. But I have some news."

"What?"

"I'm starting back to school to get my GED. I'll be in your math class, but behind you in the work. I want to be done by the time the baby comes."

"That's great. It'll be fun with you in class. Maybe we can help each other."

"Well, you can help me, but I doubt I'll be helping you. But I have some more news. I got a job."

"A job? Where?"

"At the mine. Dale told me about a half-day position keeping track of hours. I applied, and they called me Friday and told me I got it. I'll start the Monday after Thanksgiving."

Della's heart sank through the floor. "So how you gonna work and take care of a baby too? The baby could come the first of March, you know."

"Well, I could let you babysit. But then you gave him away, so you wouldn't want to. I think my mom will be glad to babysit. She lives on the way, and I could drop the baby off, then pick him up after work."

"Oh."

"Dale thinks it's wonderful. We can save money for a new car and put away some for the baby's college. See, already thinking about paying for his college."

"I'm glad," Della said, nearly choking on the words. "I hope it goes well for you."

"Oh, it will. That's why it's lucky we'll be in the same class. I'll be so busy, that's probably the only time we'll get to see each other."

"I'm happy for you," Della said even though disappointment and envy were eating her up.

"Well, I should be going. Just wanted you to know all my good news." She put her hand on Della's stomach. "Can't wait to see you, little one."

Della walked her to the door, then climbed back up the stairs. From Reggie's room came the soulful sound of a new melody. Its sadness sank into her heart, and the violin seemed to be saying, "You gave away your baby, you gave away your baby," over and over again. She covered her ears, but the melancholy tune persisted. *You gave away your baby…* Stopping at Reggie's door, she pounded on it.

The music stopped, and he opened the door. "What do you want?"

"Stop that dreadful music! I can't stand it!" she shouted.

"Well, I'm sorry, but I live here too, and I have to practice. So go where you can't hear it." He looked into her face. "Why are you crying?"

"Chris was just here. She got the job at the mine I applied for."

"Well, that's life. Go find another job you can do."

"Ain't no job out there I can do. Nothing!"

"And I told you if you don't stop saying *ain't*, I ain't gonna talk to you." He slammed the door.

Della stood there shaking, barely able to breathe, as the sad music drifted through the house.

CHAPTER 26

Thanksgiving

"Della, help me put this leaf in the table." Winnie picked up the leaf and laid it on one end of the dining room table. "Pull on the other end of the table to widen the hole. Now let's slip it in."

"Ouch!" Della's finger caught under the extension as they dropped it in the middle. She stuck her finger into her mouth and sucked.

"Come on, let's close it up."

Scrambling to the end, Della shoved, and the ends snapped into place in the leaf.

"That should do it." Winnie counted places. "Wish we could scoot the end of the table out from the wall, but if we do, it'll be too close to the door. Looks like nine places. We'll have to set a card table up in the living room for you, Brenda, and Bobby."

"The Johnsons are comin'?"

"Yes. Thea called last week and said they needed family, asked if they could eat with us. Sorry I forgot to tell you. Now if you don't mind setting the table. Be careful of the good china."

Della placed the gold-rimmed plates around the table, and then she laid a cloth napkin beside each. Opening the fancy silverware chest, she stared inside. "How do I put the silverware on?"

Winnie took a place setting from the chest. "Let me show you." She put the knife on the right side of the plate and the teaspoon beside it. On the left side she placed the dinner fork next to the plate and the smaller salad fork to the left of it. "We're not havin' soup, so the soup spoons stay in the chest."

Della finished the place settings. *I don't want to eat with the kids. It's not fair.* By the time she reached the last plate, she was angry, and without thinking, she put the dinner fork down so hard it hit the plate.

"Be careful!" Winnie rushed over and ran her finger along the rim of the plate. "No harm done, but watch it."

"Sorry," Della mumbled.

"The card table is in the sewing room. Get it and set it up in the living room. You can use our everyday plates and silverware on it."

"Yes, ma'am." She grew angrier while she retrieved the card table, washed it off, and set it. *I'm just the slave. If I'd known how hard it was gonna be, I'd never moved here. But where could I go in my condition with no man or nothing?*

"Della, can you come mash the potatoes? They'll be here any minute."

"Comin'." The steam from the potatoes hit her face as she plied the masher, stopping to add salt, butter, and milk, then mashing until she couldn't see any lumps.

"The turkey and dressing are out of the oven, so you can put the potatoes in to keep warm."

"Yes, ma'am." *It's like she's watchin' me, checkin' everything I do, even when she's not near me. Mama, why did I ever leave you?*

Sister Bess, Mother Carrie, and Chloe arrived, followed by the Johnsons. Della caught an occasional glimpse of them through the dining room door as she loaded the table with food. They were all hugging, kissing, and laughing.

"There you are," Sister Bess said, coming into the dining room. She put her arms around Della and pulled her close. "How's my girl?"

"Okay, I guess."

"My, you're getting big. What do you think? Boy or girl?"

"Don't know. *Don't want to know.* "See the new blouse I just made?"

"I like it." She inspected the hem. "Beautiful work."

"Let's get everyone seated before the food's cold," Winnie said. "Della, you, Bobby, and Brenda can stand in here with us while Nat says the blessing. Come on." Like a mother hen clucking to her chicks, she extended her hands and motioned for them to gather around.

Della stood while Nat intoned the prayer. On and on and on he went, thanking God for everyone there, for the food, for their jobs. All she could think about was sitting down and resting her legs and feet. She opened her eyes. Reggie was sitting next to Janice, and they were holding hands.

"What does it feel like to be pregnant?" Brenda asked when they had filled their plates.

"Tiring. It makes you tired." She smiled.

"Are you excited?"

"Excited? I guess so."

A perplexed look flitted across Brenda's face. "I'm excited."

"Good. Let's eat." She strained to hear the conversation from the dining room.

"Where's Carl?" Nat asked Janice.

"Somewhere in Nam. I don't know."

Carl must be her finance. Not knowing where he is would be terrible.

"Junior refused to go, and we still lost him," Ted said. "I, I mean we, miss him terribly. Life's not fair." He pushed his chair back. "This whole stupid war stinks. No heroes."

Thea wiped her eyes with her napkin. "Thanks for letting us come over. More of us here makes one who is missing seem less noticeable. Though we'll never forget him. We're praying that Carl comes home soon."

"We're prayin' for him too, aren't we, Nat?"

"Sure are."

"Grandma thinks this is the best Thanksgiving," Chloe said. "I'm glad I can be here to help her."

Della smiled. *Me too.*

"Did I tell you we heard from David C., my cousin in Charleston?" Thea asked. "Says he might come for a visit Christmas."

"Yeah, and I don't know what for," Ted said. "I don't know why a rich lawyer like him would want to come to a small town like Puttersville."

"Now Ted, don't talk like that. Says he needs to get away from the hustle and bustle of the big city, that's what for," Thea said.

"Figured since he got hired by the NAACP, he wouldn't have no use for us poor folks." Ted handed Winnie his empty plate.

"We'll be glad to see him" Winnie said as she stood. "I'm goin' to cut the pie."

So there's a lawyer in the family. Della squirmed in her seat. *Don't know why that bothers me. I'll probably never meet him.*

"Are you listenin' to me, Della? Do you want some pie?"

"Yes, please," she said, taking the piece Winnie held out to her.

"You did real good on the crust."

"Mama taught me how," Della said, smiling. She ate the pie slowly, thinking how she missed Mama. *But then the Johnsons miss Junior. Life has to go on no matter what happens.* Pushing herself up from her chair, she made her way to the kitchen with her plate and silverware, then went back to help Brenda and Bobby.

"Della," said Janice, coming up behind her. "You've worked all day cooking. Reggie and I are doing the dishes. You go sit down and rest."

She wasn't sure she had heard correctly. "You will?"

"Yes, you go rest."

"Thanks." She followed the family into the living room, but every sofa and chair was occupied. "I think I'll go to my room and rest for a little while," she said to Winnie. "Please call me before everyone leaves."

"You what? Oh, go ahead," Winnie said, never taking her eyes from Chloe. "Now as I was sayin'…"

Della climbed to her bedroom, lay across the bed, and pulled the blankets over her. *I am tired. Too tired to care if Reggie's doing the dishes with Janice.*

She wakened in a room so dark she couldn't see her hand in front of her face. Throwing back the covers, she slid out of bed and turned on the light. The clock said six-thirty. When she opened her door and went to the top of the stairs, she saw only darkness in the living room, and no light shined from the dining room doorway. An eerie silence filled the house.

She turned on the light to the stairs and made her way to the dining room. A sheet of paper lay on the table. Turning on the light, she held it up and read it. *Bess fell. We are at the hospital.* She laid the paper back on the table, then picked it up. It said *Bess*. Not Mother Carrie, but Bess. Sister Bess, the one who had taken her in, cared for her, helped her. Out of this whole family, the one she knew loved her.

The hospital wasn't that far away, maybe only two miles. She had to see Sister Bess. Slipping into her thin coat, she walked out the door and down the icy steps to the street. She turned into the wind and headed in the direction of the hospital.

She hadn't reckoned on how her worn shoes were going to navigate the sidewalks filled with snow and lumps of ice from cars. The light from houses failed to reach her path on the unlit street. Stumbling, she fell to her knees, and a shard of ice pierced her pants and scraped her leg. The toes on her right foot pushed through the holes in the end of her shoe and raked the ice as she fell. Looking down, she saw blood on the end of her toes. She dismissed the pain, got back up, and plowed on through the darkness. "Sister Bess. I've got to see her. I hope she's okay," she said as she picked her way through the ice-ridged intersection.

Headlights from an oncoming car filled the street in front of her, and she hurried to get to the other side. Breathing a sigh of relief as she reached the sidewalk, she stopped to catch her breath. The car started through the intersection, then made an abrupt u-turn. Della gasped and started down the street again, quickening her pace. The car driver adjusted his speed so the car stayed right behind her, following her.

Memories of a night when she had stayed late for a school activity filled her mind and a car followed her home. Raucous teenage boys had rolled the car windows down and jeered at her.

"Hey! Come with us! We'll show you some fun!" they had yelled.

She had turned into a driveway that wasn't her house, but they believed she was home and roared down the street. Only after they were out of sight did she dare walk the rest of the way home.

She shuddered as the car crept behind her, finally stopping.

The driver rolled down his window. "Hey, miss, need a ride?"

"No!" she shouted. Wrapping her arms around her, she hurried to get ahead of him.

"You sure?" The car sped up to be beside her.

"Yes, I'm almost home."

Her whole body shook with fear as she watched the driver turn the car back to its original direction, away from her. Gunning the engine, he roared away. She glanced over her shoulder and saw the tail lights fading.

Got to see Sister Bess. Got to see Sister Bess. She timed her footsteps to the rhythm of it. *Got to see Sister Bess. Got to see Sister Bess.*

She thought about the sermon Sunday. As usual, she hadn't heard much, but one thing Ted Johnson said was "Men ought to pray everywhere." Or something like that. *Maybe it will help if I pray.*

Lifting her face heavenward, she prayed, "God please help Sister Bess to be okay. And please help me get to the hospital. Amen."

Another car rolled down the street toward her. It passed, then stopped and backed up. The window rolled down.

"Della, is that you?" yelled Winnie. "Get in this car! Right now!"

Hurrying to the car, she opened the back door and slid in beside Reggie.

"If you was my daughter, I don't know what I'd do to you," Winnie said, twisting in her seat to stare at Della. "What in the world were you doing walking down that street this late at night?"

"Going to the hospital. To see Sister Bess." She bowed her head. "Is she okay?"

"Only a twisted ankle and a few scrapes," Winnie said. "They wrapped her ankle and sent her home with ice bags."

"We should have taken you with us," Nat said, "but we figured you was asleep."

"I was. But when I woke up and saw your note, I was so worried about her. I just had to go."

"I hope you know by now it was a stupid thing to do," Winnie said. "Really stupid. You could have fallen and hurt yourself, maybe lost your baby. Someone could've picked you up, and we'd never seen you again."

"I know. I'm sorry. I was just so worried—"

"Next time think about your own safety. A little common sense goes a long way," Nat said.

"Yes, sir."

They pulled into the driveway. Reggie hurried to open her door, and she walked into the house in front of him.

"Your feet are bleeding," Reggie said, looking down at her bare, bloody toes sticking out of the holes in her shoes. "Tomorrow I'm taking you to the store for new shoes. And some socks."

"Thanks." Tears filled her eyes as she made her way up the stairs. *He cares for me.*

CHAPTER 27

I'd Like To Know

"I think we should have a party when Della graduates." Sister Bess came through the door just as Della put the macaroni and ground beef casserole and cornbread she had made on the table. "In fact, I've thought about it all the way over here from school, and thought I'd stop and mention it."

"What do you think, Della?" Winnie asked.

"A party for me? I've never had a party just for me."

"You've worked hard to get your GED, and you deserve some recognition," Sister Bess said. "Now that my ankle's healed, we can have it at my house next Saturday. How does one o'clock sound?"

"Fine with me," Winnie said. "What do you want us to bring?"

"I was thinking I'd make some pulled pork sandwiches and potato salad. Maybe you and Della can make a cake. We'll have potato chips and drinks. Nothing fancy, just a small celebration."

"Della can make a cake. When did you say your graduation is?" Winnie looked up at the calendar on the wall."

"Next Friday, December eleventh," Della answered. "At two in the afternoon. We have a small ceremony with the awarding of certificates. The high school has a big ceremony for the seniors at seven, but we're not included in it."

"That's all the more reason to have a party," Sister Bess said. She stood. "Well, I'd better get home. Mother worries if I'm late."

"That's really nice of Sister Bess." Della sat down at the table as Nat and Reggie came in. "She's one of the sweetest people I know. I wish I could be like her."

"You will be some day," Reggie said as he sat down. "We're all God's work of art, just waiting to be more beautiful with each brush stroke."

Della bowed her head as Nat said the blessing. As soon as she heard "Amen," she asked. "Who can we invite?"

"Who do you want to invite?" Winnie asked.

"Chris for sure. And Brenda and Bobby."

"How about Janice?" Reggie's eyes met hers. "I think she'd love to come."

Della swallowed. "Okay, Janice."

"Who else?" Winnie asked.

Mama. I want Mama to be there. The thought brought tears to her eyes. "I'll have to think on it."

"Well, we'd better think on getting everything done for Christmas, too," Winnie said. "Thea invited us for Christmas Eve at their house. She wants us to bring cookies. I have a dress to finish, so Della, you're in charge of making cookies."

"Iced sugar cookies." Her thoughts flew back to when she was four and Mama let her put colored icing on the stars, bells, and Christmas tree sugar cookies. "Do you have any Christmas cookie cutters?"

"Sure do. I'll get them for you." Winnie stood. "Better get back to work on that dress I have to get done."

"Dad, I need to talk to you." Reggie glanced at Della. "In private."

"Sure, son. Let's go out back."

Della sighed. *Guess he won't be helping me with my math. Wonder what they're talking about.* She stood on the inside of the closed back door, but could hear only the murmur of their voices. Shrugging, she put the leftover food in the refrigerator. While she washed the dishes, her mind ran in circles. Was Reggie having more problems as work? Was he seeing a girl and having girl troubles? Her mind went back to the day Winnie picked her up to move her here. What did she mean when she asked if Reggie had any brothers and sisters and Winnie said "Not really"?

If the Huston family had more secrets, she wanted to know. And that included Reggie's secrets.

Reggie came back in, his face sour. He raced upstairs, came down with his jacket on, and said nothing as he went out the front door.

Something's eating at him. Guess it's a man problem. Della hung up the dishtowel and headed up to her room. Before she reached the top step, the phone rang.

"Della, it's for you," Winnie yelled from the sewing room. "Your friend Chris."

She ran back downstairs and picked up the phone. "Hi, Chris, what's up?" She listened a moment. "Okay, I'll be right there." Hanging up the phone, she stuck her head through the sewing room door. "Chris wants me to come over."

"Fine, but don't be out too late."

"Okay." She climbed the stairs, grabbed her jacket and her purse, and left. The walk to Chris's house was short, and when she knocked, the door opened.

"So glad you could come," Chris said. "I want to show you the quilt I'm making for my baby."

"Dale out?" she asked, stepping inside.

"Took his nephew bowling. I told him I'd stay here and work on this." She opened a box sitting on the coffee table. "Look at the squares I'm making." She set a pile of six-inch pastel squares on the table, then spread them out. "I'm embroidering a letter of the alphabet on each square here, and an object that begins with each letter on these.

Della picked up a square and ran her fingers over the embroidered outline of a gray kitten with blue eyes and pink tongue. "It's beautiful," she said, picking up another of a black dog with floppy ears. "Where did you learn to do this?"

"Mom taught me. It's a work of love for both of us."

Della looked into Chris's eyes. "You told her? You promised you wouldn't say anything to anyone until Christmas."

"Oh, I just told my mom, and she's keeping it a secret. She said she wouldn't tell a soul. You should have seen her face." Her eyes pleaded with Della to understand. "She can keep a secret, I know she can."

"I hope so. I don't want rumors ripplin' through Puttersville. It's no one's business but ours."

"There won't be any rumors. No one knows but you and me and my mom. And of course Dale." She laughed. "We're all so happy. You're for sure going to tell everyone Christmas, aren't you? I just have to let my relatives know by then." She patted Della's bulging abdomen. "He sure is growing."

"And getting heavier. My legs get tired after working all day. Winnie expects a lot of me. But Sister Bess is throwing me a graduation party next Saturday at one in the afternoon. Can you come?"

"Oh, I'd love to. What can I bring?"

"Just you."

"Okay. How's Reggie?"

"He's got something on his mind, but he won't tell me."

"Maybe it's his job. Some days are pretty hectic at the mine."

"I'd better get going. Promised Winnie I wouldn't be too late. Thanks for showing me the quilt. See you next Saturday at my party."

She walked back to the house remembering the glow on Chris's face as she showed her the quilt squares. A wave of envy swept over her. *It sure would be nice to have a husband to share this baby with. Wish I had some money to buy nice things like material. If only Mama could have taught me some things. But then we didn't have money.* She climbed the steps to the porch.

Lively music from Reggie's room swept down the stairs and filled the living room as Della went into the house. She stood inside the door and swayed to it, but in her mind, she and Reggie were dancing. *How can he be happy when he was so upset a little while ago?*

The music stopped, and his door opened. "Get your math. I have a few minutes to help you." He came down to the dining room.

She retrieved her book and sat down in the chair beside him. "Thanks. Math final is Monday. I have to be sure about how to do these word problems."

"Show me the ones that are giving you trouble, and I'll go through them with you."

"I thought you were too upset to help me. Appreciate it."

"Let's do the ones you're not sure about."

"I mean, if you've got something on your mind, my math can wait."

Exasperation crossed his face. "I've got helping you on my mind. Show me the problems."

"It's not so much understanding the problems, it's that I'm still unsure of how to change a decimal to a fraction."

"A decimal is a part of a whole or a sum total, just like a fraction. You always put the part over the whole. Like this." He pointed to the page. "The class used twenty-five pencils out of a bag of seventy-five. What fraction did they use?"

"So there were seventy-five pencils in all. So do I divide seventy-five by twenty-five?"

"You could. But it's easier to do it this way."

Della watched as he wrote twenty-five, drew a line under it, and put seventy-five under the line.

"What number can you divide both twenty-five and seventy-five by?"

"Twenty-five?"

"Do it."

"So the answer is one-third, right?"

"Right. What else don't you understand?"

She looked up into his eyes. "I know how to do it now. It's so easy when you explain it." She held her gaze. *Oh, if only I could wrap my arms around you!*

His eyes met hers, and for a few moments, a slight smile formed on his lips. She closed her eyes, and in spite of herself, moved her face towards his.

"I have to go up to my room and make a phone call," he said, breaking the spell. "Finish these problems, and I'll check your answer when I'm done." Turning, he ran up the stairs.

Della sighed. *We were so close.*

He returned with his jacket in hand and looked at her work. "All your answers are correct. Della, sometimes I think you want my help just to..." He put on the jacket.

"Just to what?"

"I'm going out for a few minutes." He walked to the door.

"Reggie, wait. Can I ask you something?"

"Shoot."

"When I first came to live with you, the day your mammy brought me over, I asked her if you had any brothers or sisters."

"What'd she say?"

"She said 'Not really.' I thought that was very strange. What did she mean?"

His face hardened. "Some things are none of your business, Della. When are you going to learn that?"

"Sorry." Her heart sank. "I didn't mean to pry."

"Well, then, don't." He opened the door and left.

CHAPTER 28

Graduation

"Della Renee Etter."

Della stood and made her way to the stage.

"Congratulations," the principal said as he shook her hand and handed her a GED certificate.

Della gazed into the high school auditorium while she walked across the stage. The bright lights blinded her, and she couldn't see Sister Bess and Winnie, but she knew they were there. *If only Mama could see me now.* She made her way back to her seat and squirmed while the rest of her classmates went forward to receive their certificates.

"It was a beautiful ceremony," Sister Bess said afterwards. "I wish Mother, Chloe, Reggie, and Nat could have been here to see you."

"Me too." Della turned to Winnie. "Can we go straight home so I can make the cake for my party tomorrow?"

"That's where we're headed." Winnie glanced over her shoulder. "See you all tomorrow."

"Have some cooking to do myself," Sister Bess said.

As soon as they were home, Della put Winnie's big cookbook on the table and opened it where she had left a marker for the chocolate cake she had picked out.

"Don't forget to start the chicken for dinner." Winnie disappeared into the sewing room.

"I'm a grownup now, graduated with as good as a high school diploma, ready to make my way in the world," she said to herself. Just saying it made her feel good.

Reggie bounded down the stairs. "Congratulations on obtaining your certificate. It'll go a long way in getting you a job."

"I didn't see you there." She gazed into his face, expecting a reason.

"I couldn't come."

"Are you coming to my party at Sister Bess's house tomorrow?"

"Sorry, can't do that either."

"Janice is coming."

"I'd like to be there, but I can't. Have to be at work." His face gave no hint of his feelings.

"Too bad. I'm making a huge chocolate cake."

"And I'm counting on you to save me a piece."

"I will, I promise."

"Oh, that reminds me." He reached into his shirt pocket and pulled out a small package wrapped in foil. "Here's a graduation present."

"You got me a present? Just for me?" Her heart leaped as she took it and undid the foil. A ten dollar bill fell into her hand. She stared at it, too stunned to talk."

"Buy yourself something that you really need and want."

"Oh, Reggie, I…I. Oh, I don't know what to say. Thank you." She wrapped her arms around him and gazed into his eyes. "You're so nice to me."

"Reggie, turn that music down! Neighbors a mile down the street can hear it!" Winnie stood behind Della, eyes focused on her embracing Reggie.

"Yes, Mammy." Scowling, he flew up the stairs.

"And you, girl, take those moonin' eyes off Reggie. Don't think I can't see how you look at him."

Della felt the blood rush to her cheeks, and she dropped her eyes to the recipe. "Do we have enough cocoa to make this cake?"

"And don't change the subject. I've warned you before. You and Reggie can be friends, but nothin' more. Like it or lump it." With a huff she turned and sashayed back into the sewing room.

Della fingered the bill she had hastily stuffed into her pocket. It would buy enough material to make herself some clothes after she was rid of the baby. But more than that, it meant that look Reggie sometimes gave her was more than her imagination. He liked her and cared what happened to her. Warmth filled her heart in spite of Winnie's rebuke.

She mixed up the cake, trying to keep her mind on the ingredients. In her room under her bed were the new shoes Reggie had bought her, and on her feet keeping them warm was a pair of the socks. Winnie had said nothing when he brought her home with new shoes and socks, but her face showed her thoughts. All Nat had said was "God expects us to share with those who have a need."

As soon as she put the cake into the oven, Winnie called her.

"If you're done with that cake, I have a pair of trousers that need hemmin'."

Della went to do Winnie's bidding, her mind working as hard as her hands as she thought about Reggie. What was he up to? What was it that he didn't want to tell her? Maybe someday she would know.

She finished the pants and looked at the clock on the wall. "Have to go check the cake." Going into the kitchen, she opened the oven door just a crack and glanced at the cake. It bounced back when she touched it, and she turned off the oven and set the cake on a rack.

That night she couldn't get to sleep. Her abdomen was big enough to make her uncomfortable, and the baby kept moving inside her. Tomorrow the Johnson family would all be at Sister Bess's. And of course Chloe, Nat, and Winnie. And Chris and maybe Dale. The only things to keep her party from being perfect would be the absences of Mama and Reggie.

The next morning she bounded out of bed in spite of not getting much sleep. Reggie was in the shower, so she crept down the stairs and raised the cover from the cake she had iced the night before. The flowers she had drawn with yellow and white icing stood out on the dark brown icing, and she admired her work.

She heard Reggie come out of the bathroom and go into his room. *Better get my shower and get dressed.* Halfway up the stairs she met Winnie coming down.

"Hurry up. Just because we're havin' a party don't mean we can skip Saturday cleanin'."

"Yes, ma'am." She grabbed her clothes and took a short shower. After dressing and eating breakfast, she did the dishes, then dusted and swept. Her most hated Saturday chore was mopping the kitchen, dining room, and the bathrooms. Just for today, she wanted to forget it, but she knew how strict Winnie was, so she got the mop bucket and mop and started working.

Reggie ran downstairs whistling, wearing his dress coat and trousers and flipping his black and gold toboggan into the air. "Later." He grinned and leaped over the mop bucket.

"Why are you wearing your good clothes to work? At least that's what…" She stopped. He was out the door. He couldn't be going to work. He never wore his Sunday best to work.

"Where's Reggie goin'?" she blurted out when Winnie came into the dining room. "He sure did look spiffy. Wasn't goin' to work."

"Watch what you're doin'," Winnie said, pointing to the puddle of water spreading out from the mop on the floor. "You'll ruin the wood floors putting that much water on them."

"Sorry." Della sopped up the water and wrung the mop out.

"The sooner you get done, the sooner we can go over to Bess's. I'll be ready when you are."

"Yes, ma'am." Winnie went back into the sewing room, and Della swished the mop across the floor, singing 'Crazy'. *Maybe I am crazy lovin' Reggie. Every time I look at him, Winnie gets upset.* She finished the living and dining rooms and headed for the bathroom.

"Della, would you mind cleanin' the bathrooms before you mop?" Winnie yelled. "I just don't have the time."

"Okay." Sighing, she grabbed the sponge and bent over the tub, scrubbing the mat and sides. "Ouch!" she screamed as she straightened up and grabbed her stomach as another sharp pain coursed through her abdomen. "Guess I'm crowding him too much." She dropped to her knees and cleaned the bottom and sides of the toilet. Tears filled her eyes. *As soon as I'm rid of this baby, I'm going to get a job and move out.*

By the time she finished cleaning and mopping the bathroom, she dragged herself up to her room and looked through her clothes. "Not my Sunday dress that I have to wear every week," she muttered, thrusting it to the end of the closet. She chose the first shirt Sister Bess had helped her make. It still made her feel loved and special. Slipping into a pair of slacks, she combed her hair and went downstairs.

I lost Mama, but Sister Bess loves me. She's always there, rootin' for me and takin' my place. Tears filled her eyes as she remembered saying goodbye to Mama.

"You all ready?"

She raised her head to see Winnie waiting for her at the bottom of the steps. "Yes, ma'am, ready and rarin'."

"You don't look rarin'. What's botherin' you, child?" She handed Della the cake.

"Just missin' Mama. We ain't never done anything to find her. But she's probably dead of cancer."

"You'll probably never find her." She reached for her coat and slipped into it.

Della pulled her coat from the hall tree. One of her hands caught in a hole inside the sleeve. As soon as she buttoned it, the bottom buttons flew back out of the worn buttonholes because of her extra girth.

"Come on. Nat's already warmin' the car up."

Della said little as they drove the short distance to Sister Bess's house. She gazed out the window at the new fallen snow, brighter than diamonds in the sun, yet as cold as Winnie's remarks about Mama.

Nat lined the car up behind the Johnson car in Bess's driveway. Winnie was the first one out of the car. Nat held the door open for Della as she struggled from the confines of the back seat, her hands clasping the cake.

"Sorry, we're later than I thought we'd be," Winnie greeted Sister Bess at the door.

"Well, come on in. Thea and Ted and family already come."

"You can put the cake in the kitchen," Sister Bess said to Della, then turned to Winnie. "Did I tell you David C.'s coming for Christmas?"

Della passed through the living room. Ted and Thea hardly looked her way, but Brenda and Bobby ran up to her.

"We wanna see the cake," Brenda said, peeking into the pan. "Ooh, it's pretty. Look at the flowers."

"Thanks," Della said. "I decorated it myself."

"Where's Janice?" Winnie asked Thea.

"Oh, she went somewhere with Reggie. Didn't say where, but you probably know," Thea said. "Poor girl, she just needs a little company, someone her own age."

Poor girl! Della's heart sank to her stomach. Reggie had lied. He wasn't going to work, but on a date with Janice. She stiffened her upper lip and sank her teeth into it, holding back the words that rushed onto her tongue.

She found a spot on the end of the counter for the cake. A ham studded with cloves sat on the other end, and potato salad, Jello salad, rolls, and iced tea filled the remainder of the counter top. A flowered table cloth adorned the dining room table, and Sister Bess's best china decked the matching placemats.

A warm glow pushed its way past the hurt in her heart. Sister Bess had gone to a lot of trouble for her.

Sister Bess came into the kitchen, took Della by the shoulders, and pushed her against the refrigerator. "You!" Scorn filled her eyes. "If I had known what I know now, we wouldn't be having this party!"

"Why? What'd I do?" Della gasped.

"I just learned that you're giving away your baby. Thea told me before you all got here. Said she heard it from a trusted source. How could you?"

"I…I." Della turned and lay her head on her arms against the refrigerator, sobs shaking her frame.

CHAPTER 29

What If?

The next morning Della woke late. She hadn't slept but a couple hours. The night passed like an interminable nightmare, scenes from the day before tormenting her. Reggie out with Janice and not coming home until bedtime. She hadn't seen him, but she heard him come in and run up the stairs, whistling. Sister Bess hadn't spoken to her after her outburst, not even saying goodbye as she left. Brenda and Bobby huddled next to their mama on the sofa, their eyes following her when she dared go into the living room. The stony silence of Nat and Winnie as they drove home.

"You ready for church?" Winnie yelled up the stairs.

Della got out of bed and opened the door. "I'm not feeling well. Not going." She lay back down, raised the blankets up to her chin, and stared at the picture of the forest she had cut out of a magazine and hung on the wall. The trees in the photo morphed into people—Sister Bess, Nat and Winnie, and the Johnson family, all standing around pointing a finger at her. She turned over and buried her face in her pillow, but they reappeared. Chris wasn't among them, but she hadn't come to the party, either.

"I can't stand it." She threw back the covers, grabbed some clothes, and headed for the bathroom. After showering and dressing, she poured the rest of the coffee into a cup, then spied the covered cake pan on the counter. One piece remained, and she scooped it out with her fingers, and standing over the sink, ate it and drank her coffee.

The house was hers, all hers, but she couldn't revel in the quiet and solitude. The walls closed in on her like prison doors, and the aloneness smothered her. Throwing her coat around her shoulders, she opened the door. The phone rang.

She picked up the receiver. "Hello, Huston residence."

A woman's voice asked, "Is Reggie there?"

"No. May I ask who's calling?"

"Rose. Please tell him Rose called."

"Rose who?"

The receiver clicked as the caller hung up.

Della put the receiver back. The questions flew through her mind like arrows shot from a bow. *Who's Rose? What if Reggie has another girlfriend? What if he's been meeting with her?* She opened the door and stepped onto the porch, then walked through the drips of water falling from gleaming icicles hanging from the eaves.

The snow had melted from the sidewalks, and she walked along them, not thinking about where she was going, but eventually finding herself at Chris's house. "I wonder if she's home," she muttered, turning onto the walk leading to Chris's front door. She knocked, and the door opened.

"Hi, Della. I was going to call you this afternoon. Come in."

"I missed you at my party," she said, stepping inside.

"I'm sorry. I should have told you that I couldn't come, but I was so busy getting ready I forgot. Some of the people who work in the office at the mines decided to have a Christmas party. At the last minute. Dale and I had to go."

"How was it?"

"Okay, I guess. They gave us each one of these." She picked up a mug from the table. "A cup of hot chocolate mix with marshmallows and a candy cane stuck in it. They said it was our Christmas bonus. I hope not."

"Me, too," Della said. "Not much of a bonus."

"No. Besides that..." Chris blushed and sighed.

"What?"

"Tom and Dick Hyers. You know, the mine owner's son and nephew. I shouldn't say anything, but they bothered me. Especially Tom."

"Bothered you? How?"

"Tom had this cigarette lighter. Slim, silver, and on its side a red circle on it with a red, white, and blue shield with a torch. It had his initials on it. Said his grandpa gave it to him for Christmas. He kept turning it on and holding it up in front of my face. You should have seen the look in Dale's eyes. I thought he was going to attack him. I think he would have if Reggie hadn't sat down to talk to him. We left early."

"Reggie talked to the Hyers? What about?"

"I didn't listen to them. We just wanted to get out of there."

"I'm sorry that happened."

"So how was your party?"

"Not so good."

"Why? What happened?"

Della looked Chris straight in her eyes. "Who all did you tell about my giving you my baby? Seems like everyone there knew, and boy, was Sister Bess upset at me." A lump rose in her chest, and try as she might to prevent it, tears spilled down her face. "She hates me now. Didn't even tell me goodbye."

Chris grasped Della's hands. "I told my mom, just like I said. No one else. And I asked her not to say a word to anyone."

"Well, she must've said something to someone. And they blabbed it to another person, who told someone else, and..." She sighed. "Now the whole world knows."

"I'm so sorry. I'll talk to Mom."

The door burst open, and Dale walked in. He stopped halfway into the living room. "Della, good to see you. I didn't realize you were here." Without giving her a chance to answer, he turned to his wife. "Did I tell you I asked about getting the baby on our insurance at work last Wednesday? Thought I'd better get all that in order."

"Who'd you talk to?" Chris asked.

"Tom Hyers, of course. He takes care of the insurance."

"And I suppose you told him where the baby's coming from? That's probably who's telling everyone in town."

"Oh, I didn't think of that." Dale's face fell, and he sank into a chair. "I guess I didn't have to tell him, but he asked. I didn't think. Just trying to make conversation, keep the boss happy."

"The boss has a big mouth." Della stood. "Should go. I told them I was too sick for church, so I'd better be there when they get back."

She plodded home. It didn't matter that everyone in Puttersville knew. She hoped Sister Bess would forgive her, but their relationship would never be the same. "Soon as I get rid of this baby, I'm going to find me a real job," she muttered. "Find me a place so I can have my privacy and be my own boss." She'd said it before, at least a hundred times, but saying it out loud made it seem more real, right around the corner.

She entered the house. Reggie sat in the living room stuffing some books and papers into a bag.

"You been out," he said, not looking up.

"You left church early."

"Yes. An appointment for lunch." He stood and put on his coat, then stepped across the room toward the door.

"Rose called."

He dropped the book in his hand. "She did? What'd she say?"

"Nothing. Hung up when I said you weren't here." Hurt and anger rippled through her. She didn't try to stop the words spilling out of her mouth. "I thought you liked me. But I guess your mammy means more, and you're minding her. It isn't fair."

"Let me remind you. Life isn't fair. You don't know anything about fair, not even what happened last week."

"What?"

"Thursday a week ago Martin Luther King, Jr. was awarded the Nobel Peace Prize for his work in civil rights."

"Oh, that's fair. From what I hear, he deserves it."

"You bet he does. Now tell me what other important thing happened this week."

"I don't know." She glared at him. *Why does he always have to act like I'm an ignoramus?*

"The Heart of Atlanta Hotel versus the United States Decision. The Supreme Court said private businesses have to abide by Title II of the Civil Rights Act. All public places have to allow blacks to use public facilities."

"Oh. So what's all that got to do with Rose? Is she your girlfriend?"

"Something else you should know. I will go out with whomever I want. I will like whomever I want. And no one's going to tell me whom to love." He stood and walked out the front door, slamming it behind him.

Well! I wish Winnie could've heard that. She pondered the thought. Reggie telling his mammy that. She could see Winnie's face turning red with anger and hear Nat say, "Now, now, dear. Reggie didn't mean it, did you, Reggie?" And Reggie would have replied, "You bet I meant it. Tired of you all treating me like I'm a teenager. I'm old enough to do what I want."

But it would never happen. Reggie was too sweet to say something like that to his mammy. His loyalty to his parents, family, and friends couldn't be questioned. Only in her imagination. And that was probably the only way she could ever be his girlfriend.

But who wants a girlfriend whose stomach is so big she's hard to kiss? Who would marry someone who has a baby that's not his? Shame poured over her. *Who wants a wife who's been dirtied by her daddy? No man in his right mind.*

Her stomach rumbled, and she glanced at the clock. Twelve-fifteen. Nat and Winnie should be home any minute. She gasped. *Was I supposed to make something for dinner?* No. Winnie had not said anything before leaving and had not left a note.

Nat and Winnie had not returned by 12:45, so she made herself a sandwich and carried it up to her room. After eating, she lay down and pulled the blanket up. It seemed only a few minutes until the front door slammed, jarring her awake. Footsteps sounded on the stairs, then a tap on her door.

"Della, you awake?"

"Yes, ma'am." She recognized Winnie's voice. "What is it?"

"May I come in?"

"Yes."

Della swung her legs off the edge of the bed and sat up as Winnie settled on the bottom edge of the bed.

"How are you feelin', child?"

"Better. I'm sorry I didn't make it to church."

"You missed a great sermon on forgiveness. Ted told a story of how he was angry at a friend when he was in high school, and the friend died in a car accident before they could make up. Everyone there was wipin' their eyes." She reached out and took Della's hands in hers. "Look at me."

Della lifted her eyes to Winnie's face.

"Bess invited us for lunch, expectin' you to be with us, but when you weren't, she said she was comin' over at three to talk to you. Do you feel like comin' downstairs?"

"Yes, ma'am. Just need to brush my hair." She picked up her brush and stroked her hair back and front. Winnie left, and she followed her. The doorbell rang as soon as they reached the living room.

Sister Bess came in and handed Winnie her coat. Walking to Della, she wrapped her in her arms, then tilted Della's face upward. "I'm sorry for treating you the way I did last night. Do you forgive me?"

Tears rolled from Della's eyes as she hugged Sister Bess. "Yes. I'm sorry I disappointed you. But I can't keep no baby."

"You know your friend Chris well enough to know she'll be a good mama?"

"I think so. She's lost two babies, you know, and she really wants one. Her husband already put the baby on their insurance. They're good people. They drew up the adoption papers, too, and they can't wait."

"The adoption papers? They hired a lawyer?"

"I…I don't know." Della took a few steps back. "They said the papers they had were just fine."

"David C. is coming. He'll be here for Christmas. He just got hired by the NAACP, so he's good. We'll get him to look at the papers."

What did Dale and Chris say about the adoption papers? Della couldn't remember. What if they weren't legal? A lump of fear filled her throat.

CHAPTER 30

David C.

The day after Christmas Della woke to a bright room. She had forgotten to close the curtains. Limping to the window, she peered outside. A new coat of snow covered everything, at least three inches of glistening whiteness. She closed the curtains and climbed back into bed.

Christmas Day was a bust, at least in her eyes. The Johnsons had David C., and they elected to celebrate at home, so it was just the four of them and Sister Bess, Mother Carrie, and Chloe. She and Winnie cooked enough food for an army—a ham and a turkey and all the trimmings and two pies and a cake—and she had been on her feet and doing most of the serving and the cleaning up. All that work would have to be her gift to them, for she had nothing more to give.

Yes, she loved the watch from Sister Bess and the blouse Winnie made her, but she was a bit put off by Reggie's gift, a book on civil rights. She was so disappointed she couldn't bring herself to look inside it. He had put his hand on her shoulder and said, "Some things in there you need to know."

But even that wasn't the cause for the deep ache that clung to her inside and out, the feeling that something was missing and keeping Christmas joy away. Lying there looking at the window curtains, images of Christmases past flashed through her mind, and she knew what the hurt meant. No Mama. No sweet voice singing carols as she cooked breakfast, no homemade fudge, no handmade gifts. The thoughts of those gifts—a handmade teddy bear, bows for her hair, and a stapled-together scrapbook Mama had glued family pictures in just for her. She had not remembered any of them when she hurried away to leave before Daddy got home.

"Oh, Mama," she whispered. "This was our first Christmas apart. Oh, I miss you. I would give anything if we could have one more Christmas together."

"Della, you gettin' up today? Come on, girl, we have work to do. David C. is comin'."

Oh yes. David C. was coming. Thea had probably told him about her giving away her baby. He would ask her to see the adoption papers. The problem was she couldn't remember the adoption papers. Surely she had a copy, but if she did, she didn't know where it was. She would look for it again as soon as she had a free moment.

"Comin'!" she yelled. She threw back the covers, picked out some clean clothes, and headed for the bathroom. After dressing, she went downstairs. Reggie sat at the table, whistling a tune from one of the works he had played on his violin.

"You look worried. Anything wrong?"

"I lost something I need. At least I think I lost it. I'll have to look later."

"Oh. Anything I can do to help, let me know. I'd better be off. A few of the kids from church are cleaning up from the Christmas party, and I'd like to be there to help."

"Okay." She hadn't gone to the party, had barely known about it. "Who all's comin' to help?"

"Brenda and Bobby for sure. Maybe Danny. I don't know who else. Want to come?"

She shook her head. "Winnie's already tellin' me to help clean. Remember we're havin' company."

"That's right. Ted and Thea and that lawyer cousin are coming. I'll be back for lunch. And I'll help."

"Sure thing," she said, sighing. *If only I could go.* She scraped the rest of the oatmeal and raisins into a bowl and ate them without sugar or milk, then washed the dishes.

"I'm taking the remainder of the day off from sewing," Winnie said as she came into the kitchen. "Reggie around?"

"No. Just left to help clean up at church. Said he'd be back for lunch and would help us."

"Just like him. We'll be done by then." She opened the refrigerator door and perused the contents. "Don't know if they'll be here for dinner, but if they are, we have enough."

Nat rushed through the front door, panting, his boots shedding chunks of snow all over the floor. "Where's Reggie?"

"Said he was going to go help clean up at church, right, Della?"

"Yes, ma'am, that's what he said.

"I was down at church, and Reggie's not there. No one's seen him. Stopped in at the drug store and heard there's a sit-in down at the mine. Sheriff is headin' down there. If he's at the mine protestin', and he gets thrown in jail, he can rot in there. I ain't bailin' him out."

He ain't no little kid! Della wanted to say it, but one look at Nat's face warned her to keep quiet.

Winnie glared at him. "If Reggie's at the mine protestin', you should be proud. He's standin' up for our people's rights, somethin' you never did."

"He's goin' to lose his job at the mines, that's what'll happen." He turned and stomped out of the house.

"Wonder what he's protestin'," Della said as she wiped up the melting snow on the floor. "He never said anything about protestin' at the mine."

"I heard some of the women at church talkin'," Winnie stated. "Said they knew some safety measures were not in place. They's worried about their men, that's what. Nearly every able-bodied man in this town's dependent on their jobs diggin' up that coal."

The ache in Della's feet and legs was worse by the time she mopped the floors and cleaned the bathrooms. Winnie wiped the kitchen cabinets and countertops, but Della wished she would go back into the sewing room. She had to call Chris, had to find out about the adoption papers and get a copy if she could, and she didn't want Winnie hearing and poking her nose into her business.

Her chance came at last when Reggie came home.

"Come into the sewin' room, need to talk to you," Winnie told him.

The minute Della heard the door shut, she picked up the phone and dialed Chris's number. She counted fourteen rings before she hung up. *In a way it's a relief. If I don't have the papers, David C. can't say they're wrong. But what if he insists that I get them and show them to him?*

David C. came with Ted and Thea right after lunch. Della was still cleaning up the dishes, and after greeting them, she went back to her task. When she finished, she took a kitchen chair and sat it in the living room corner where she was mostly hidden behind a bookcase. They were discussing safety at the mine.

"Reggie heard about it," Nat said.

"Tell me what happened." David C.'s eyes darted toward Reggie. He slid his glasses from the top of his head with one hand while he searched his briefcase with the other, pulling out a manila folder. "I've been working on a case from the mines down south."

"Nothing happened," Reggie said. "I stopped at the grocer to pick up some snacks for the kids at church. Mr. Dobbs, the store's owner, said his son Tye and another miner were meeting Mr. Hyers to discuss safety concerns. I took the cookies and drinks to the church building, but since no one was there, decided to go down and see what was happening. When I arrived, I parked a ways down the road. No one was there except the sheriff and Tye Dobbs and another man.

I'd know Tye anywhere with his bushy brown beard, but couldn't quite make out the other guy. They went in and talked to the Hyers. I think all three of the Hyers were there—the owner Steve Hyers, his son Tom, and his nephew Dick—but all Tye, the other man, and the sheriff did was go in and talk to them, and then they went home. I turned my car around and left as soon as I saw them come out with the sheriff. Don't think they saw me. When I got to the church building, everyone was there, ready to work."

"How many miners are there?" David C. extracted a notebook and pen.

"One hundred sixty-five at the Puttersville No. 1 Mine. This spring they plan to open No. 2 Mine. I overheard the Hyers planning it last week. They thought they had closed Steve Hyers' office door, but it wasn't completely shut. He said they would employ over fifty new miners to start and more later."

"Do you have any idea what the miners are wanting?"

"No. I'm not told what goes on between the miners and the boss."

Winnie cleared her throat. "Sister Brown at church said there's more coal dust in the air than should be. They're savin' money on limestone spread. And methane fills every inch of that mine. The fans don't work half the time. They're pushin' so hard for more production that on one has time for safety. Said her husband was real worried."

"Her brother's wife said she's heard some talk of a strike," Thea added. "Can you help the miners here?"

"Probably not." David C.'s mustache twitched, and he closed his notebook and pen and put them back into his briefcase. "But I have a friend who might be able to do something. He's one of the executives at United Mine Workers."

Della watched David C.'s eyes probe the room. She shrank down in her chair as far as she could and stared at his shiny black shoes, thinking that if she didn't look at him, he wouldn't see her in the corner.

But he did. "You must be Della," he said. She wanted to run, but his eyes pinned her to her chair.

"Yes, sir."

"I hear you're letting another couple adopt your baby." When she didn't answer, he asked, "That right?"

"Yes, sir. I am."

"The state has rules about adoptions, you know. Will you go get the papers and let me have a look at them?"

"I…I don't have them. The Bakers are going to make me copies, but they haven't yet."

"I'm leaving in a week." His gaze pierced her whole body. "Get them for me, and I'll check them out for you. You don't want to take any chances with legalities."

"No, sir." Her hands shook, and she stuck them between her knees, sure everyone believed she was an idiot for not having a copy of the papers. No, they knew she was stupid. *How could I not have the papers? I barely remember what they said when we made the agreement.*

David C. stood, his shoes catching the rays from the ceiling light fixture. His pant legs didn't have one wrinkle in them, not even from sitting, and he turned and brushed his chair off with his hand before setting his briefcase on it. Nat stood beside him, a head taller.

"Oh, it's after four," Winnie said, looking at her watch. "Why don't you all stay for an early dinner? Won't take long to get it on the table."

"Sorry, but I have a meeting," David C. said. "We'll take a raincheck. We'll come back when Della has her papers for me to see." He put his hand on Winnie's shoulder. "Call and let me know."

Winnie nodded. "She'll have them soon, won't you?"

"Yes, ma'am." Della said her goodbyes, and as soon as they left, she ran up to her room, and throwing herself across her bed, covered her head with her pillow. After a few minutes she rolled over and tossed the pillow away. Crying wouldn't do any good. Neither would the anger that stirred in her breast. Anger at her circumstances. Anger at everyone who stuck his nose into her business, including Winnie and David C. Mostly, though, anger at herself. How could she believe that her arrangement with the Bakers could be her and their little secret? Why hadn't she considered that the adoption papers might not be legal?

She reached under the bed and pulled out her old suitcase, hauled it up onto the bed, and undid the latches. Sticking her hand inside, she clasped the pouch containing her coin. She slid it into her hand and ran her fingers over its strange letters.

"Mama, I don't know if you planned for me to have this, but I thank you. Maybe I'll never know what it means, but you do. It reminds me of your love, and I'll never let go of it." She stared at it a few more seconds, then slipped it inside the bag and tucked it under the bottom suitcase strap. Feeling more in control, she redid the fasteners on the suitcase and tucked it back under her bed. She'd better go down and help with dinner. She was halfway to the door when a gentle knock sounded.

"May I talk with you a minute?"

Reggie's voice.

CHAPTER 31

New Year's Party

She opened the door a crack, and he pushed it and came into her room. "I could tell David C. upset you. I'm sorry. But he's right. The papers have to be legal."

"I know. It's been several months since we did them. I…I don't think they hired a lawyer."

"Then tomorrow after church you go get them so David C. can have a look. You need to get his help while he's here."

She sat down on the bed and sighed. "Okay."

"There's something else I wanted to ask you. Do you want to go to the company's New Year's Eve party with me? It's next Thursday night."

"Me?" She looked up at his face, so full of warmth and acceptance. "You want to take me? In this condition?" She placed her hand on top of her abdomen. "What will your mammy say?"

"I already told her I was going to ask you. She said I ought to go to the church party that night. I think she was unhappier about my not going to church than she was that I was taking you."

"But why me? You've got a good education. You should have lots of girlfriends, not somebody like me. Why aren't you taking Janice?"

He bit his lip. "I told you, Janice and I are just friends. Sure, sometimes I take her places. But really, she's like my sister."

"But me? Why?"

"Della..." He took her face in his hands and looked into her eyes. "I see your struggle. I know how hard you work here. And I know that you don't think much of yourself. It wasn't your fault what happened to you, and God still loves you. Will you go with me because we're friends?"

"But I don't have anything to wear. Nothing fancy like everyone else."

"Wear the new blouse Mammy gave you for Christmas. You are pretty enough without fancy clothes. And I'm real proud of you, learning how to speak like an educated person."

"Yes, I'll go with you." She looked up at him. "What do you mean, like an educated person?"

"Things like not leaving the endings off your words. You just said *taking* instead of *takin'*.

She laughed. "Guess you're rubbing off on me. And I'd love to go with you."

"Okay, it's all set. We'll leave here Thursday evening at six-thirty, so be ready." With that, he backed out the door and closed it.

After church and lunch the next day, she walked to Chris's house and knocked on the door. No one answered, and after knocking several times, she turned homeward. *Maybe they went visiting. I'll call them tonight.*

Not even worrying about the adoption papers could squash the joy that leaped into her heart every time she thought about Reggie's invitation. He admired her, perhaps loved her. He cared about her feelings and what happened to her, so much that he was willing to buck his mammy's wishes.

By Tuesday evening she had still not procured a copy. Chris didn't answer her phone calls, and she had not found them home Monday evening. Wednesday she busied herself washing and ironing her clothes, making sure to hang her best pair of pants and her blouse in the closet where they would not be crowded and wrinkled.

Thursday her stomach fluttered with nerves. While the family ate dinner she stood in the bathroom trying to get her hair to curl. In the last few weeks, all it did was hang straight.

"Changes in your hormones due to your condition," Bess told her at church last Sunday.

Della pinched her cheeks to make them rosy, and then she twisted strands of her hair around her forefinger so it would curl, but when she let loose, it fell limp onto her shoulders.

Winnie passed by the open bathroom door and stopped to stare at Della's efforts to curl her hair. "You know I'm unhappy."

"That I'm going out with Reggie?"

"He could at least take you to the church party where you'll be safe."

So you can keep an eye on us. "We'll be okay. My hair won't do anything. Won't curl."

"It'll never be noticed on a galloping horse."

"But I'm not a galloping horse!" Della said, making a face.

Winnie let out a long cackle, then held out her hand. "Thought you might like to try these. Some Avon samples I can't use. Some lipstick and blush."

"Thanks. I…I've never had any makeup."

"Well, just experiment with them and see what you can do. I think this pink lipstick will look good on you." She turned to walk away.

"Winnie."

"Yes?"

"I was thinkin'…thinking my going out with Reggie would make you angry, and here you are giving me makeup." She put her arms around Winnie and hugged her. "Thank you."

"Girl, when you have children, you'll see that there's times to step back and let them be their own person. I'm tryin' to learn how to do that. Besides, I think you've both earned some fun time. I just wish it was at church. And I remind you both that you're only friends. Nothing else."

"Yes, ma'am."

"Did you get a copy of the adoption papers?"

"Uh, no. I've called several times. I've walked to their house three times. No one answers the door, and no one answers the telephone. I think they must've gone out of town."

"I told David C. we'd have them by Friday. They're comin' for dinner Friday evening, so you be sure and get them."

"Yes, ma'am. I'll try real hard."

"Good girl. See what you think of that makeup." She walked out the door, leaving Della to her own experimentations. At six-fifteen she gave her hair one last swipe and walked down the stairs.

Reggie rose from his seat on the couch. He didn't whistle, but Della felt his approval as he took her hand in his. The blush she had brushed onto her cheeks deepened as she walked through the door he held open for her.

"Your mammy said she reminded you that we were only friends," she said as he climbed behind the steering wheel. "She made me promise the same thing."

"Well, we are friends, aren't we?" He smiled down at her, his eyes saying more than the words he had spoken. "Of course we're friends. We don't need to tell her anything else."

Her heart pounded, and she looked down, blushing, sure he could hear it. "*Anything else,*" he had said. What else was there to tell?

They arrived at the Event Center at the hotel. Cars flashing their lights and blaring their horns assaulted them with their drivers' revelry.

"I was afraid of this," Reggie remarked. "People aren't waiting until midnight to hit the booze. Maybe we should go to the church party. What do you think?"

She shrugged. "It's up to you."

He grinned down at her. "You too. Oh, what the heck. Let's go in. We can always leave if it gets too rowdy." He opened the car door for her and helped her out. His large hand wrapped around hers as he led the way into the building.

A real date! Reggie's taking me on a real date! Della's eyes brimmed with tears of happiness. A few days ago she would have never guessed it possible. She would do her best to remember every second of this wonderful night.

"Happy New Year, Reggie. Come on in and enjoy," Steve Hyers greeted him at the door. His eyes lit on Della, and his visage changed. "This your girlfriend?"

"Happy New Year, Mr. Hyers. This is Della. We're just friends."

"I see." He raised his glass of beer. "Don't get too friendly."

Anger flashed across Reggie's face, and he let go of her hand. "If he weren't my boss, I'd tell him a thing or two, and it wouldn't be 'Happy New Year.' Want to get some refreshments?"

"Sure."

They wound their way through tables and chairs. In one side of the room a man played records, a number of couples danced, and nearby a line of people danced single file, twirling with each beat of the music.

Reggie handed her a plate, and they walked along the table gathering sandwiches and cookies. Two large glass bowls filled with red punch stood on the end of the table. Reggie filled a dipper and brought it to his nose, then shook his head. "Spiked," he said, smelling the punch in the other bowl. He poured the dipper full from the second bowl into a glass and handed it to her.

"Oh, there's Chris and Dale." Della pointed to a table across the room. "Let's go sit with them."

Chris's eyes lit up as they approached the table. "I was hoping you'd be here, Della. Sit down." She pulled a chair out and patted it. "Hi Reggie," she said as he put his plate on the table. "I'm Chris. The last time I saw you, I was sitting in your math class, but you probably don't remember. This is my husband Dale." She held her hand out to Reggie. "You work in the office, right?"

"I do. Nice seeing you. So you're the ones adopting Della's baby?"

"Yes, and we can't wait."

Della sat down. "I'm so glad you're here, been trying to reach you for a week."

Chris raised her eyebrows. "Something wrong?"

"Remember when I signed the adoption papers? I need a copy. A lawyer friend is here, and he wants to see them."

"I can get you a copy, but not until at least Saturday, maybe Monday."

"Saturday, I hope."

Tye Dobbs arrived, plate and drink in hand. "Mind if we join you? This is my wife Debbie, for those of you who haven't met her."

"Sure, have a seat," Reggie said. "What's going on with you lately?"

Tye shrugged so hard that his shoulders touched the edges of his brown, bushy beard. "Can't say much." He spoke in a near whisper. "Worried about the mine. Old Hyers so tight with his money he's skipping out on safety measures. Number One's going to blow if he doesn't get the fans fixed and more limestone powder down."

"Every day he goes down there I'm praying he comes home," Debbie said. "Isn't fair what they're doing to us. We got us a little one on the way."

"You do?" Chris reached across the table to take Debbie's hand. "Congratulations."

"Just found out," Debbie said, smiling. "Due next July. Told our folks last night, and they're so excited. It'll be their first grandchild."

"Oh, that's great," Della said. "Wish my mama was here."

Reggie turned to Tye. "Heard you were down at the mine talking to Mr. Hyers a few days ago."

"Yeah, me and one of the other miners went down to talk to the boss. Showed him some things we all wanted. I got over a hundred of the men to sign it."

"You sign it?" Reggie asked Dale.

"Of course."

"What'd Hyers say when you showed it to him?"

"I think we're going to have to contact the union. Said he didn't give a—" Dale snorted. "I can't believe his son Tom's one of the safety inspectors."

"Shh," Chris warned as Tom Hyers headed toward their table, beer in one hand and plate in the other.

"Everyone enjoying the party?" Tom asked.

"Great party," Reggie said.

"Wonderful food," Chris stated.

"Good." Tom sat down in the chair next to Chris, who scooted her chair as close to Dale's as she could.

"Glad you like the food, honey," Tom said, sliding his hand toward her.

Dale shot him a warning glance. "Be nicer if everyone behaves himself. There's nothin' like New Year's to have people drunk and out of their senses."

"Of course we're behaving ourselves, aren't we, sweetie?" Tom raised his hand to Chris's shoulder, but missed and hit her chest. "Oops. That was a mistake. Let me try again."

Chris stood. "I'm going to throw these things into the trash can."

Dale jumped up and followed her.

"So you and your friend thought you could scare Dad into making some changes," Tom said to Tye, a sneer on his face. "Please, Mr. Hyers, our lives are in danger," he whined, pantomiming a sad and worried face. "We're going to the union." He burst into raucous laughter.

Debbie reached for Tye's arm. "I'm cold, honey. Would you please go out to the car and get my coat?"

"I have to go to the restroom," Reggie said. "Come on, Della."

She followed Reggie to the outside hall where the restrooms were located, and they each went into their place. Della dawdled as much as she dared, combing her hair, putting on more lipstick, and washing her hands. *Reggie's probably wondering what happened to me. I'll suggest we go home or to the church party.*

Hearing a commotion, she opened the door. About a dozen people stood at the end of the hall, all talking at once.

"Someone's killed Tom Hyers!" a voice shouted. "Call the police!"

CHAPTER 32

In Jail

"Let's go before the police get here," Reggie said as he came up behind her. "I don't want to get involved in this mess." He took her hand, and together they ran to the car. Reggie drove out of the parking lot and headed down the street when two police cars passed them with their lights flashing and their sirens wailing.

"I wonder who did it," Della said. She shivered. "Tye was awful mad at him."

"Doesn't mean he did it. He went to his car to get Debbie's coat, remember?"

"He could've come back in."

"There were lots of people upset at Tom. Unhappy with all the Hyers. Anyone could have done it. Will be interesting to see if they arrest someone." He took her hand. "Let's go to the church party. It's only a couple blocks away."

"Okay. What're they doing at the church party?"

"Oh, board games, snacks. We'll see."

She couldn't get her mind off Tom's murder. "Did you see him? Did you see Tom lying there dead?"

"No. I came out of the restroom after you. I just wanted to get out of there."

"Me too. But I'd liked to have seen him. Wonder if someone stabbed him or shot him."

"Let's talk about something else. Have you read the book I gave you for Christmas?"

"Sorry, no. Haven't had the time."

They pulled into the church parking lot and parked. Bobby saw them and ran to their car, waving and yelling as he reached them. "Reggie! I'm so glad you're here. You got to come in and play games with us."

"We're coming, we're coming," Reggie said as he got out. He opened Della's door and whispered, "You have to read it." He smiled down at her. "Remember, there's something in there I want you to know."

"Okay, I will." She took his hand as they walked into the church building with Junior.

"Promise?"

"I promise."

"Good."

Thea Johnson spied them as soon as they stepped through the door. "So glad you two made it," she said. "There's still some goodies on the table."

Winnie and Nat left their game. "Told you it'd be more fun here," Nat said. "Glad you came."

"It is more fun," Reggie said. "Someone killed Tom, the owner's son. We just got out of there as quickly as we could."

"Tom Hyers? He's dead? What happened?" Nat asked.

"We don't know. We were in the restrooms, and when we came out, he was lying dead in the hallway."

"You didn't see or hear anything?" Winnie set her glass down and put her hand on Reggie's arm. "Nothing?"

"Not a thing," Della said.

A crowd gathered around them, and several people asked more questions, but Reggie couldn't tell them any more than he had already said. "I just hope they find out who did it. Could have been anyone there. All the miners are upset at the Hyers, and Tom was drunker than I've ever seen him."

"Tye Dobbs was really mad," Della said. "You should've seen what Tom did—"

"Don't go into that." Reggie said in a stern voice. "No use in spreading rumors."

Della's face turned red. "Sorry."

"You two want to join us in a game of Scrabble?" Winnie asked. "We'll start over if you join us."

"Want to?" Reggie took Della's arm and steered her to the table. Taking his coat and toboggan off, he tossed them onto a nearby chair. "Come on. It's an easy game to learn. All you have to do is make words."

The door opened, and two police officers burst into the fellowship hall. "Reginald Huston," one of the said. "We're looking for Reginald Huston. Is he here?"

"Right here," Reggie said, standing. "What's up, officers?"

"We're arresting you for the murder of Tom Hyers. Steve Hyers said he saw you running from the scene of the crime." They stepped over to Reggie, and one of them grabbed his arms and twisted them behind his back. Della heard the clink of handcuffs snapping shut around his wrists.

"No! I didn't do it! I was in the restroom when it happened!" Reggie shouted. "You have to believe me!"

"You're coming with us," one of the policeman said as they shoved him toward the door.

"Call David C.!" Reggie yelled as the door shut behind him.

Nat and Winnie yanked the door open in time to see the police car speeding from the parking lot.

"Come on, Winnie and Della, we're going to the police station!" Nat said. Anger and disbelief filled his face, and his eyes sparked with determination. "Nobody's goin' to arrest my son for nothing."

"We're coming, too," Ted said. "Be down there just as soon as we call David C. from the church office."

Della got into Nat's truck. "Reggie didn't do it," she sobbed. "I swear. We were both in the restroom, and we don't know who did it."

Winnie handed her a tissue. "Stop cryin'. Be brave for Reggie. We know he didn't do it, and they'll find out who did. David C.'s comin'."

Nat parked at the police station, and they went inside.

"Where's my son? I want to see my son," Nat said to the policeman sitting at the desk. "What're they doin' to Reggie?"

"Questioning him," the officer said. "I wouldn't wait around here if I were you. Your son won't be coming home tonight."

Ted and Thea rushed into the station with David C. He hoisted his briefcase onto the desk. "I want to speak to Reggie Huston. I'm his lawyer."

"You can't see him until we're done with our investigation," the officer said.

"*The Sixth Amendment* of the *United States Constitution* gives him the right to have his lawyer present during questioning. Take me to him." David C. spoke in a commanding tone.

"Not in this town it don't. Take it to the judge, to the district attorney, to the state supreme court if you wish. You'll get a chance to speak with him, but not until we're finished."

David C. motioned for the Hustons and the Johnsons to follow him outside, and when they had gone out and shut the door, he said, "Best if we don't aggravate the situation. My advice is for you all to go home and get some sleep. You'll need to be rested tomorrow."

"They can't keep him in jail, can they?" Winnie asked.

"He didn't do nothing. I know my boy," Nat stated.

"I'm afraid they can keep him. Reggie's their scapegoat, and until he's proven innocent, they'll keep him locked up."

"But that's unfair. He didn't do it!" Della said. She fought back tears. *Reggie wouldn't want me to cry.*

"I know he didn't," David C. said. "I'll stay here and talk to him when they let me, and I'll let you know what happens as soon as I can."

"You and Della go home," Nat said to Winnie. "I'm waitin' here with David C."

"We'll take you," Ted said. He put his arms around them. "Gather around, everybody. Let's say a prayer."

They gathered in a circle, arms around each other.

"Heavenly Father," Ted prayed. "You are God Almighty who knows everything. You know our brother Reggie didn't murder Tom Hyers. Please help him, Father, while he is in jail. Let him rely on You and keep him in Your care. Please, we pray, be with David C. as he works to prove him innocent. In Jesus' holy name. Amen."

"Amen," they all repeated.

Della turned to go, and David C. tapped her shoulder. "I still need to see your adoption papers. Tomorrow?"

"Chris said they would try to have them for me tomorrow or Saturday. Chris and Dale were at the party, so please talk to them."

"I plan to. First thing. Now you all go home and try to sleep."

Nat put his arm around Winnie. "Reggie will be okay. Don't worry."

"Keep praying," Ted said. "We'll be seeking God's help for your boy."

When they were home, Winnie turned on the television. "Something to keep me awake 'til Nat gets home," she said. "You go on up to bed."

Della looked at the clock. A little after ten, her usual bedtime. She should be tired, but every nerve in her body felt wide awake. She sat down beside Winnie. "No use in my going up there. I can't sleep for worrying."

"I know what you mean, but won't do us no good. We have to trust in God to protect Reggie and show the world he's not guilty.

Maybe you can tell me what happened at that party," she said, getting up and turning off the television.

Della related how Steve greeted them at the door half drunk, their talk about the mine workers' problems, and Tom's making fun of Tye at the table. "Everyone kept their cool. We all got up and walked away, just left Tom sitting there. That was the last time I saw him alive. When we came out of the bathroom, he was lying dead at the end of the hallway. A crowd had gathered, but no one knew what happened."

"Where did Tye go?"

"Outside to get his wife's coat."

"Where were Dale and Chris?"

"They had gone to the trashcan, but I don't know where they went after that."

"Are you sure Reggie was in the bathroom?"

"I saw him go in. But I didn't want to be around those people, so I stayed in the bathroom a little while. When I went out, I heard someone shout that Tom was dead. And Reggie came out of the bathroom and came up behind me. That's all I know."

Winnie turned the television back on. *The Tonight Show Starring Johnny Carson* was playing. They watched for five minutes, and then she turned it off.

"Wish I knew what was happening down there," Della said. "Can't bear to think of Reggie facing those policemen. He's all alone."

"Not really alone. God is with him."

"Then why doesn't God do something? Right now?"

"Be patient, child. God's time is not always our time."

"But I wish He'd hurry."

"I know it's hard, but we have to trust in God." She blew her nose. "Just have to trust."

The front door opened, and Nat came in. His shoulders drooped. "Hi Honey, Della."

Winnie ran to him and put her arms around him. "How did it go? Did you get to see Reggie?"

"Only for a few minutes. David C. asked him how much he told them. Reggie said, 'Nothing. Nothing to tell.' Then David C. told him about his *Fifth Amendment* right to silence. Reggie knows he doesn't have to say anything at all if he doesn't want to, especially anything that might incriminate him. As David C. said, too bad the Puttersville Police Department doesn't know our rights. Anyway, Reggie knows David C. is a good lawyer and is goin' to help him."

"Wonderful. Let's go to bed and get some sleep."

"I vote for that. Come on, Della, you too."

Halfway up the stairs, they heard a loud thud on the outside wall of the house, and then a terrifying explosion ripped apart the night quiet.

Della gasped. "What was that? Is somebody shooting at us?"

"Sounded like a firecracker," Nat said, crossing the room and turning on the porch light. He peered outside, then stepped onto the porch. He returned holding a rock four inches in diameter. A string secured a note to one side of the rock. Nat unwrapped the string and unfolded the note.

"Reggie Huston, you killed Tom Hyers," Nat read. "You will pay."

Nat handed the note to Winnie. "I'm glad he's in jail. It might be the safest place he can be."

CHAPTER 33

The Prognosis

A knock sounded on the door before Della finished her breakfast the next morning. Nat had gone to the back yard and Winnie was in the sewing room, so she went to the door and opened it. A policeman stood outside.

"Are you Della Etter?"

"Yes."

"I need to talk to you."

"I don't have to talk to you."

"You talk, or I'll get a search warrant. Is that what you want, the police coming in and going through your things?"

"What do you want?" she asked, stepping back.

"Were you with Reginald Huston at the Puttersville Mine party last night?"

"Yes."

"Did you see Tom Hyers?"

"Yes."

"Did you talk to him?"

"No."

"Did Reginald talk to him?"

"I don't remember."

"Don't remember, or won't say?"

"I don't remember."

"Where were you when Tom Hyers was killed?"

"In the bathroom."

"Where was Reginald?"

"In the bathroom."

"Are you absolutely sure? Did you see him in the bathroom when Tom Hyers was killed?"

"I…I—"

"What's goin' on here?" Winnie charged into the living room. "What do you want?"

"I'm investigating Tom Hyers' murder."

"Well, this isn't a court of law." She took Della by the arm. "Go to your room, girl. I'll handle this."

"Yes, ma'am." Della fled as far as the top of the steps, where she stopped. Trembling, she peered down into the living room."

"Officer, you want to question anyone here, you better do it at the station. Now get out!" Winnie slammed the door behind him.

Della crept down the stairs, her stomach churning.

"What'd you tell him? Winnie asked.

"Nothing. Only that Reggie was in the bathroom when Tom was killed. Then he wanted to know if I saw Reggie in the bathroom. How could I answer that? He said he'd get a warrant if I didn't talk to him."

"Then he'll have to get a warrant. We're goin' to the jail in a bit to visit Reggie. Want to come?"

"Yes."

Nat came in through the back door. "I saw a police car drivin' past the house. Were they here?"

"Yes," Winnie said. "They wanted to talk to Della. Said they'd get a search warrant. I told them to leave."

"You should've got me." He turned to Della. "Don't you ever let an officer in or talk to him when you're alone, understand?"

"Yes, sir." Her voice trembled.

Winnie put her arm around her. "Then let's get the breakfast dishes done. We need to be back by two as David C.'s comin' over."

Della poured out the rest of her oatmeal and rinsed her bowl. Filling the sink with hot water, she let her hands wash and dry while her mind raced. *What if there's a trial and I have to testify? There will be a trial. That's for sure. What I say might mean jail time, even death for Reggie. But what can I say if they ask me that question? Of course I didn't see him in the bathroom. But someone else could've seen him in there.*

Winnie came into the kitchen. "I know you've already told it, but tell me again. Who else did you see at the party?"

"Dale and Chris were at our table. So were Tye and Debbie Dobbs. You know, Tye's the one Reggie saw take some papers to Steve Hyers, the boss. We were talking to them about the miners' concerns about safety when Tom came over. He was drunk and acting wrong toward Chris."

"Did he say anything to anyone?"

"He mocked Tye's efforts to bring the miners' concerns to Steve Hyers' attention. Got up and made fun of Tye."

"What did Tye do?"

"He went out to his car to get Debbie's coat. Chris and Dale took stuff to the trash can on the other side of the room. Reggie and I got up to go to the bathroom. We all just wanted to get away from Tom. Nobody said anything to him or did anything. When Reggie and I came out of the bathroom, Tom was dead. We didn't see what happened, so we left. We didn't want to be there when the police came."

"I sure hope they find out who killed Tom so Reggie can come home. I told Nat we'd bring him a ham sandwich. Let's make Reggie one and take him some cookies. And make us one for an early lunch, would you?"

"I'll make the sandwiches," Della said. She piled extra ham and cheese on and spread the bread with mayonnaise. Finding a paper bag, she put the food inside it and sat it on a shelf in the refrigerator.

Nat came into the kitchen. "Ready to go? Winnie's already in the car."

"Coming." Della grabbed the bags of sandwiches from the refrigerator and hurried to catch up with Nat, who was holding the truck door open for her. She settled into the seat as he got in and pulled onto the street.

The police station housed the small Puttersville jail. Nat's truck pulled into the parking lot behind them, and they walked in together, Winnie carrying the sack of food.

"We're here to visit Reggie Huston," Nat told the officer at the desk.

He looked them over, eyeing the sack in Winnie's hand. "What's in there?"

"We brought him some lunch," she said. "Two sandwiches and some cookies. That's all."

"You can't take that in there. Not allowed."

Winnie dumped the sack out on his desk. "You can see for yourself. Nothing in here but food."

"And how do I know there's not a knife in those sandwiches? You can go in, but not the food. You got fifteen minutes, and it started when you stepped in here."

He showed them through a door into a narrow hallway. At the end of the hall were three cells, all empty except the one Reggie was in.

"Reggie, are you okay?" Winnie clasped his left hand through the cell bars, and Della grabbed his other hand. "Are they treatin' you okay?"

"We tried to bring you some food, but they wouldn't let us," Nat said through clenched teeth.

Reggie turned toward them. He left eyelid was swollen over his eye, and a cut crossed his brow.

"What happened to your eye?" Nat asked.

"What'd they do to you? What'd they do to my boy?" Tears rolled down Winnie's face. "They hurt you."

"I wouldn't talk," Reggie said. "They tried to make me, but David C. said I didn't have to. My *Fifth Amendment* right. So I haven't told them a thing."

"Good for you," Winnie said. "A policeman came to the house this morning and tried to make Della talk, but she didn't."

"I was afraid," Della said, squeezing his hand. "Oh, Reggie I'm so sorry they hurt you."

Reggie looked into her face with an expression of pain and love. "Don't talk to them again," he said. "Don't let them in the house."

"We're not going to, son. We'll do only what David C. tells us. That's all," Nat said. "We want you home soon."

"I wish I could hug you," Winnie said. She reached up to clutch his arm. "I miss you."

"I'll be out of here soon, Mammy. Don't you worry."

"Time's up," the officer said. "Let's go."

"Love you. We'll keep prayin'," Winnie said.

"Love you," Della mouthed after Nat and Winnie headed for the door. She let go of Reggie's hand and followed.

"You can come once a week to visit," the officer said as they passed his desk. "Our usual visiting day is Wednesday. You can come for your fifteen minutes any time between one and two o'clock in the afternoon."

Winnie stalked out and grabbed the bag of sandwiches as she passed the desk, but once they were outside, she burst into tears. "They hurt him bad," she said. "And we can't take him any decent food."

"Don't worry. David C. will have him out soon," Nat said, putting his arm around her. "We'll keep prayin'. You too, Della, keep prayin'. I'm takin' the rest of the day off. Want to hear what David C. says."

"Let's go home and make the place presentable, Della." Winnie opened the car door for her. "From now on, everything we do is for gettin' Reggie home."

They finished sweeping, dusting, and putting away Reggie's coat and toboggan left on the sofa. Della held his coat to her face and drew in his scent. *They didn't even let him take his coat.* She recalled the last time she saw him between two officers practically being dragged from the church.

David C. knocked on the door a few minutes after two.

"Come in and have a seat," Winnie said, ushering him through the door. "Can I get you some water or coffee?"

"Nothing, thanks." He sighed as he sat on the sofa and put his briefcase on the floor beside his feet. "We have a lot to do to get ready for the arraignment."

"What's that?" Nat asked.

"The court hearing where Reggie will be formally charged. It's on the court calendar for two Fridays from today. The police detective is out working on the case even today, New Year's Day. They have to find enough evidence to make the murder charge stick."

"A policeman was here asking Della questions this morning," Winnie said. "He threatened to get a warrant to search the place if she didn't talk."

"I'm surprised they haven't already been here with a warrant," David C. said. "If I were you, I'd search Reggie's room. See if there is anything they can use as evidence against him."

"What are we looking for?" Nat asked.

"Any kind of weapon Reggie might have. Get rid of it."

"He doesn't have one." Nat stood. "I've never seen anything in his room, not even a penknife."

"Anything he might have written, then, especially anything about work or the Hyers. If you find anything, get rid of it. And be careful not to let it slip that you found it, not to anyone. If word gets out, they can charge you with tampering with evidence. That can mean jail time."

"What else should we do?" asked Winnie.

"I have hired a private detective, someone I know in Charleston. Keep that to yourselves. His name is John Quaid. He's helped me with several cases, and he's good. Very thorough. He'll be here to talk to you early next week." He turned to Nat. "He'll come in the evening if you can't take time off from work."

"We went to visit Reggie this morning. He had a black eye. They beat him up to get him to talk, but he wouldn't." Winnie blew her nose. "Soon as this is over, I'm goin' to sue them."

"I'll talk to them," David C. said. He extracted a pad from his briefcase and wrote on it. "I'll see what I can do."

"Appreciate that," Nat said. "How much is all this going to cost me? The cost doesn't matter if you can clear my boy. Just curious."

"Don't worry about the cost. We'll work it out." He stood and picked up his briefcase. "Need to go. I have some investigations to make."

"Thanks a bunch," Winnie said, resting her hand on his shoulder. "Just get our boy out of that stinkin' hole fast as you can."

David C. paused at the door, his face sober. "Don't expect a miracle. I'm afraid this is going to take some time. Maybe a long time."

CHAPTER 34

More Questions

Two weeks later, Winnie came downstairs, dressed in her Sunday suit. "Della, get those dishes done now! I know the baby slows you down, but not like molasses goin' uphill. Today's Friday the fifteenth of January. Reggie's arraignment, and we got to be in court."

Reggie's being in jail's really getting to her. As if it's not getting to me, too. All I can do is think of him. "Yes, ma'am." More than being seven months pregnant was slowing her down. She daydreamed of the good times she and Reggie had spent together. Playing his records. Being with the young people at church. Even their arguments were preferable to his absence and her constant longing for him. The thought that he might never come home made her shiver. She dried the last dish as Winnie popped through the sewing room door.

"We're leavin' for the courthouse in ten minutes. If you want to go, be ready."

"Just a minute," she said, climbing the stairs. Yes, she wanted to go. But to hear Reggie being arraigned for a murder he didn't commit, no. She ran her hairbrush through her hair and grabbed her purse, then went back downstairs.

Nat waited on the porch, and Winnie was standing at the front door with her coat on. "Won't hurt to be there a tad early. Maybe we'll get a chance to speak with David C. Maybe there's something more he can tell us than what he said when he was here yesterday."

Della doubted that they would see him. Before leaving their house a few days ago, David C. had taken Reggie's dress pants, shirt, jacket, tie, and shoes. He was probably with Reggie now, helping him and talking with him. They spoke little during their drive to the courthouse, each in his own thoughts.

"There won't be a lot of people at the courthouse," David C. had told them. "But if there is a trial, this place will be mobbed. Probably everyone in Puttersville will be there."

Nat parked in front of the courthouse, and they got out and walked up the courthouse steps together. As they entered, David C. met them in the foyer.

"Reggie is ready," he said. "He's calmer than I am. Let me show you where to sit." He led them to a room inside. Reggie was seated in front, and Della wanted to run to him, but David C. held her back. "You can't talk to him."

Della took a seat beside Winnie, who sat so erect she may as well have been tied to the straight chair back. She held her head high and looked forward, her face set. Nat had on his work clothes, but his face carried a look of dignity.

He put his hand on Winnie's arm. "Remember, God's on our side. We know Reggie's innocent."

"He is." She glanced his way and nodded. "They'll prove it."

"There's Mr. Allen, the prosecution lawyer, in the red tie," David C. said. "Sitting behind him are Steve Hyers, Dick Hyers, and other members of their family. The judge will be here soon, so I'll go." He went to sit beside Reggie.

"All rise," the Bailiff announced. "Honorable Judge Timothy Hall, presiding."

Della stood. From the corner of her eye she caught a glimpse of Ted and Thea Johnson sitting in the seats behind them. She nudged Winnie and pointed, and Winnie nodded, but didn't look back.

"Be seated," the Bailiff said.

Judge Hall swiped his hand through his white hair. "We are here today to see if there is enough evidence to try Reginald Huston for the murder of Tom Hyers. How do you plead, Mr. Huston?"

Reggie stood. "Not guilty, Your Honor."

"Very well. Let the court recorder so note." Judge Hall addressed Mr. Allen. "Does the prosecution have any evidence that Mr. Huston is guilty?"

Mr. Allen stood. "We do, Your Honor. Mr. Huston's whereabouts during the time the murder took place are unknown. Mr. Thorn, who discovered Tom's body, saw Mr. Huston running from the scene of the crime."

"No, Your Honor, that is not true!" Reggie shouted. He stood and waved his fist in the air, shaking his head. "I was not running from the scene of the crime." A low murmur filled the room.

"Order! Order in the court!" Judge Hall banged his gavel.

Reggie sat down and whispered to David C., who whispered back.

"That seems small evidence on which to accuse someone of murder," Judge Hall stated. "Is there any corroborating evidence?"

"Several witnesses saw him running out the door," Mr. Allen said. "I recommend that this case go to trial."

Judge Hall turned to David C. "What does the defense say about Mr. Allen's allegations that Mr. Huston ran from the scene?"

"Mr. Huston swears that he was not running from the scene because he murdered Tom Hyers," David C. said. "Running, yes, but not for the reason given by Mr. Allen. I will prove that he is not the murderer."

"I see," Judge Hall said. "Although I do not think running away is a proof of guilt, it seems to be Mr. Allen's word against the word of the defense. This court then declares that Reginald Huston shall be tried by a jury of his peers for the murder of Tom Hyers," Judge Hall said. "The court will set a date for the trial. Due to the gravity of the charge, there will be no bail bond. Guard, please return Mr. Huston to prison."

"No! Reggie's innocent!" Winnie jumped up and ran to Reggie, but before she reached him, the guard whisked him out the door. He had time only for a quick glance back at Winnie, who collapsed into a nearby chair and sobbed.

Della reached Winnie first, and she put her arms around her. "Reggie's innocent," she said. "We all know that."

"God will save him," Thea said, handing Winnie a tissue.

"Don't you worry none," Ted said. "Our God is mighty to save those who trust in Him."

Nat took Winnie's arm. "Come on, let's go home. Get in the car, Della." He turned to Ted. "Thank you both for coming."

They got into the car. No one said a word on the way home. Winnie wiped her eyes several times and blew her nose. Every time Nat shifted gears, he had to remove his hand from hers.

Della sat in the back seat, her mind racing. Reggie, accused of murder. Reggie, in jail and not able to prove them wrong or do anything to clear his name. Over and over, the look on his face as the guard led him away, his eyes pleading for help. She used her coat sleeve to wipe away the tears sliding down her face.

Nat pulled into their driveway. "I didn't expect David C. I think that's his car in front of the house."

"It is David C.," Winnie said. "He's gettin' out."

David C. waited for them on the porch. "I know it's time for lunch, but I need to talk to Della. It'll take just a few minutes."

"Come in," Nat said. "Winnie will fix you a sandwich, and we can talk while we eat."

"Thanks." He took off his coat, and Della hung it up on the coatrack, then went to help Winnie.

"Did Reggie ever give you an indication that he didn't like Tom Hyers?" he asked Della as they gathered at the table.

"He said Tom and Dick, the boss's nephew, let him do all the bookkeeping while they went into the back room and drank and played cards. Reggie worked many Saturdays to keep the books up to date."

"Did you ever hear Reggie say he wished bad luck for them? Or that he wanted them to move away or be dead?"

Della gasped. "No. Reggie would never say anything like that." She took a bite of her sandwich, and stared into David C.'s eyes. "What he did say was one day he would be the white man's boss, the one everybody else looked up to. He wanted to make something of himself."

David C. finished his sandwich before continuing. "Think about the New Year's Eve party. Can you tell me everyone who was there? Everyone you knew, that is."

"I didn't know very many. Only the ones at our table, Dale and Chris Baker of course, and I met Tye and Debbie Dobbs and Tom Hyers."

"Was Steve Hyers there? How about his nephew, Dick?"

"We spoke to Steve Hyers. I never saw Dick. I don't think he was there. Reggie would have pointed him out to me."

"Detective John Quaid will be here Monday," David C. said. "He's going to talk to you first, Della. Please don't be upset if he asks you some of the questions I just asked. But he's an expert, and he'll know where to look for clues."

"Thank you both for lunch," he said to Nat and Winnie. "I'm going to go talk to others."

"And I must get back to work," Nat said. He took David C.'s coat off the rack and handed it to him. "I'll walk you to your car."

"Why don't you go rest?" Della asked Winnie. "I'll clean up these few dishes."

"Thanks, but I couldn't rest if I tried. I need to keep busy." She headed for the sewing room.

Della finished the dishes and stood in front of the television. Winnie wasn't the only one needing something to keep her mind busy. She navigated through the four available channels, then back down, finding nothing that interested her.

A knock at the door sent fear rippling through her chest. Another policeman? Someone there to threaten them? She opened the door a tiny crack and peered out. Chris stood on the porch, holding a bag.

"Come in, Chris. I wasn't expecting you."

"Here. I made you some cookies." She handed the bag to Della. "I'm so sorry for everything you're all going through. And I finally got the adoption papers copied for you." She took them from her purse. "Here they are."

"Thanks. I have to show them to David C."

"Who's that?"

"Reggie's lawyer. He wants to take a look at them and make sure everything's okay."

"I...I hope they are. We didn't get a lawyer, you know. Dale went to the library and looked everything up, though. They should be fine."

"I'm sure they will be. Right now, all I can think of is proving Reggie innocent. The police were here asking me questions, and I don't think they were on Reggie's side. They're looking for evidence to use against him."

"I'm so sorry. Anything I can do to help?"

"Not unless you saw someone murder Tom and can prove it. What did you do after you went to the trash can?"

"Stayed in there. They were playing 'Duke of Earl,' my favorite, and everyone was dancing, clapping, and singing along."

"Were you and Dale dancing?"

"No. Just standing there singing and watching everyone else. Come to think of it..." She stared into the distance. "Come to think, Dale didn't stay for the whole song. When it was over, I looked around, and he was gone."

"When did he come back?"

“I saw him come in right before they found Tom dead.”

“Where’d he go? Where had he been?”

“I don’t know. At the time, I didn’t think it was that important.”

“Come on, Chris, think. Maybe he saw something.’

“He would have told me if he’d seen what happened. I know he would.”

“Go home and ask him. Then call me and tell me. I have to know.”

“He had to go help his mom, and he said he wouldn’t be back until later. But I’ll ask him as soon as he gets home.” She stood. “Have to stop at the store, so better get going.”

Della stood inside the open door and waved goodbye. “Be sure and call,” she yelled as Chris got into her car.

A blast of cold air pushed the door into the doorstop, and Della shivered as she closed it and headed up the stairs to get her sweater. Inside her room, she opened the closet door. On the shelf near the top of the closet she could see the book Reggie had given her for Christmas, the one she had promised to read. She reached up and took it in her hand, and turning on the light, sat down on her bed and opened it.

On the inside of the jacket flap she found a sealed envelope with her name printed on it in Reggie’s neat handwriting. She unsealed the envelope and pulled out a note. Her heart nearly stopped. *Dare I open it? What if it’s something I don’t want to see?* Slowly she unfolded the note and read.

> Dear Della, I have admired you ever since I met you, but you know what Mammy says. I hope that someday soon she will change her mind. I’m hoping to be able to tell you why she feels the way she does soon. I’m anxious for that day. Yours, Reggie.

Della let the note drop into her lap and sat there, too astonished to move. *So that's what Reggie wanted me to know. If only he were here to explain.*

CHAPTER 35

More Clues

Della listened for the phone the rest of the afternoon and evening, but Chris didn't call. Maybe she forgot to talk to Dale, she told herself. Maybe Dale didn't see or hear anything, so she didn't think to call back. Then a frightening thought—maybe Dale killed Tom, and they weren't telling anyone. Dale had reason to be angry at Tom. Very angry if Tom was not going to follow safety procedures. She shuddered.

By the time David C. came over Saturday afternoon, she had convinced herself that Dale was the murderer. She had no proof, but she had a gut feeling. Where else could Dale have been during the few minutes he was gone?

"I spoke with the Bakers," David C. said, sitting down and propping his briefcase between his feet. He pulled out a notebook and opened it.

"Did Chris know where Dale went right before Tom was killed?" Della asked. "Or maybe it was at the same time, or maybe after—"

"Whoa!" David C. interrupted. "Dale said he went to the restroom during that brief time. Someone had just found Tom's body when he came out."

"But Reggie said no one else was in the restroom," Della said.

"Dale said it was probable that Reggie didn't hear him enter. The toilet flushed as Dale walked through the door."

"I also spoke with Tye and Debbie Dobbs," David C. said. "Tye said he was very upset at Tom's mockery. Debbie could tell and asked him to get her coat from the car. Tye said it was dark outside, and he didn't see anything. Debbie swears he was back inside three minutes after he left."

"Is there anyone else you can think of that I should speak to?" David C. asked. He turned to address Nat and Winnie. "Does Reggie have any enemies? On the other hand, is there anyone to talk to who knows him well? Besides the Johnsons, of course."

The owner of the drug store came to Della's mind. No. She wasn't sure he was Reggie's friend.

"The rest of the church members," Winnie said. "They all know and love Reggie. Talk to everyone at church."

"They'll tell you what a kind, responsible person our son is," Nat added.

"The court will set the trial date next week."

"When will the trial be?" Winnie asked.

"I don't know, but probably not for a few weeks, maybe a month. I need time to investigate, and so do the police. And I heard that there are a couple trials before Reggie's." David C. rose and picked up his briefcase. "My detective John Quaid has been delayed, but he should be here to help next week. I have one more person to talk to today, and it's getting late."

As he left, Della muttered "You didn't even ask me about the adoption papers."

"Did you say something?" Winnie asked.

"Nothing important." Della headed up the stairs. Halfway up she stopped and reviewed the scene that had stuck in her mind since they left the party. Someone else besides party goers had been in the hallway when she came out of the bathroom. A crowd had gathered around near Tom's body, but in the other end of the hallway she had glimpsed a man pushing a wide broom. His back curved, and he was so bent over that his chin nearly touched the top of the broom handle every time he swept.

He had to be the janitor. How long had he been there? Maybe he had seen or heard something. Nat and Winnie huddled on the sofa. They couldn't call David C., but she had to let them know. She retreated down the stairs, her mind whirling with excitement.

"Hey, I just remembered someone else who was there. Someone I didn't tell David C. about."

"Who?" Winnie asked.

"The janitor of that building where we had the party. At least I think he was the janitor."

"The party was at the old Brown Hotel, right?"

"Yes. In their Event Center."

"I know the janitor there." Nat stood and grabbed his coat. "Matt Turner. Used to work with him. Maybe he was the one workin' that night. Come on, Della, we're goin' to go talk to him. Want to come, Winnie?"

"No. I've got work to do. You guys can be the detectives. Be home for dinner in a couple hours."

Della lifted her coat off the stand near the door and put it on. She caught the door as it closed behind Nat and hurried to catch up.

"We'll try the hotel first. If he's not there, I know where he lives," Nat yelled as he got into his truck and started the engine.

Della put one foot on the running board and pulled herself into the seat.

"I brought you along because you can identify him if he's the man you saw workin' that night," he said. "Please let me do the talkin'."

"Okay." *Can I identify him?* She tried to picture him as he swept. She didn't remember his face, but she couldn't mistake his curved back.

In a few minutes they pulled into the Brown Hotel parking lot. Della slid out of the seat and ran to catch up with Nat.

He reached for the door and held it open for her. "Remember, I do the talkin'."

She nodded and followed him inside.

They entered a small room. In the front a woman sat typing, and she looked up. "Can I help you?"

"I'm looking for Matt Turner. Is he here?"

"I'll check and see." She left through a door in the back of the office.

Nat drummed his fingers on the counter and shifted his weight from his left foot to his right. "Wonder where she went?" he asked after a few moments.

The receptionist came back. "Mr. Turner will be here in a few moments. You can wait for him here."

Della waited in the corner of the small room, while Nat paced in the space between its walls. The back door of the office squeaked open, and a gray-haired man stepped into her office.

"Mr. Turner, these folks want to talk to you."

"If you can spare a few minutes," Nat said.

"Let's step outside," Turner said. "I'll meet you out front."

"Sure." Nat said. "C'mon, Della."

Matt Turner came around the outside of the building and faced them. "What'd you need to talk to me about?"

"Remember me? Nat Huston? I worked at the high school when you used to work there." Nat held out his hand. When Turner didn't return the gesture, Nat continued. "This is Della, who was at the mining company's New Year's Eve Party here. Were you workin' that night?"

"So what if I was?" He stuck a cigarette in his mouth and pulled a slim silver lighter out of his pocket and lit the cigarette.

Della could tell that he was the same man with the twisted body she had seen that night. What held her interest was the slim, silver cigarette lighter he twirled in his fingers. A red circle with a red, white, and blue shield with a torch on the side of the lighter caught the rays of the sun. *Just like the lighter Chris said Tom Hyers's grandpa gave him for Christmas.* She started to ask him where he had gotten it, but recalling Nat's instructions, she said nothing.

"Guess you've heard about Tom Hyer's murder," Nat said. "Were you here the night he got killed?"

Turner scratched his unshaven chin. "Yeah, guess I was. Why do you want to know?"

"My son is in jail for that murder. A murder he is innocent of. I want to know if you saw anyone or heard anything at the time Tom was killed."

"Sure didn't. I had just come into the hallway when I saw a bunch of folks gathered 'round."

"You didn't get there before the crowd?" Nat asked.

"Nope. I gotta get back to work now if you don't mind."

"Thanks for talkin' to us," Nat said, but Turner was already walking back around the side of the building.

"Well, that wasn't much help," Nat muttered. "Let's go. Time for dinner."

"Maybe it was some help," Della said after getting back into the truck. "Did you notice his cigarette lighter?"

"I saw he had one. What about it?"

"Chris told me Tom Hyers got one for Christmas. He had it at their Christmas party. It looked just like what Chris told me about Tom's lighter. Silver with a red circle holding a torch."

"Probably lots of lighters like that. Anyone could have one."

"Chris said Tom's had his initials on it."

"Still doesn't mean much, especially since you didn't see the initials."

"I almost asked Mr. Turner about it."

"Thanks for not askin'." He turned the truck toward the street. "Soon as we get home I'll call David C. and tell him."

Back home they sat down to a dinner of cornbread and beans cooked with ham. As soon as Nat asked the blessing, Della told

Winnie, "We saw the janitor. He had a cigarette lighter just like the one Chris said Tom Hyers had. The exact same one."

"Della, you don't know it was the exact same one," Nat said. "You said Tom's lighter had a monogram on it. Did you see a monogram on the one Mr. Turner had?"

"No. But that doesn't mean it wasn't the same lighter."

"Sounds like you're jumping to conclusions," Winnie said. She handed Nat a piece of cornbread. "Ted and Thea are coming over around seven. Said they had some news."

"I hope it's good news." Nat sighed. "I spend most of my time thinkin' about Reggie, just wonderin' how he's doin'. Wish we could visit him more'n once a week."

"I know, honey." Winnie touched his arm. "Doesn't seem fair."

Della saw the tears in Winnie's eyes. "When we go see him there's always that officer, standing there hearing everything," Della said. "And we can't take him anything."

"Well, let's finish dinner and see what the Johnsons have to say." Ted scooped the last of his beans into his mouth and took his plate to the sink.

Della barely finished the dishes before Ted and Thea arrived.

"God is with us in our fight," Ted said. "Our heavenly Father will fight for Reggie." He hugged Winnie and put his hand on Nat's shoulder. "How you doing, Brother?"

"We're holdin' up. Sit down."

"We went to the grocery store this morning," Thea said. "Always busy on Saturday morning. You know the grocery store owner, Earl Dobbs?"

"Know who he is. Talked to him once or twice," Nat said.

"Well, he was in the produce section," Ted stated. "Had a bunch of men gathered around him. I know they were talking about the troubles at the mine. I stopped to listen, but pretended I was looking for something on the shelf. One of the men lowered his voice. Said he went into the office to take care of some paper work. The door to

Steve Hyers's office was closed, but this guy said he could hear real loud shouting and arguing coming from behind that door."

"What were they sayin'?" Nat asked. "Did he hear anything?"

"Said he heard one of them yelling he was going to file a complaint with the UMW Safety Department in Washington, DC. That's all he could make out at the time. He didn't want to be seen standing by the door."

"Wonder when this happened?" Winnie said.

"Talked like it was the week after Christmas," Ted said.

"Thanks a bunch." Nat stood and shook Ted's hand. "That makes two things I got to talk to David C. about."

CHAPTER 36

Don't Talk

David C. did not return to Nat and Winnie's house that week or the next week. John Quaid didn't come. By then, Della couldn't eat or sleep.

"Thea said he's working on the case," Winnie told her. "We shouldn't worry, and we can't bother him." She put her arm around Della. "I know how hard it is to wait for news."

After dinner the last Friday of January, David C. knocked on their door. Beside him stood a man who towered over him. "My detective John Quaid," David C. said. "Sorry I couldn't get him here before now, but he's been very busy."

"Come in," Nat said. "Mr. Quaid, pleased to meet you. This is my wife Winnie and Della, who is staying with us."

"Reggie's trial is the first Monday of March," David C. stated as he and Quaid sat down on the sofa. "I'm sorry it's so far away, but it gives us more time for investigating."

"But aren't the police doing their own investigation to help us?" Winnie asked.

"Who do you think is the richest man in Puttersville?" David C. asked. "Who pays the most taxes? Who hires the citizens of this town and pays their wages?"

"I see," Nat said. "The police don't work for the little guy."

"No. If Quaid and I don't work on your side, no one will. He has training in forensics, and right now, that area looks the most promising in Reggie's defense."

"It's been nearly a month since Tom's death, and no one has said how he died," Nat said. "The papers don't even mention his murder, and back when they did, they said nothing. Do you know?"

"There's a gag order for everyone on the investigation," David C. said. "That means no one involved in the case can say anything, even if they know. That's why the newspaper can't get any information to print."

"Do you know?" Della asked.

"We have an idea, and it figures heavily in our investigation. But I can't talk about it."

"People at church are always askin' me about the investigation, but I don't know what to tell them. Probably shouldn't say anything anyway," Winnie said.

"Winnie's correct," David C. stated. "I'm asking you all not to talk about the case to anyone, not even among yourselves. That way, no one can blame you for saying something that's not true. Can you do that, Della?"

"I think so."

"I hope you *know* so. It's important that we don't spread rumors. You want to do what's best for Reggie, right?"

"Yes, sir."

"Good." David C. turned to Quaid. "I believe you have some questions."

"Let me start with Della," Quaid said. "I know you've told David C., but please tell me everything you can remember about your and Reggie's time at the party New Year's Eve."

Della took her time to rehearse the events, including seeing the janitor, Mr. Turner.

"Do you remember what Reggie wore that night?" Quaid asked.

"His clothes? Let me see." Della tried to picture Reggie. "Some black pants, his black shoes, and I believe his light blue dress shirt."

"Did he have on something he wears all the time?"

"His West Virginia State University toboggan," Winnie said. "He graduated from there, you know, and he's proud of that toboggan."

"May I see it?"

"It's right over here on the coat rack," Winnie said, walking over and taking it off one of the hooks. "He wears it everywhere." She handed it to Quaid.

"Thanks. May I keep it a while?" He faced Nat. "Mr. Huston, did Reggie talk to you about problems with his job at the mine?"

"Some. During his first month he considered quitting. Said he didn't have no respect and got stuck with most of the work."

"Do you feel he was angry enough to kill Tom Hyers?"

"No. Reggie would never think of such a thing. He knew there are better ways to handle problems." Nat stared at Quaid and ran his hand over his chin. "That's what an education does for you. Gives you alternatives. Besides, Reggie was a believin' Christian. He would never do anything to destroy that. Reggie did not murder Tom Hyers."

Quaid turned to Della. "Do you think either Dale Baker or Tye Dobbs killed him?"

"They were both very angry at him," she said. "But I don't think either one would take their anger out on him by killing him. I know Dale better than I know Tye, but both seem to be hard workers and good men."

Quaid stood. "Thanks for your time. We have more investigating to do. Your input has helped, and I may need to ask you more questions."

"I'll be in touch with you," David C. said as he picked up his briefcase. "Try not to worry. Bye now." He and Quaid left.

Winnie sighed. "I was hopin' Reggie would be declared innocent by the end of January. But it's here, and he isn't, so guess I'll get back to work sewin'." She headed toward the sewing room.

Della needed some time to herself, and she started up the stairs to her room.

A knock on the door. Della paused halfway up the steps and waited for Nat to see who it was.

"Hello, Matt, what can I do for you?" Nat asked.

Della couldn't hear the reply.

"Come on in," Nat said.

Matt Turner came in, and Della crept down the stairs and stood beside the television, listening.

"When y'all came by the hotel, I got scared. Something I should've told you." His voice trembled. "I was scared I'd get blamed for Tom's murder. 'Fraid you'd call the police right then and there."

"What is it?" Nat demanded. "What'd you see?"

"Didn't see no more than I told about when Tom was killed. Didn't see no one there. But earlier that morning, Tom and Dick Hyers was at the hotel office. They was arguin' about who would pay for the New Year's Eve party. Seems like Tom was the one who talked his dad into havin' the party. Tom told his dad he and Dick would pay for it. Dick was madder'n an old wet hen when he found out. They shouted and hollered all the way back out to the parkin' lot."

"So who paid?"

"Don't know." Turner shrugged. "One of our guests had a leaky toilet, and I had to go fix it. Didn't see who handed over the cash." Matt lifted his cane and set it down with a thump.

"Will you be willing to testify about what you saw and heard at my son's trial?" Nat asked.

"Will if I'm able. Back's gettin' so bad I have to have surgery." He walked to the door, his cane tapping with every step.

Nat let him out. "Thanks for comin' by to tell us." He shut the door.

"Maybe Dick Hyers killed Tom," Della said.

"Don't go jumpin' to conclusions. He wasn't at the party, remember? How could he have killed Tom if he wasn't there?" Nat sighed. "Just wish this whole thing was over and Reggie was back home."

Della went up to her bedroom. Just Nat mentioning Reggie's name sent her heart into a tailspin. She longed for his smile, his soft voice telling her she was pretty and what happened to her wasn't her fault. Remembering the touch of his hand on her chin as he lifted her face up that day he invited her to go with him to the New Year's Eve party brought tears to her eyes. He loved her. Was it a sisterly love, or was it the kind of love that every girl dreamed of, that she longed for? If only she knew.

She pulled her old suitcase out from under her bed and took her coin from its hiding place. Clutching it, she put it to her heart. "Mama," she said. "Mama, where are you? I need your help."

But Mama wasn't there, not even her voice telling her things would be okay. Fear shot through her heart. Was Mama slipping from her mind? She tried to recall the sound of her voice, the smell of her, the smile on her face, but for some reason, she couldn't. Sliding the coin back into its pouch, she put it in the suitcase. She kicked off her shoes and lay down, pulling the blankets over her shoulders. For a long time she stared into the darkness. Closing her eyes, she drifted off to sleep.

A pounding on her door and Winnie's voice wakened her. "Della, Mother Carrie's had a stroke. They're takin' her to the hospital. Get up and get dressed if you want to go."

"What? What?" Della sat up in bed. "What'd you say?"

"Mother Carrie's at the hospital. Come on, we need to go!"

Della flung back the blankets, climbed out of bed, and looked out the window. A mere hint of the rising sun filled the horizon with a soft glow. She gathered clean clothes and headed for the shower. In twenty minutes she descended the stairs. Nat and Winnie stood by the door with their coats on.

"Hurry up, girl. We should've left," Winnie said.

Della grabbed her coat and put it on as she followed them to the car. She climbed in and gripped the seat. Nat sped to the hospital. He hit the potholes and skidded through patches of frozen ice, and Della was sure a police car would pull them over. She breathed a sigh of relief when they half slid into the hospital parking lot.

Sister Bess met them inside the hospital. "She got up to use the bathroom about five," she said as she led them down the hall. "Just as we reached the bathroom door, she went down, and I couldn't get her up. I'm sure she's had another stroke, and this time, it's a bad one."

Della recalled Mother Carrie's words at Thanksgiving. "I won't be here next year."

"Let's wait in here," Sister Bess said, opening the door marked Emergency Waiting. They sat down, and Sister Bess continued, "She's not been herself lately. Not eating well. No interest in anything, wouldn't watch her television shows. Wouldn't talk to anyone. I wanted to take her to the doctor, but she wouldn't go."

"I'm sorry." Nat put his arm around Sister Bess. "You should've told us."

"Didn't want to worry you. You have plenty of problems of your own." Sister Bess glanced at Della. "When is your baby due?"

"Middle of March." Della rubbed her extended abdomen. "He sure has been kickin' a lot."

"And you still want to give him away?"

"Yes. Can't support no baby." Della's face tingled as the blood crept into her cheeks, and she looked away. "Just can't."

"I hope you're doing the right thing," Sister Bess said. "Mother doesn't approve, and you know what I think."

Della nodded.

"Last night Mother woke up around two and called for me," Sister Bess said. "When I went to check on her, I took her hand, and she grasped mine so hard it hurt. "Saw your pappy," she said. "Standing right there, young and handsome. A big smile on his face, and his arms reaching to take me."

"It was a dream," I told her. "Go back to sleep, you need your rest."

"No! No dream!" she shouted. "I tell you, he was right here. He told me he'd see me soon. And guess who was standing there right beside him?"

"Who?"

"Why, Jesus, of course. So glistening white and so...so full of love and warmth and understanding."

"Go back to sleep, Mother," I said. "We'll talk about it in the morning." Sister Bess buried her face in her hands. "I should have been more loving, more supportive."

Ted and Thea walked through the door. "You were tired, and you did what you could," Thea said, wrapping here arms around Sister Bess. "God knows you did your best."

"I heard what you just said about Mother Carrie's dream," Ted said. "Only wasn't a dream. Those who are dying often see Jesus and loved ones before they go. I think it's a special welcome home gift from God."

Dr. Richards came into the room. "Your mother has had a bad stroke," he said to Sister Bess. "I'm sorry, but I don't expect her to live. You can go into the Intensive Care Unit and see her."

Della was the last one in line as they passed through the ICU door and stood in the crowded space around Mother Carrie's bed.

Sister Bess took Mother Carrie's hand and looked into the vacant eyes. "I'm sorry, Mother," she said. "Sorry I didn't listen to you." She put her other hand on Mother Carrie's forehead. "I love you," she whispered.

The shallow breaths came farther and farther apart, and as they stood there, they stopped. Mother Carrie passed into eternity.

CHAPTER 37

What They Wanted

Two weeks after Mother Carrie's funeral, David C. called while they were eating dinner. "Two weeks until the trial. It's about time we heard from him," Nat said after hanging up. "No wonder we didn't, though. He's been in Columbus, Ohio, and other cities doin' some investigatin'. Says this is far more complicated than he thought. He's comin' over to talk at seven."

"What's he going to talk about?" Della asked. "I don't understand why this trial thing is taking so long."

"We don't either," Winnie said. "We just have to be patient and keep trustin' in the Lord to make things right."

"Things don't ever seem to be right." Della's eyes filled with tears as she stared at the spaghetti on her plate. "All this praying everyone's been doing for Reggie, and I don't see God helping him."

"Wait till we see what David C. has to say," Nat said. "He might have some good news."

They finished dinner. Della was glad that Winnie helped her with the dishes, and they finished just as David C. knocked on the door.

David C.'s face was grim as he sat down and fingered through his briefcase. He extracted a manila folder. "Do you all know who Chet Hobbins is?" he asked.

"Sure. President of United Mine Workers," Nat answered.

"Yes. Not a very popular man, at least among the local miners. They think he's crooked, maybe even got his hand in the till. But he's powerful, and right now, they can't get rid of him."

"What's that got to do with Tom's murder?" Nat asked.

"Maybe nothing. Maybe a lot. John Quaid is looking into some things. Did any of you ever hear Reggie talking about United Mine Workers?"

Nat shook his head. "Not about the UMW."

Della thought back. "After Christmas he told me about Tye Dobbs and some other man going to talk to Steve Hyers about safety issues at the mine. Said they might have to go to the union."

"I see." David C. poked through his briefcase and brought out another folder. "Did he ever say anything about Tom Hyers running for president of the local union?"

"No, never. Reggie didn't want to get involved with local mine politics," Winnie said. "He had his eye on bigger fish."

"I need to find out as much as I can about what's happening at the mine," David C. said. "My success in this investigation depends in part upon all of you keeping what we discuss to yourselves. I know I can count on you not to speak of the trial or anything I've told you to anyone. True?"

"You know Winnie and I won't talk," Nat said. "You neither, right, Della?"

"Of course not. I won't say a word to anyone."

"Good. I have several more people to question. I feel I'm on the right trail." He picked up his briefcase, then turned to Della. "I've been so busy I forgot to look at your adoption papers. May I see them?"

Della's heart leaped. "Yes, sir. I'll get them." Her legs trembled as she went to her room and took them from the bottom drawer of her dresser. She took the stairs down slowly, reading them as she went. "Here they are." She handed them to him.

He scanned them without commenting, then handed them back to her. "This isn't worth the paper it's written on," he said. "You need to go to the courthouse and fill out the proper papers. Both you and the Bakers." His eyes travelled to her middle. "And from the looks of you, I'd say the sooner the better."

"We'll probably need a lawyer, and they cost a lot of money." She looked up at him, her eyes begging.

"Sorry, I can't. No time. I have only two weeks to finish this investigation. Less time than I need." He stood. "Need to go write up some notes."

Nat showed him out the door. "David C. sure does sound mysterious," he said when he returned.

"Just as long as he's onto something that will prove Reggie is innocent," Winnie added. They walked into the kitchen, their arms around each other's waists.

Della breathed a sigh of relief as she went to her room. Nat and Winnie hadn't yelled at her about the papers. They hadn't said anything. Maybe they were discussing how they could help her. Maybe they'd even pay for a lawyer. If they didn't, she'd ask the Bakers if they would pay for one.

Two weeks until Reggie's trial. She rubbed her abdomen. The baby could come early, maybe before or during the trial. *I hope not. I have to be there to be a witness for Reggie.*

The next day was Saturday, and she got up late, dreading what she knew she had to do. Talk to the Bakers about the papers and ask them to help. She thought of her own meager savings, the ten dollars

Reggie had given her for graduation. It would be a tiny portion of the lawyer's fee.

After doing the breakfast dishes, she stuck her head into the sewing room. "I'm going to visit the Bakers. Have to see what they want to do about the adoption papers."

"Good idea," Winnie said. "Call before you go to make sure they're home."

They were home. Thoughts whirled through her mind as she walked to their house. *What if they won't pay anything? What if I have to keep the baby? What will I do?* She rang their doorbell with trepidation.

Chris opened the door. "Come in. Is something wrong?"

Della got the papers from her purse and handed them to her. "The lawyer Mr. Huston hired for Reggie says these papers are no good. He says we need a lawyer to draw them up proper."

"Oh." Chris looked over the two sheets. "What's wrong with them?"

"He said they need to be done in a court with a lawyer according to state law."

"I see." Then her face brightened. "So. You have a lawyer. Make an appointment for us all to meet at the courthouse Monday."

"Reggie's lawyer is not my lawyer. I asked him, and he said he doesn't have time. So we have to hire our own lawyer."

"How much will that cost?"

"I don't know," Della said. "I'm hoping you can find out. And…," She turned her eyes to Dale. "I'm hoping you can pay for a lawyer. All I have is ten dollars."

"Well, I don't know. We just spent most of our savings on a new, safer car."

"We can get my parents to loan us the money," Chris said. "Please, Dale. I really want this baby, and I thought you did, too."

"Oh, Chris, of course I do." He wrapped his arms around her and pulled her close to him. "You know I do. I'm wondering where we can get the money, that's all. But we'll get it, even if we have to take out a loan from the bank."

"Whew! Thank you, both of you." Della wrapped her arms around Chris. "You know I want you to have this baby. I just can't do it by myself."

"Don't worry. We'll look into getting a lawyer Monday. We promise." Chris took her hand. "We won't let anything happen to our chances of having a baby, will we, Dale?'

"No, we won't." He bent over and kissed his wife. "Never."

Della said goodbye and headed toward home. She didn't feel as happy about Dale's promise as she thought she would be. The adoption was a sure thing. Had she cradled some small hope deep within her heart that she would have to keep the baby? Self-loathing enveloped her. What kind of a person was she to give away part of her flesh and blood? Reggie said that what happened to her wasn't her fault. Was she adding to her sins by not keeping the child?

A picture of Daddy filled her mind, and she shuddered. No, she was doing the right thing. This child was Daddy's doing, not hers, and she wanted no reminder of him. She wanted Reggie to love her, but how could he? No one who knew what happened to her would ever love her.

The house was empty when she returned. On the table was a note from Winnie. *The jail changed their visiting time to ten o'clock Saturday. We'll be back in time for lunch.*

She sank into a chair and stared at the note. Visiting Reggie was the highlight of her week. *I won't get to see Reggie. Oh, how I miss him.*

A knock sounded on the door. She went and opened it a crack to see who it was. Two officers stood outside. What was it that Nat had told her about police? Not to let them in unless he was there? She shut the door and hurried into the kitchen.

Another knock on the door, this time louder. Then another, and another, harder and louder. She crept to the door and opened it.

"Are you Della Etter?"

"Yes."

"We need to talk to you about Tom Hyers' murder. May we come in?"

"You already talked to me about it."

"Listen, Miss Etter, we got more questions. Either you let us in or you can come sit in our car while we talk."

She opened the door, and then she took refuge on the sofa.

They came in and stood in front of her. One fingered the club hanging on his belt. The other stared at her abdomen. "How long have you known Reginald Huston?"

"About eight months."

"Where'd you meet him?"

"He was my math teacher at the high school."

"Oh, so that's his baby you're carrying. Doing that to a student is enough to put him away for a while," the officer said, sneering.

"It's not his baby."

"Prove it."

"I can't. It's my…" Shame rolled over her like a hot blanket, and she couldn't go on.

"Whose baby is it?"

"It doesn't matter. The daddy is dead."

"So were you with Reginald Huston on the night Tom Hyers died?"

"Yes. We were at the miners' New Year's Eve party. Reggie worked for them."

"Did he like Tom Hyers?"

Della knew it was a leading question. "Tom was his boss. One of them besides Steve Hyers and Dick Hyers."

"What did he do?"

"He was one of the bookkeepers."

"So he handled company money."

"No…no. I don't think so."

"So he could have taken some of the company's money."

"Reggie would never do that. They trusted him."

"How do you know they trusted him? Did they ever tell you they trusted him?"

"No. But Reggie told me."

The other officer laughed out loud. "Reggie told me," he said, imitating her voice. "Reggie told me. What a story. You would've believed anything he told you, wouldn't you?"

She looked up at him. What could she say? Of course she would have believed Reggie's every word, but what difference would it make if she said it? She shrugged and said nothing.

"You two! Get outta my house! Now!" Nat stood in the open doorway, his face twisted in anger. "I told you never to come here again!"

"Just doing our job, man, just doing our job. We got what we needed, though. Plenty to bring up at the trial."

CHAPTER 38

Testimony

On the first Monday of March, the day of Reggie's trial, Della woke up earlier than usual. A dull ache across her back drove her deeper under the covers. Knowing that she wouldn't miss Reggie's trial, she forced herself out of bed. She dressed and went to the kitchen where Winnie was frying bacon.

"My back's bothering me," she told Winnie.

"Probably all the extra weight carryin' your baby. Then this cold front snuck through in the night with snow. March comin' in like a lion. Do you feel like setting the table? We need to eat and get to the courthouse by nine." She hummed as she mixed eggs to scramble. "Today's the day my Reggie is gettin' out of jail. Just know it."

After eating breakfast and doing the dishes, Della climbed the stairs to put on some makeup and brush her hair. Nat and Winnie were waiting for her in the living room, their coats on.

"Reggie's gettin' out today," Winnie said. "Our God is good."

"Hope so," Nat said. He put his arm around her. "We shouldn't get our hopes up. Come on, Della, let's go."

"I'm trying. Stairs seems steeper today." She threw her coat around her shoulders and followed them to the car.

They arrived at the courthouse and found a crowd of people on the courthouse steps, waiting for the doors to open. Ted and Thea were standing at the top of the stairs near the doors, and they joined them.

"It's going to turn out okay," Ted said. "I been praying and praying."

The Bailiff unlocked the doors from inside, and they entered and sat down. David C. came into the courtroom from a side door, and behind him, the sheriff led Reggie, handcuffs around his wrists, to a chair in the front.

Della stared at the people in the jury box. She didn't know anyone. No one from church. No one at school.

Nat was looking, too. "Don't know any of the jurors," he whispered to Winnie. "None of our friends, that's for sure."

"All rise," said the Bailiff. "His honorable Judge Timothy Hall presiding."

Judge Hall took his place. "You may be seated. Will the defendant rise?"

Reggie and David C. stood.

"Reginald Huston, you are charged with the premeditated murder of Tom Hyers. How do you plead?"

"Not guilty, Your Honor," Reggie said, his voice loud and clear, his head held high.

"Let the records so indicate," Judge Hall stated. "The prosecution may state its case. Mr. Allen, are you ready?"

"Yes, sir." Allen stood. "On the night of December 31, 1964, Reginald Huston was at the Puttersville Mine Operations New Year's Eve party. He had an altercation with Mr. Tom Hyers, then excused himself and disappeared. Fifteen minutes later, Tom Hyers' body was found in the hallway. Reginald Huston fled the scene. I can prove that he killed Tom Hyers because of what witnesses are saying." Allen took his seat.

"Mr. Chambers, what do you have to say for Reginald Huston?" Judge Allen asked.

David C. faced Judge Hall. "Your Honor, Reginald Huston was proud of his job with Mr. Hyers. He did not flee the scene, as Mr. Allen stated. He is innocent of the murder of Tom Hyers. I believe I can prove that Reginald Huston did not kill Tom Hyers."

"Record Mr. Chambers' statement," Judge Hall said. "Mr. Allen, you may call your first witness."

"Yes, sir. I call Mr. Steve Hyers."

Steve Hyers took the stand, and the Bailiff swore him in.

"Mr. Hyers, please state your name and your occupation for the court records."

"Steven Hyers, owner and president of Puttersville Number One Mine Operations."

"Tell us how you know the defendant, Reginald Huston."

Hyers glared at Reggie. "I hired him to help my son Tom and my nephew Dick with the bookkeeping. I shouldn't have. He has a record, you know, but I thought I'd give him a chance to make it in the world as he seemed good with figures."

"Was Mr. Huston a good employee?" Allen asked.

"After he caught on to our system, he did okay. At first he worked hard, even came in on some Saturdays. But then things turned sour."

"What do you mean turned sour?"

"Seemed like he took offense at how Tom and Dick worked. Started spreading rumors about them among other employees."

"What kind of rumors?"

"Said they didn't do their share of the work. Said they played cards and drank. We don't do those things at Puttersville Mine Operations. I hired that lying nigger, and now I've paid the price. My Tom is dead." He buried his face in his hands and sobbed.

"You're dismissed, Mr. Hyers. Your Honor, I reserve the right to recall this witness."

"Does the defense want to cross examine Steve Hyers?"

"Not at this time, Your Honor," David C. said.

"Then I call Dick Hyers to the stand," Allen said.

After Dick was sworn in, Allen asked, "Did you ever hear Reginald Huston say anything to anyone about Tom Hyers?"

"Yes, sir. Tom and I came down to the mine office one Saturday, right before Thanksgiving. Reginald was working on the books. He looked up from his work and said to Tom, 'Bout time I had some help,' meaning Tom didn't do his share. From then on, Huston saved a lot of his work for Tom, and we had to work extra hours or we would've been down there Christmas Day."

Della gasped. *That's not true! Reggie worked late Monday through Wednesday before Christmas so the miners could get their paychecks early before Christmas!*

"Mr. Allen, do you have any more questions for Dick Hyers?" Judge Hall asked.

"No, Your Honor, but I may call him to the stand later."

"Do you have anyone else you'd like to testify?"

"Not at this time, Your Honor."

"Mr. Chambers, do you want to question this witness?" the judge asked.

"No, Your Honor. I ask Steve Hyers to take the stand."

"Remember that you are still under oath, Mr. Hyers," Judge Hall said as Steve went up.

David C. walked in front of the witness chair and pointed to Steve Hyers. "Mr. Hyers, you stated that Reginald Huston has a record. What kind of record?"

Steve cleared his throat. "He was arrested last summer. Charged with disorderly conduct. That's why he lost his job teaching math at the high school. I shouldn't have given him that second chance."

"How do you know he was arrested and charged with disorderly conduct?"

"Said so. In the police records."

"I checked the police records. There are no records of any kind for Reginald Huston."

"Then why did he lose his job at the high school?" Hyers asked.

"I talked to the high school principal. He told me that they let Mr. Huston go to save money. They had another teacher already on staff who would work for less money."

Della's chest swelled with pride. Reggie was a good teacher. He didn't do anything wrong.

"That's all the questions I have for Mr. Hyers," David C. said. "I now call Christine Baker to the stand."

The bailiff took Chris's oath.

"Please state your name and occupation," David C. said.

"Christine Baker. I work in the office at Puttersville Mine keeping the records for the miners' work hours."

"How long have you worked there, Mrs. Baker?"

"Since the week after Thanksgiving."

"Did you work with Reginald Huston?"

"Not in the same room. I worked in the small office next to the bookkeeping office."

"The bookkeeping office where Mr. Huston worked with Tom and Dick Hyers?"

"Yes."

"Could you hear what Reginald Huston, Tom Hyers, and Dick Hyers said to each other?"

"Most of the time. I mean, I concentrated on my own work, but I could hear if I wanted to."

"Did you ever hear Mr. Huston speak to any of the Hyers men in a disrespectful or derogatory manner?"

"No, sir. Never. He almost never spoke unless they spoke to him."

"Did you ever hear Mr. Huston say anything bad about the Hyers men? Any of them?"

Chris thought for a moment. "No, sir, I don't believe I have ever heard him say anything bad about them."

"Did you see Tom Hyers at the Puttersville Miners New Year's Eve party?"

"Yes. He was eating at our table."

"Did Tom Hyers say or do anything to you?"

"Objection!" Allen shouted. "No relevance to this case!"

"Your Honor, I believe Mrs. Baker's testimony has relevance to what happened at the party," David C. said.

"You may answer the question, Mrs. Baker," Judge Hall said.

"Yes. He…he touched me inappropriately." Chris shielded her face with her hands and looked down as she related what Tom did.

"Can you tell me what happened after that?"

"He started making fun of Tye Dobbs. Tye and Debbie were at our table, too. Tom Hyers mocked Tye because he and my husband Dale had taken a paper signed by many of the miners to Steve Hyers and talked to him about safety concerns at the mine. Tom Hyers represented our men on the Safety Committee."

"Then what happened?"

"I could tell my husband was seething. The New Year's Eve party wasn't the first time Tom Hyers acted inappropriately toward me. He did at the Christmas party, too. So I suggested to my husband that we go throw away the paper plates. Debbie Dobbs asked her husband Tye to go out to the car and get her coat. Reggie and Della went to use the restroom. No one wanted to stay and listen to Tom Hyers."

"Thank you, Mrs. Baker. You may step down. I now call Mr. Tye Dobbs to the stand."

When Tye was sworn in, David C. said. "Please state your name and occupation."

"Tye Dobbs, miner at the Puttersville Mines."

"Thank you. When you went to get your wife's coat, did you come right back in?"

"Yes, sir. Mr. Steve Hyers was standing at the door when I left. I spoke to him. He was still there when I returned."

"Then where did you go?"

"I went back into the room and gave Debbie her coat. We joined a group of people who were clapping and dancing to 'Duke of Earl'."

"Did you leave the room before Tom Hyers' body was discovered?"

"Yes. I went to the restroom."

"Did you see Mr. Huston in the restroom?"

"No. But someone was in there. Someone with a black and gold toboggan. They left it on the sink. When I came out of the toilet, the toboggan was still there."

"Do you mean this toboggan?" David C. pulled it from his briefcase and held it up, then handed it to Tye.

"I think this is it. Yes, I remember this picture of the yellow jacket bee on it. This is the toboggan."

"Did you hear that Tom Hyers was dead when you came out of the bathroom?"

"Yes. There was a crowd gathering at the end of the hall. I went up to the crowd and stood beside Della. Reggie came out of the restroom and stood behind us."

"You may step down, Mr. Dobbs. I now call Mr. Reginald Huston to the stand."

Reggie approached the witness chair, his handcuffed wrists and hands in front of him. The bailiff swore him in and nodded to David C.

"Please state your name and occupation," David C. said.

"Reginald Nathaniel Huston. I was a bookkeeper at Puttersville Mine Operations."

"Is this your toboggan?" He tossed it to Reggie.

Reggie caught the toboggan in his arms. "Yes, this is my West Virginia State University Yellow Jackets toboggan. I wore it the night of the New Year's Eve party."

"Did you take it into the restroom with you?"

"Yes, I sure did. I take it everywhere."

"Do you know anyone else in Puttersville with a toboggan like it?"

"No sir, I don't. Only other person who lives here and attended West Virginia State University is my Aunt Bess. And she doesn't have one."

"Thank you, Mr. Huston. You may step down."

Judge Hall banged his gavel. "This court will take a recess until 1:30, when it will reconvene."

Della stood and looked around. Chris rushed up to her. "We got a lawyer, and he helped us fill out the papers. All you need to do is step around the corner and sign them in front of the notary. Can you do it now?"

"Sure." Della caught up with Winnie and told her where she was going, and she joined Dale and Chris as they walked down the hallway to an office.

The clerk recognized the Bakers. "You're here to sign the adoption papers," she said.

"Sure are. This here's Miss Etter, who's letting us adopt her baby."

"Here are the papers." The clerk retrieved them from a file cabinet. "Let's walk over to the notary's desk.

Della signed her name on several sheets as the clerk explained each one. The last line she signed was below a line that said, "It has been explained to me that I have ten days to change my mind about forfeiting my child." Her heart jumped as she signed her name. *If only…*

"Let's go celebrate," Chris said. "Della, we're taking you out for lunch."

"Thanks," Della muttered. Her stomach was churning, and she didn't feel as if she could eat.

CHAPTER 39

Condemning Evidence

Della ate only half of her hamburger as she listened to Dale and Chris chatter about the nursery they were decorating.

"I love the light blue walls," Chris said. "Mom's bringing a mobile to hang over the crib tonight. The one we picked out with all the little animals on it." She reached to take Dale's hand in hers. "Oh, I'm so excited." They were still holding hands as they walked from the diner.

A pang of envy swept through Della. What would it be like to have someone to love, someone to help you, support you, and be a father to your children? Even if Reggie were proven innocent, he could never fall in love with her. Because of what had happened to her. Because of Winnie's not allowing him to.

"We better get back to the trial," Chris said, glancing at her watch. "Don't want to miss anything."

Della followed her and Dale out to their car. In spite of the short drive to the courtroom, they slid into their seats in the court room just as the trial restarted. Mr. Allen called Steve Hyers to the witness stand.

"Mr. Hyers, I have only one question," he said. "What motive do you think Reginald Huston had for killing your son?

Hyers lifted his head in pride. "As many of you know, I've been president of Puttersville Miners' Union since it was founded. And that was right after I opened Mine Number One here and started hiring. I'm getting older and have more responsibilities, and I just can't find the time to carry out all the duties. Tom was planning to run for president of the Puttersville Miner's Union. He had my full support." He stopped and glared at Reggie. "However, I don't think he had Mr. Huston's support. In fact, I believe Mr. Huston planned to run for president himself. He wanted rid of Tom, and that's why he killed him. I'm glad he's in jail. Don't want a nigger as president of our union."

"And now we have a clear motive," Allen said. "Thank you, Mr. Hyers, you may step down. I don't need to call any more witnesses, Your Honor."

David C. stood. "I would like to call Tye Dobbs to the stand."

"You may take the stand, Mr. Dobbs. Remember, you are still under oath."

"Mr. Dobbs, will you tell the court your plans for next year? Your plans that have to do with the Puttersville Miners' Union?"

"Yes, sir. I filed in this court and with the headquarters of the UMW that I would be running for the office of President of the Puttersville Miners' Union this year. I think I can be proactive in bringing about changes that will ensure the safety of the miners."

"Do you have the support of the miners at Puttersville Miners' Union?"

"I believe I do. Almost every one of them signed the petition Dale Baker and I took to show Steve Hyers."

"Thank you, Mr. Dobbs. You may step down," David C. said as Judge Hall banged his gavel to silence the loud murmur spreading through the courtroom. When the crowd grew quiet, David C. said, "You see, Your Honor and members of the jury, Tye Dobbs was running for president, not Reginald Huston. I now ask Della Etter to take the stand."

Della gasped. *Why me?* "Yes, sir," she said as she made her way to the front. She sat down, and the bailiff swore her in.

"Miss Etter," David C. said, "Where were you at six o'clock on New Year's Eve?"

"I was at the Puttersville Mine party. I went with Reggie."

"Were you at the same table with the Bakers, the Dobbs, and Tom Hyers?"

"I was."

"Did you leave the table with Mr. Huston to go to the restroom?"

"Yes. We went together. Not in the restroom, of course. I went in the women's bathroom. I stayed in there a little while to fix my hair."

"Did you see anyone in the hallway when you came out?"

"The crowd gathering around Tom Hyers. And I saw the janitor. He was sweeping."

"What was he using to sweep?"

"A broom. If I remember, it had a blue handle."

"Bailiff, may I have Exhibit B?" David C. asked.

"Like this broom?" David C. said as the Bailiff handed it to him. He held up a blue-handled broom with a wide row of black bristles."

"Yes, I think it was just like that one."

"When you came out, was Mr. Huston waiting for you outside?"

"No. He was still in the restroom. He came out of the men's room right after I came out of the women's."

"What did you see when you came out of the women's restroom?"

"There were a bunch of people, maybe about ten, huddled at the end of the hall. I heard them say, 'Tom Hyers is dead!'"

"Then what did you do?"

"I looked around for Reggie. That's when I saw him come out of the restroom. He came up behind me."

"Thank you, Miss Etter. You may step down. Your honor, I'd like to call Mr. Matthew Turner to the stand."

Della searched for Turner as she went back to her chair. She didn't see him in the courtroom. As she sat down she saw him coming to the front, accompanied by the Bailiff, who helped him to the witness stand.

After the Bailiff swore Turner in, David C. faced him. "Will you state your name and occupation for the court?"

"Matthew J. Turner. I work as a janitor for the hotel here."

"Were you at work the night of the Miners' New Year's Eve party?"

"Yes."

"Are you the great uncle of Tye Dobbs?"

"Yes."

"Were you upset because Tom Hyers was running against Tye for president of the local miners' union?"

"I didn't know Tye was running."

"Bailiff, may I have Exhibit A?"

The Bailiff handed David C. something wrapped in clear plastic, and David C. gave it to Turner. "Is this your cigarette lighter?"

Tuner examined it. "No."

"How do you know it's not yours?"

"It…it doesn't have the correct engraving."

"So you have a lighter like this one?"

"No."

"Would you stand and turn your pockets wrong-side out?"

"I can't stand."

"Bailiff, will you help Mr. Turner stand?"

The Bailiff and an officer approached Turner, and taking hold of him under his elbows, stood him up.

"Mr. Turner, please empty your pockets."

Turner fumbled as he took out the contents of his pockets. A lighter fell to the floor.

"Is that your lighter, Mr. Turner?" David C. asked.

Turner stared at the lighter but said nothing. The Bailiff picked it up.

"Will the Bailiff see if there are any initials on that lighter?" David C. asked.

"Let me see. There are, right here," said the Bailiff. "TSH."

"TSH. Thomas Steven Hyers," David C. said. "Mr. Turner, how did you get Tom Hyers' lighter?"

"I found it on the floor at the hotel."

"When?"

"That night. New Year's Eve."

"Did you try to find out who it belonged to?"

"No."

"Why not?"

Turner shook his head. "I don't know."

"Your Honor, may I ask the court to present Exhibit C?"

The Bailiff brought out a broom with a blue handle, wrapped in clear plastic, and held it up.

"Hold it up higher so everyone can see it," David C. said. He turned to the people sitting in the courtroom. "I want Your Honor, the jury, and the good people here to know that this is not the broom that was Exhibit B. Is there anyone here who can tell me about this broom?"

A police officer came forward. "I believe I can."

"Please tell the court your name and occupation."

"Phil Talbot. I am the Chief of Police for the Puttersville Police Department."

"What do you know about this broom, Chief Talbot?"

"I went with my officers when the call came out about Tom Hyers. We searched the hotel where he was killed. We found this broom in the boiler room closet in the basement of the hotel."

"What is different about this broom?"

"The handle has blood on it. We scraped off a sample and sent it to our lab. The blood is AB-negative, the rarest type of blood. Only one percent of people have AB-negative blood. Tom Hyers had

AB-negative blood. I can almost say for certain this broom handle has Tom Hyers' blood on it."

"Matthew Turner, did you kill Tom Hyers?" David C. asked.

Turner stared at the floor, then raised his head and shouted, "No. I did not kill Tom Hyers! I swear!"

From the back of the courtroom came a shout. "You did kill Tom Hyers! I saw you!" Della gasped as a woman ran to the front of the room and faced Turner. "I saw you beating him with that broom!"

Chaos swept through the courtroom. People left their seats and raised their fists as they ran to the front of the courtroom screaming, "Killer! Murderer!"

Judge Hall banged his gavel. "Order! Order!" he shouted. "Order! Everyone, sit down and be quiet!" When the people returned to their seats, Judge Hall stared at the woman. "Who are you?"

"My name is Rose Hanson. I am Dick Hyers's fiancé. He couldn't go to the party, so he sent me to give his dad a message. I stayed and talked with Steve a few minutes, then decided to use the restroom before returning home. When I saw him…" She pointed at Turner. "When I saw him beating someone with that broom, I didn't go into the restroom. I turned and ran. I didn't know it was Tom. I couldn't see the person he was hitting."

Della looked at Winnie, who buried her face in her hands and sobbed. "Oh, Rose, oh, Rose, why are you here?" she asked. "Why, why?"

Judge Hall turned to Dick Hyers. "Do you know this woman?"

"Yes," Dick said. "She is my fiancé. I did not know she saw Turner hitting Tom." He faced Rose. "Why didn't you tell me?"

"Dick, I'm so sorry, I didn't know it was Tom." Tears streamed down her cheeks as her eyes sought his, pleading. "Please believe me. I didn't know it was Tom."

Hall addressed Rose. "Why didn't you go to the police?"

Rose dropped her head. "I was afraid. I was the only other person in the hallway, and I thought Turner would tell the police, and I would be accused."

"Why did you believe that?" Judge Hall asked.

"Because, because I've been in some trouble with the law, so who would they believe? But when I heard it was my brother Reggie who was accused of murdering Tom, I had to say something. That's why I came here today."

Judge Hall's eyes riveted onto Turner. "Matthew Turner, did you kill Tom Hyers?"

"Someone offered me a thousand dollars to do it."

David C. stared at him, a look of astonishment on his face. "Someone offered *you* money to kill Tom? You, bent over and crippled? Who?"

"Someone high up in United Mine Workers who didn't want Tom Hyers movin' up in the

ranks. I needed the money for my back surgery. They asked me to find someone to do it," Turner said. "You see, I used to live in Chicago. Got mixed up with the Mafia. I know people."

"But you didn't find someone. You did it yourself," David C. stated.

"I saw my opportunity. Tom was so drunk he fell and hit his head on the wall. He was out cold. I just finished him off."

Phil Talbot and several other policemen handcuffed Matt Turner and led him from the courtroom.

"This case is dismissed," Judge Hall said. "Reginald Huston, you are free to go."

Reggie held out his hands, and a police officer unlocked the cuffs and took them off. Jumping up, he threw his fist high in the air, and shouted, "I'm free! I'm free! Thank you, Lord Almighty!"

CHAPTER 40

Rose's Story

Della joined the crowd rushing toward Reggie. Nat and Winnie threw their arms around him, hugging and kissing him. Della struggled to get close to him, but all she could do was hold onto the lower part of his arm as he hugged his parents.

"Thank You, God," Nat said, tears streaming down his face. "Thank You, Thank You."

"I knew you'd be free today," Winnie said. "Just knew it."

"Let's take our son home," Nat said. "Come on, Reggie, let's go home and plan a big party. We'll invite all our friends. Celebrate big time." He turned to Ted and Thea. "You're all invited to our house tomorrow night to help us celebrate."

Cameras flashed as they left the courthouse, and reporters shoved microphones toward Reggie as they stood on the steps.

"Mr. Huston, I'm a reporter with *The Dominion News* of Morgantown," said a man taking pictures. "How does it feel to be a free man?"

"I knew I would be exonerated," Reggie said. He shouldered his way through the crowd. "Now I'm a free man, and I'm going home." Surrounded by family and friends, he walked to the car.

"Mama! Mama! Wait!"

Winnie stood beside the open car door and stared at Rose, who was running toward her. "I ain't your mama," she said as Rose drew near. "Haven't been for a long time."

Rose stopped and held out her arms to Winnie. "I know I don't deserve to be your daughter," she said. "I beg you to forgive me. It wasn't easy growing up as the daughter of Wally Diamond. He was as mean to his wife Ginny as I heard he was to you."

Winnie sagged at the sound of the name she had for so long tried to forget, and Nat reached out and took her arm to steady her. "Sit down in the car, Baby. It'll be okay."

Winnie slid into the car seat and stared at Rose with tears in her eyes. "He took my baby away from me. I never saw you again 'til you were grown. He had no right." Tears slid down her face. "Then he taught you to drink, and he brought all sorts of bad people around, and you got all mixed up with them. Then you had to marry a proven thief, that William Hanson, and look where it got you."

Rose stepped closer. "I paid for my crimes. I did my time. I won't ever go back there. Did I tell you I divorced William?"

"Should've never married him," Winnie said.

"Where did you meet Dick Hyers?" Reggie asked.

Rose hung her head. "In a Morgantown bar."

Winnie snorted. "See, you ain't changed your ways one bit."

"I was working as a waitress in a restaurant that had a bar in it," Rose said. "I had to serve him, and we got to talking. You have to understand how low I felt, like a stinkbug trying to come clean. But I was hungry for love, for anyone who would listen to me."

"Just like the scum bug you were," Winnie said. "And for all I know, still are."

"I'm sorry." Rose searched the faces of those standing around the car. "But you got to know that when I heard Reggie here," she said, resting her hand on Reggie's arm, "that my little brother was being charged with murder and might go to jail for life, I had to show up at that court house and help him."

"So how long you been livin' here?" Nat asked. His eyes smoldered. "How long you been livin' here, spyin' on us?"

"Haven't been spying on you. I swear. And I live in Morgantown, not here."

"How long?" Nat demanded.

"Only four months. I moved here to look for a job. I work at a restaurant."

"And you never tried to contact me one time?" Winnie asked as she wiped her eyes with her handkerchief. "Didn't even want to talk to me?"

"No. I knew how you felt, and I didn't want to upset you, but I called Reggie." She walked closer to Winnie, her eyes pleading. "I know I done wrong. But you don't know how hard it was, Dad bringing in one girlfriend after another. Of course they left as soon as he came home drunk and beat them up. And none of them wanted a brat to take care of. The second girlfriend, I think her name was Mary, tried to send me back to his ex-wife Ginny, but she couldn't find her. One gal wanted to send me to an orphan's home, but when Dad found out she had started the paperwork, he nearly killed her. She left, and Dad took me to the bar where he worked and kept me in the back."

"Didn't you go to school?" Reggie asked.

"I went when I could. Not very often. When I was fourteen, I ran away. Got hooked up with a gang of street kids who lived by stealin'. That's how I met William. He was the leader of the pack. They called him 'Wolf'."

Winnie bent over her knees, her hands on her face, and as she rocked back and forth in the car seat, and sounds the likes of which Della had never heard came from her—moans and crying punctuated by "He took you…and he didn't even want you. He mistreated you, and threw you away like trash. Oh, my baby, my baby! You were all I had, and I loved you so. Oh, why didn't I fight harder for you when he sued for custody? Forgive me, Lord, please forgive me."

Rose stepped up to the open car door, bent over, and put her arms around Winnie. "I'm sorry. I never had a mama, but I've been dreamin' about you ever since I learned you were my real mama. Please take me back."

Winnie raised her tear-stained face. "You goin' to be around here for a while? Goin' to marry Dick Hyers and live here?"

"No. Dick just asked me to return the engagement ring he gave me. Said he didn't want to be married to anyone connected with Reggie."

"I'm sorry, but you're better off," Winnie said. "He ain't no good."

"I know that now." Rose took Winnie's hand and pulled, and she got out of the car. Rose wrapped her in a hug. "May I call on you?"

"Why don't you come have dinner with us?" Winnie asked. "We'd be glad to have you."

"Can't. Have to go to work. If you'll give me your phone number, I'll let you know when I have some time off. We'll get together."

Winnie reached into her purse and found a piece of paper to write her phone number on. Rose took it and waved goodbye, and they stood and watched as she walked down the block.

"Let's get home," Nat said after she turned the corner.

Della climbed into the back seat of the car beside Reggie. She looked up at him and blushed as his eyes met hers.

"Thank you for helping me, Della. If you hadn't seen Turner using Tom's lighter, if you hadn't said anything about that, it probably would have turned out differently." He reached across the seat to take her hand.

"I would've done anything to help you," she said. "All I could do is think about you the whole time you were in jail."

Winnie turned around in her seat to stare at them. "You two love bugs remember to give God the glory," she said, smiling. "Our God answered our prayers." She smiled at Della. "Thanks for helping Reggie. I'm sorry I've treated you so roughly." She stared at Della's feet. "You can't imagine the fright that took hold of me when I found out about your father. Just like Wally Diamond, drinkin' and runnin' around. I couldn't think of you lovin' Reggie 'cause I thought you'd turn out just like Rose. Please forgive me."

Tears filled Della's eyes. "I thought it was because he's black and I'm white. Thanks to Sister Bess and you, I did okay. And I forgive you."

"You're like my daughter, Della. Now I have two daughters." She strained to put her arms around Della, but she was too far away, so she patted Della's leg. "And I love this little one that's comin'."

"I've been dreaming of this day for a long time." Reggie put his hands on his parents' shoulders. "We have much to celebrate." His eyes met Della's, and he took her hand. "Much."

Nat pulled into their driveway, and Reggie got out and ran around the car. A smile covered his face as he opened Della's door and took her hand to help her out of the car. Waiting for his parents to walk through their front door, he whispered, "I don't think Mammy minds us holding hands."

Della put her feet outside the car and let him pull her up. As her feet touched the driveway, a searing pain ripped through her back and into her abdomen, and she grabbed her stomach and moaned.

CHAPTER 41

The Little One

Della gasped as Reggie half carried her into the house. "I just had the most painful cramp. I think my baby's coming."

Winnie stopped and stared at her. "Probably just indigestion. It hits hard when you're this far along."

"That didn't feel like any indigestion I've ever had."

"Well, we'll wait and see. If you have any more, we'll start timin' them."

"Welcome home, Son," Nat said.

"Come in and have some beef stew," Winnie said. "I made it yesterday just for you. And Della made you a cake."

Reggie grinned at her. "You all went to a lot of trouble. And you weren't even sure I was coming home."

"I was sure," Winnie said. "I put my trust in God, and He took care of you."

Della's stomach churned as she set the table. She put half a dipper of stew into her bowl and sat down even though she didn't feel like eating.

Nat gave thanks for the food, for Reggie getting out of jail, for their being together, for God's care, for David C., and for their friends who stood by them. Then he launched into another long request for the well-being of everyone involved in the trial.

Della felt the searing cramp starting in her back, then hitting her front. She bent over and put her sweat-covered face in her hands as Nat said "Amen". When she looked up, Winnie was staring at her.

"You had another one, didn't you?"

"Yes. Oh, it hurts. I don't think I can eat."

Winnie looked at the clock. "It's five-fifteen. We'll see how long it is before you have another one."

"I'm sorry," Della said. "It's not fair to Reggie. This is his time to celebrate."

"Oh, don't worry about that," Reggie said. "What a great honor to have your baby born on the same day I got freed. If it's a boy, are you going to name him after me?"

Tears filled Della's eyes. "I don't get to name him, remember?"

"Oh, sorry." Reggie took a bite of his roll. "Mammy, can I help you with the dishes so Della won't have to?"

"Why, of course."

Nat put his hand on Reggie's shoulder and gazed into his eyes. "God is so good."

Della pushed her bowl back and stood. "I'm going to go to my room and lie down." Something warm trickled down her leg, wetting her pants and shoes. Suddenly, another cramp streaked through her abdomen, and she bent over. "I'm leaking all over. Someone help me!"

Winnie was at her side. "Looks like your water's broken. We better get you to the hospital. Nat, will you call the Johnsons? Sorry, Reggie, but you may have to do the dishes alone." Reaching into a nearby closet, she grabbed an old blanket, and then pulled Della's coat from the stand and wrapped it around her shoulders. "Come on, girl." Outside she opened the front passenger door and put the folded blanket on the seat. "In case you leak some more."

As Della got in, another cramp wracked her body. "Oh! Another one. Oh, it hurts. Tears streamed down her cheeks, and she wiped them on the tail of her coat with shaking hands."

"You're trembling," Winnie said. "Are you cold?"

"Not cold. It hurts so much. And I'm scared. What if things don't go right? What if the baby dies? What if I die?"

"Think of the millions of women who have given birth. Think of all those who didn't have a hospital to go to, but had their babies at home. You'll be fine."

"I'm sorry. Guess you're right."

"Of course I'm right."

They were at the hospital. Winnie parked close to the emergency entrance. "Can you walk?"

"I think so." She opened the car door and twisted in her seat to get out, but as she did, another cramp made her sit back and moan.

"I better go tell them to bring out a wheelchair," Winnie said. "Those cramps are comin' real close together."

Della closed her eyes. *Oh, if only the baby was here. If only I could be my old self and never have to think of what Daddy did to me again. Today's my day of freedom, too.* A rattling noise came toward her, and she opened her eyes. A nurse pushing a wheelchair was outside the car.

Winnie pulled the car door open and took her hand. "You can do it. Easy, now," she said, helping her out of the car and into the chair.

"They're calling Dr. Haskins," the nurse said. "She should be here before the baby comes."

Della held her abdomen as the wheelchair bumped over the parking lot and over the threshold. With each jolt she felt a stab of pain up her back, and she clenched her teeth and groaned.

"Here's your room," the nurse said. "And your bed. You can put this gown on. Take off your clothes and put them in this bag. I'll be back in a bit."

Della put the gown on and lay down on the bed. Another cramp descended, and she clutched the pillow and cried. "Mama, Mama, I need you!"

Winnie took Della's hand and rubbed her back. "Relax. You'll be okay."

The nurse returned. She took Della's temperature and blood pressure. "You're doing fine. Your baby will be the first one born in March. Did you bring some baby clothes?"

Della shook her head. "I'm not keeping the baby."

"Oh." The nurse dragged a chair across the floor. "For you, ma'am," she said to Winnie. "Dr. Haskins is on her way. If you need me, just punch this button."

Five minutes later, Dr. Haskins came into the room and examined Della. "You're dilated almost all the way. Do you remember the breathing exercises we practiced?"

"Yes."

"Good. The next time you have a contraction, try breathing. And try to relax. It will ease the pain."

"Okay," Della said. "Here it comes!" She tried to breathe and count as she had practiced, but in the end, she clutched the bed's side rails and screamed. "I hate him! I hate him for doing this to me! Ohhhh."

The nurse came back in and put Della's feet in stirrups.

Dr. Haskins examined her again. "That was fast," she said. "The baby's crowning."

"What does that mean?" Della asked.

"I can see the top of your baby's head. It'll soon be all over. The next contraction, remember to breathe and count."

Della tried, but the pain was so excruciating she couldn't concentrate. "Help! Winnie, help!" she screamed.

Winnie had backed up to the other side of the room to give Dr. Haskins room. "I'm right here, Della," she said.

"The next contraction you have, you need to push," Dr. Haskins said. "Push as hard as you can. Get that baby out of there."

The next contraction came in giant waves. Della pushed as hard as she could, sobbing. As soon as it stopped, she tried to relax, but another contraction followed.

"Push, push!" Dr. Haskins said. "Give it all you've got!"

Della clenched her teeth and her fists and gave one huge push. The next thing she heard was the wailing cry of the baby.

"There, there, it's all over. You have a beautiful little girl. Do you want to see her?"

"No. She's not mine."

"Are you sure? You need to see her."

Della lay back, every muscle in her body aching. "Okay. But I'm tired, so just one peek."

"Here she is." Dr. Haskins wrapped the baby in a blanket and laid her on Della's chest.

The nurse placed one hand on the baby and raised Della up by putting pillows behind her. Della steeled herself and glanced at the baby. Light brown hair covered the baby's tiny head, and her dark eyes looked upward as if to say, "Here I am."

"She looks just like Mama!" Della gasped. She reached her finger toward the infant's hand, and the baby clutched it. Della jerked her hand away. The little one's mouth opened, and out came a pitiful cry.

"Here, please take her," Della said, turning her face away.

A nurse took the baby.

"I need to go home and rest," Winnie said. "And spend some time with my son. I'll see you tomorrow."

"Thanks for being here," Della said. "What happens now?" she asked the nurse.

"Just a minute, and we'll have you ready to go to a room." The nurse washed her and helped her into a clean gown. Then she brought a wheelchair in and took Della's arm, guiding her into the chair.

Della thought about the tiny one she had birthed. Even crying, she looked just like Mama. "Harriet," she mumbled. "Your name should be Harriet. Just like Mama's name."

"What'd you say?" the nurse asked as she pulled the blankets down and helped her into bed.

"The baby's name should be Harriet." Tears fell on her pillow, and she wiped her face. "I didn't know it would be so hard."

"You don't have to give her away, you know. You can change your mind."

"I can't keep her. I don't have no baby clothes. No job, and no money." Tears rolled down her cheeks. "I couldn't keep her if I wanted to."

"Oh, yes you can. I'll help you." Sister Bess stood in the doorway. "Winnie called me and let me know about the baby. She asked me to call Dale and Chris, but I didn't. I wanted to make sure." She neared the bed, and her arms surrounded Della.

Della buried her face in Sister Bess. She tried to stop crying, but the tears kept coming. "I never thought she would look like Mama. I…I just can't give her away. I want to be her mama. Oh, Mama, I wish you were here!"

"Shh. Sister Bess is here. Would you like to go see her? The nurse left the wheelchair."

Della nodded. "Maybe for just a little."

Sister Bess wheeled the chair to her bed. "Come. We'll just go take a peek." She helped Della into the chair and rolled her out the door. "I know where they keep the babies."

They passed through the hallway. The nurse who had been present during the birth looked up from her station in surprise, but she said nothing. They came to a door marked Nursery, and Sister Bess held the door open with one foot as she pushed Della through. Inside was a room separated by a large glass window low enough for Della to see inside.

Della raised herself up and stared. A soft light illuminated six tiny cribs and the three front cribs holding babies. "*Baby Boy Whipkey, Baby Girl Stevens*," Della read. "All born yesterday." The third crib said only *Baby Girl*. She sucked in her breath and held it, not able to breathe. *My baby doesn't even have a name!*

"Is that your baby?" Sister Bess asked, pointing to her.

"Yes. She's beautiful, isn't she?

"You don't have to give her away."

"But I promised."

"The state says you can go back on your promise."

The door to the Nursery opened, and Chris and Dale ran through it. "We heard our baby was born!" Chris said. "Where is she?"

CHAPTER 42

Sweet Mama

"Your baby?" Della's trembling hand pointed to the window. "In...in there," she said.

"I want to see her." Chris stepped up to the window. "Oh, she's adorable! Can I hold her? Can we take her home now?"

"Chris," Della mumbled, then said it louder. "Chris, I can't give her away. You remember, the paperwork said I could back out. I can't give her to you. I want to keep her."

"You can't do this to us! We've waited so long, planned...and now you're saying we can't have her?" Chris took Dale's arm, steadying herself, her face ashen.

"I'm sorry, but I can't let her go," Della said, not daring to look into Chris's face. "She looks just like Mama. My mama that I lost." She lifted her head to meet their eyes. "I'll pay you back for the lawyer, every cent."

"I should have known you couldn't let your baby go," Chris said. "Even though you promised, I didn't think it was in you." Then her face softened. "What you can do is give me back my maternity clothes. We just found out I'm expecting again. The baby will be here around next Halloween."

"I'm so glad," Della whispered. She tried to stand, but her legs gave way, and she sank back into the wheelchair.

"We'll stop by and pick up the maternity clothes tomorrow," Dale said. "Come on, Chris, let's go home so you can rest." Turning, they walked out the door.

"Sister Bess, what have I done? Poor Chris. I don't know what to say."

"You did what was most important. You want to keep your baby. I'm proud of you. Shall we go tell the nurse?"

The nurse saw them coming. "What name shall I put on the birth certificate?" she asked.

"Harriet. Harriet Ann Etter," Della said. "But how did you know?"

"A little bird told me. Sign here," she said, sliding a paper in front of Della.

"That was Mama's name," Della said, her eyes meeting Sister Bess's eyes. "Only Mama's middle name was Grace. That's what my real father called her."

"By the way, Miss Etter, you'll be going home tomorrow. Do you want me to bring little Harriet to you in your room?"

"Yes, please."

Sister Bess left as soon as the nurse brought the baby. She lay in the crook of Della's arm, swaddled in a pink blanket. Della ran her fingers gently over her soft head.

"My sweet little Harriet," she whispered. "How did I think I could not keep you? How could I?" She sang a lullaby she remembered Mama singing to her.

The baby squirmed and made a soft noise that grew louder and more persistent. Soon she was sucking her fingers and crying.

Della rang the bell for the nurse. "I think she's hungry," she told the nurse. "What do I do?"

The nurse showed her how to nurse the baby. After the baby ate, the nurse took her back to the Nursery. Della turned on her side and fell into a deep sleep.

The next morning Dr. Haskins checked on her and signed the release papers. "You and the baby can go home as soon as someone comes to get you."

Della sat on the bed, holding little Harriet and gazing into her face. Her heart filled with a love she had never known. "I almost lost you," she whispered. "But you're mine, all mine, and I'm going to take you home and take care of you, little Harriet."

"Well, look who we have here." Reggie walked into the room. "Mammy and I came to get you two." He picked up Harriet, his large hands holding her and supporting her head as if he'd always known how to handle a baby.

Winnie came in and took the baby from him. "My turn," she said. For a few moments she stood cradling the baby in her arms and gazing into her face. "My, she's pretty," she said. "You did good, Della. I brought you some clean clothes. We'll go as soon as you get dressed."

"Thanks." Della's heart swelled. "I didn't think it would turn out okay, but now I know it will. I have to find a job so I can take care of her."

"Your job *is* taking care of her," Winnie said. "We'll make it, all of us working together. Let's get you home."

After Della dressed, the nurse wheeled her out to the car, and she climbed in the back seat and took the baby, holding her against her chest, feeling her soft breath, and watching her sleep. "You're my little angel," she said.

When they got home and went into the house, Winnie took the baby from Della's arms. "We bought you something. A gift from all of us."

Reggie carried a bassinet from the dining room. Pink blankets lined its sides and covered the mattress. "Harriet won't have to sleep in a dresser drawer."

"It's beautiful. Oh, thank you," Della said. She took the sleeping bundle from Winnie and laid the baby in the bassinet.

Nat came through the front door. "Anything for lunch? Someone forgot to pack me a bag." He stopped in front of the bassinet. "Well, lookie what we have here." He smiled at Della. "You have a beautiful baby."

"Thanks," Della said, putting her hand on the sleeping baby. She couldn't take her eyes from her little miracle.

"Bess brought us some soup on her way to school, so we'll have soup and sandwiches," Winnie said. She put the soup on the stove to heat.

Della started gathering the bread, meat, and cheese from the refrigerator, but Winnie stopped her. "Sit down and rest. As soon as you eat, I want you to take a nap. You need to take it easy for a few days. Besides, that baby's goin' to be keepin' you up at night."

"Yes, ma'am. Thank you." After Nat said the blessing, she downed the soup and sandwich. Sister Bess's good soup. She thought of Sister Bess and Mother Carrie, and the anguish and fear she felt when she couldn't keep the soup down, knowing that she was in the family way. *If I had only known what I know now, I wouldn't have been so fearful.*

A knock sounded on the door, and Nat rose to see who it was. "Della, come here. Somebody to see you."

"Someone to see me?"

"Come in, won't you?" she heard Nat say, and she looked up.

"Mama! Mama!" she screamed. Mama stood there with her arms outstretched, and Della flew into them. "Mama, oh, Mama, I thought you were dead! Oh, Mama, where have you been?"

"I looked for you, Della. When I was able, I searched for months, but no one knew where you were. Marie helped. This morning we saw your picture in the Morgantown newspaper. Standin' on the courthouse steps here in Puttersville. We read about the trial and saw you were with the Hustons. They're in the phone book. We came as soon as we could."

"But Aunt Marie wasn't home when I got to her house," Della said. "I had nowhere to go. Then Sister Bess took me in."

"I put my house up for sale, and I went to get Harriet. I had to get her away from Gus, but I didn't know what bad shape she was in 'til I got there." Aunt Marie stepped forward. "She would have died if I had not taken her to a hospital."

"Cancer kills a lot of people," Winnie said as she entered the living room.

"Harriet didn't have cancer," Marie said. "She had tuberculosis, which can be cured, only Gus drank up all the money and wouldn't get her any help. I was moving to Morgantown, so I took her there and put her in the hospital. When she was strong enough, I transferred her to a nursing home to get completely well. It took her four months to get strong enough to come home with me."

"And who are these people?" Mama asked.

"This is Winnie," Della said, pointing. "And her husband Nat, and their son Reggie. Oh, Mama, they have been so good to me. First I lived with Sister Bess and Mother Carrie and Chloe, but now I live with them, and now I have..." She took Mama's arm and guided her toward the bassinet. "Mama, her name is Harriet. She looks just like you."

"She's your baby?" Mama put her arm around Della's shoulders. "You're a mother?"

"Yes, Mama. She was born yesterday. I was going to give her away, but I couldn't."

"I'm glad you didn't. Who's her father?"

Della hung her head and whispered, "Daddy. Mama, the terrible things he did to me. I wanted to tell you, but you were too sick."

"That's why I sent you away. I didn't know it had happened. I would have had him arrested. But he is in God's hands now." She glanced at the faces of Della's friends. "Thank you for takin' care of my daughter. All of you."

"Della has been a lot of help," Winnie said. "You should see how she can sew. She made the blouse she has on."

"But Sister Bess found me first, and she is so nice, and Mama, you have to meet her," Della said. "Oh, I'm so glad you found me."

"That's a beautiful blouse," Aunt Marie said. "Would you like to come home with us?"

"Oh, yes, I would!" Della stopped and looked at her adopted family. "If Winnie and Nat and Reggie don't care."

"That's a silly thing to say." Reggie laid his hand on her shoulder. "They're your family. We'll miss you, but you're free to go, right, Mammy?"

"Of course. If you all didn't live in Morgantown, I would hire her to hem clothes for me. She does an excellent job." Winnie wiped her eyes. "She has been like a daughter to me, though. I want you to know that."

The door opened, and Sister Bess walked in with Chloe. "Chloe wanted to see the baby," she said. "Oh, you have company."

"Sister Bess, Mama's here! And Aunt Marie."

"I'm so glad to meet you," Mama said. "I can never thank you enough for rescuin' my daughter."

"I did what my heart told me to do," Sister Bess said. "She has been a blessing to our family."

"Just as you have blessed her," Mama said. "Oh, the baby's cryin'."

"She's probably hungry again." As Della turned toward the bassinet, the room spun around her. "Oh," she said, sitting down on the sofa. "I don't feel so well. All of a sudden, I'm too tired to stand. Mama, can you carry Harriet up to my room so I can feed her?" She grasped the bannister and pulled her way up the stairs behind Mama.

"I believe Della's too tired to make the trip to Morgantown today," she heard Sister Bess say to Aunt Marie. "Why don't you and Harriet let her rest here tonight? I have an extra room, and you can stay with me."

When Della wakened the next morning, she felt a renewed energy, even though she had slept on the sofa and was up twice to feed and change the baby. Something else she had done after everyone was in bed. She had slipped the coin from its bag, drawn a picture of it, which she left in the little bag, and put the coin in her purse. As happy as she was for her and her little one to be going home with Mama and Aunt Marie, it would mean saying goodbye to Reggie. Would she ever see him again?

After checking on the baby and eating a bowl of cereal, she headed upstairs to start packing. She met Winnie at the top of the stairs.

"I hope you don't mind, but I took the liberty to pack your things," Winnie said. She carried Della's worn suitcase in one hand and a couple boxes under her other arm. "I know how tired you were last night, so I let you sleep in. The maternity clothes are in this box. I'll give them to Chris for you."

"Thanks for all you've done for me." She went into the bathroom and brushed her teeth and hair, and then she ducked into her bedroom for one last look. Nothing there but her purse, and she slung the strap over her shoulder. Opening the door of the bedroom, she came face to face with Reggie. It was a moment she had been dreading.

He placed his hands on her shoulders and pulled her close. "You're starting a new page in your life, Della. Please don't carry shame and anger with you. Remember to go to church and trust God. And take little Harriet with you."

"I will. I promise."

"And don't be a stranger. Please come visit us."

"I will if I can. What are you going to do? Are you going back to work at the coal mine office?"

"No. I'm joining the army. I've been reclassified as 1A since I'm not in college."

Della's heart felt like a heavy stone inside her chest. "You can't. You'll get killed!"

"It's okay. You've heard me practice on my violin. I can play the trombone just as well as I play the violin, and I'm pretty good on the clarinet. After Christmas I auditioned for the army. I received a letter saying I would be stationed at Fort McArthur to play in the army band. It's in California. I'll be okay."

"You'll be far away."

"I'll be home for a visit after basic training. Think of the benefits I'll get when I finish my stint. Money for housing. Help with college. I can get my Master's Degree. Lots of other GI benefits."

"I don't want you to go."

"I'll write to you, and you can write to me. It'll be fine."

"I won't. But I want to give you something." She pressed it into his hand. "My lucky coin. Keep it so you'll remember me."

"I'll never forget you. I'll see you after basic. For sure. I love you, Della."

"And I love you." Their eyes met, and she stood on her tiptoes to reach his lips as he bent towards her."

"Della. Your mama and auntie are here," came Winnie's voice from the living room.

One quick kiss, and she headed down the stairs, her eyes filled with tears.

"We got the bassinet folded up," Aunt Marie said. "Good thing I brought my truck."

Della nodded and took baby Harriet from Mama. "Bye. For now. We'll come see you soon."

"Please come," said Winnie.

Della turned to Reggie. "What's the name of that song you always play? You know, the happy one."

"That's 'Ode to Joy' by Beethoven. It's a tribute to joy, love, and friendship among all people all around the world. I love it."

"Me too," she said, smiling up at him. Here's my little love and joy." She snuggled little Harriet close to her breast.

As she followed Mama and Aunt Marie out the door, she heard violin music coming from Reggie's room. "Ode to Joy," the tune that reminded her of the good times they had spent together, filled her with happiness. Her heart sang as she thought of the future with little Harriet, Mama and Aunt Marie. And Reggie.

OTHER BOOKS BY DONNA WITTLIF

World Eternal Series by Donna R. Wittlif
Book 1 World Eternal: Promises
Book 2 World Eternal: Proselytes
Book 3 World Eternal: Perils
Heart of A Family Series: Finding Her Heart

Available online at Amazon and Barnes & Noble

CONNECT WITH DONNA

Website: **www.donnarwittlif.com**
Facebook: **www.facebook.com/authordonnawittlif**
Twitter: **www.twitter.com/DonnaWittlif**
Bublish: **www.bublish.com/author/view/6560**

If you enjoyed *Finding Her Joy*, please find it on Amazon or where you bought it and do a review for me. All it takes is your saying what you liked about it.
I appreciate your help.
Donna Wittlif